Love to the Women

~ A Novel ~

by

Heather Trefethen

Love to the Women
Copyright © 2013 by Heather Trefethen

All rights reserved.

Cover Design and Interior Design Consultant
David Edmonds

FIRST EDITION

ISBN-10: 148273351-X
ISBN-13: 978-1482733518

to

Grace and Helen

1

As I looked around the empty office, it suddenly dawned on me: Christ, I hope Jayne can still stand me. She and the girls were set to pick me up in Boston at around two, along with a welcoming committee of neighbors with pickup trucks to help haul my ridiculous amount of luggage back to the house. Frankly, I dreaded the flight home from London, but the thought that it would be my last was a huge consolation. I eyed the clock. Another hour and I'd be officially retired.

"Mr. Sheridan?" Priscilla squeaked. She was our newest junior secretary here at Donovan-Davis and was trying desperately to get the hang of things. What she lacked in experience, though, she made up for in her ability to brew a really good cup of coffee.

"Yes?"

"Your wife just called," she said, carefully handing me a

fresh cup of dark roast as she juggled a stack of manila file folders.

"Jayne called?" I replied, more than a little alarmed. "It's two o'clock in the morning over there. Is everything alright?"

"Yes, Mr. Sheridan. Everything's fine, sir," replied Priscilla, now strangling her folders in a double death-grip as if they were stuffed with a pack of pythons bent on escaping. "She wanted to tell you not to expect her this afternoon. Something about a shipment of fabric."

"At two in the morning?"

"I'm sorry, sir," she frowned. "It's what she said."

"Thanks, Priscilla," I sighed. And with that, she scrambled off to asphyxiate another bundle of paperwork.

I missed Jayne terribly. It killed me to be away from her and the girls all the time, but this was it. I was done. No more traveling. I'd be home for good now and we could all spend time together just like I'd dreamed.

I gazed at the lonely calendar, barely believing how much time had passed. The last fourteen years had gone by faster than I could have imagined, the most recent being nothing short of a blur. It hadn't always been fun and games though. Especially in the beginning.

Jayne and I married in the summer of 1933 with me fresh out of college and not a job to be had. Work was scarce back then, the Great Depression still looming over the country like a dark cloud, and I had to go wherever I could draw a paycheck. I still remember how exhausting it was moving every two or three or six months. It went on like that forever.

I did a lot of design work for the WPA, the TVA, and

any other Government Works Project I could get my hands on. The pay wasn't always that great, but it was better than living off the dole. Plus, the experience I gained was better than any regular static office job could ever hope to offer. The downside, though, was always the traveling.

Jayne and I maintained our nomadic existence for over a decade, running here and there, never lighting long enough in one spot even to make good friends. We didn't dare start a family either for fear I wouldn't be able to provide for them. It took its toll on both of us more than I had ever realized; but Jayne, especially, bore the brunt of the load. She felt so alone.

It was during a trip to Nevada that my poor wife finally broke down, along with the car. She cried endlessly, dreading the thought of confessing to yet another new neighbor, "No, we don't have any children." That was practically unheard of in those days, unless there was something wrong with you. Even the poorest of souls had children. I knew, then, that we had to settle down.

With that singular thought, we abandoned the car and headed back to Boston. I hated the thought of having to live with Jaynie's meddling parents in nearby Milton, though. So with what little money we had, we rented a one room flat in the city and I immediately hit the bricks scouting for work. I'd heard that Richards & Fielding, a promising new firm, was looking for a new architect and I did all I could to land the job. I guess I'd made a bit of a name for myself with all the government projects I'd worked on since Mr. Fielding hired me on the spot. I couldn't believe it. Neither could Jayne. It seemed too easy. Great pay. Steady employment. A paid vacation every year. We could buy a house. We could have a family. It was perfect.

Of course, there was a downside: Travel. Lots of travel.

I thought Jayne would balk at the idea at first, especially since she was eventually going to be in a big house all by herself with a new baby. Then, two babies. Then, a third. However, she took it all in stride, trying her best to be stoic for the neighbors while I was out pressing the flesh with clients as far north as Portland, as far south as Miami, and as far west as Los Angeles. I even headed overseas a few times.

When I traveled, I always made a point of bringing back a nice gift for Jayne and something special for our little girls to make up for my absence. The presents from Europe always went over the best, though, since they were usually the fanciest. Donna, for instance, doted over her Wedgwood children's tea set for a year and Jayne wore her pearls everyday, just like the Queen.

It was while at a seminar on bomb shelter design back in '45 that I saw an opportunity to expand our business overseas. I quickly pitched the idea to Mr. Richards and his partner, keenly pointing out how great it would be to get in on London's post-war rebuilding boom and how equally great it would be to work with the group of architects I'd met from the west end firm, Donovan-Davis. I also raved about Page, their secretary, who'd saved me from myself when I got caught up in an air raid on the way to my Covent Garden hotel and hadn't a clue what to do.

"If you're going to wander about lost, do it in here," she kindly ordered as she gently, yet firmly shoved me into the tunnel of the shelter.

It took some convincing on both ends - not to mention several more trips overseas - but in the spring of 1952 our firm officially merged with Donovan-Davis. Mr. Fielding was so thrilled with the idea of finally having an enterprise in

Europe he asked me to head across the pond to manage the new branch on a permanent basis. It was an easy decision for me, especially since the offer came with a hefty promotion, but it was a tough one for Jayne. She loved the house in our quiet little Quincy neighborhood and, as much as she hated to admit it, didn't want to leave her mother and father behind who kept threatening to retire to Florida. The girls didn't want to leave their friends either and they were all afraid they'd have to eat steak and kidney pie at every meal.

"Donna says they drive on the wrong side of the road over there," said little Penny, dirt on her face, shoe untied, curls akimbo.

"That's true," I told her as I laced up her sneaker. "But, don't worry. I'll probably be taking a taxi cab most of the time."

"Do *they* drive on the wrong side of the road, *too?*" she asked, her big green eyes wide with alarm.

"Yep."

"I bet they must crash a lot," she added. I can still see her trying to visualize the carnage in her mind, her little brows converging in on each other as she thought long and hard. You could practically hear her tiny gears turning.

Jayne and I finally agreed to keep the house in Quincy and I would head to London on my own with the understanding that I would come home at least every six weeks for a visit. The boss crunched the numbers and oddly enough agreed it would be more cost effective to put me up in a small one bedroom flat in the city than to relocate the entire family to a big house in the country. And so became the plan.

As business grew, my every six weeks turned into every three months, which turned into every four months, which turned into once in a blue moon. Being busy, the time flew for me, but dragged for my wife and daughters. Penny, my baby, wrote me everyday. Ruthie, once a month. Donna, my eldest, never. She was so mad at me for leaving she could have spit.

I called Jayne every Friday night like clockwork. Half the time, we'd lose our connection and I'd never get it back. I missed her so much. The guilt took some getting used to. All I wanted was to be able to provide for my family. But now, after all these years, I was beginning to see that Jayne and the girls had created a life without me and it was going to take some getting used to having me around the house for good. To my own credit, I'd given them the opportunity to become strong, independent women. I only hope I hadn't done too good a job. I only hope they can still stand me.

I eyed the clock again. Not long now. I was waiting for Page to come in and bid me adieu, with one of her infamous ribbings included. I'd already made the rounds upstairs to say my goodbye's to the Accounting Department, stopping in quick to see Wiggy, the chap in the mailroom. He was set to retire, too, in about a month or so. At 76 years old, he was as spry as a teenager, and just as unruly. He could run circles around us all.

"Mr. Sheridan?"

"Yes?"

"Your daughter just called," said Priscilla, peaking her head in the doorway, files still in a choke hold.

"Which one?"

"Donna, sir."

"Donna? At this hour?"

"Yes, sir. Sorry, sir," Priscilla apologized. "She wanted

to tell you not to expect her this afternoon. Something about a nail appointment."

"Nails…" According to Jayne, Donna's latest fetish was something called "French tips", which apparently were quite expensive. Everything was expensive when it came to Donna. I cringed at the thought of her upcoming nuptial, which was on track for becoming the wedding of the century. I loved my daughter dearly but, at the same time, wished she'd start spending some of her own money instead of mine. "Well, far be it from me to keep her from her appointed rounds," I sighed.

"Oh, and she mentioned the Monaghan's would likely be absent as well," Priscilla added. "Something about a good haul, whatever that means."

I knew exactly what that meant. Billy and Skip Monaghan, our neighbors, were seasoned lobster fishermen and when they were hitting them, they were out round the clock. That meant Penny would be there, too. She and Billy were practically inseparable.

"Great," I feigned, "trumped by a lobster, no less."

"I'm sorry, sir," frowned Priscilla. "It's what she said."

"Well, no worries. It won't be the first time I've had to take a cab."

"Yes, sir. I mean, no, sir. I mean… Good luck, sir."

"Thanks, Priscilla," I sighed, and off she went only to return a split second later.

"Sorry, sir… Forgot to mention it…" she said, shifting her weight from side to side as she adjusted her gasping files.

"Let me guess," I smiled. "Ruth's not coming either."

"No, sir. I mean, I'm not sure, sir. No word. But there was a message from Penny, sir," she reported. "She said she'd be there. With bells on. Her words. Not mine, sir."

"Well, that's great news," I said. "I was hoping not everyone had abandoned the Sheridan ship."

"Yes, sir," she beamed. "Me, too, sir. Bye, then." Those poor file folders.

I had a small hope that Ruth, my middle daughter, would still be there, too, but I didn't count on it. She'd likely be singing somewhere and I certainly didn't want to keep her from that.

I walked over to the big floor-to-ceiling windows and peered out onto the bustling street below. I was going to miss the shrill sound of the taxi cab's worn brakes, the bark of the fish mongers and street merchants, even the occasional police siren. Still, with each minute that passed, my longing for home grew stronger. I couldn't wait to embrace a more favourable routine, one that involved lots of free time where I could just kick back with a cold one and relax, go to the movies with my daughters, or make love to my wife over the course of an entire blissful afternoon. It was going to be great, just like I'd planned.

"Having second thoughts?" came a soft, familiar voice.

I looked over my shoulder. "I beg your pardon…" I crooned.

"You heard me."

In the doorway stood Page Reynolds, the ever-dedicated Donovan-Davis secretary. She was a tall, attractive woman who always maintained a deliberate, confident stride and had the best posture of any woman I'd ever known. She was gently pushing 70 now, but didn't look a day over 45, attributing her youth to plenty of rest, a glass of wine every night, and a very active sex life. God bless her husband.

"I was just thinking about Jayne and the girls, how nice it'll seem to be home for good," I said, tearing off another page from my page-a-day calendar. It was the only thing besides the furniture left in the room and I couldn't help but fiddle with it one last time.

"You assume they'll be able to tolerate you," quipped Page, easing into the office.

"That's my fear you know," I quietly confessed, "that they won't be able to stand me."

"I know, love. But don't worry," she said as she straightened my tie. She was always straightening my tie. "One look at you and they'll forget all about being cross."

"I sure hope you're right," I said, tossing the calendar page into the waste can. "The year went by so fast, though. I still can't believe it's the middle of August already."

"Neither can I. And it's 1965, not 1964. That's what you get for buying your calendars from the street urchins, you know. I'm surprised you never caught on."

"I wondered why I was always getting my days mixed up. Why didn't you tell me?"

"I can't hold your hand *every* step of the way."

"Shit," I sighed, tossing the rest of the calendar into the can.

Page had such a polite way of teasing you that you hardly even noticed. I'd gotten used to the jibes, the jabs, the winks. At the same time, she knew when to be serious. Beyond Jayne, she was my number one confidant. I could tell her anything and I did.

"Come on, love," she winked, taking my arm in hers, "there's some people that want to kick you in the shins before you go."

"I hope they don't kick too hard," I grinned.

"Brace yourself all the same."

Ralph Sanders, my replacement, was scheduled to arrive

that afternoon and everyone was on pins and needles hoping for an easy transition. The well-seasoned hot shot had been pacing the floors of Richards & Fielding for almost a decade and a half waiting to inherit the throne. He must have called a hundred times.

"Take care, ladies," I said as I peeked my head into the secretarial office.

"Take care, Mr. Sheridan," a trio of voices sang out. "It won't be the same here without you." Priscilla waved from her desk then clenched her pencil with both fists so tight I thought for sure it would splinter in two. I was going to kind of miss her.

Over the years, we'd grown from one secretary to three, plus two full-time accountants, Page in charge of them all. She ran a tight ship, which Mr. Fielding especially appreciated. Our stable of British architects had grown as well, now numbering nineteen, including Mr. Donovan and Mr. Davis, and we had our hands into everything from modern high rises to modest chalets. It had been one hell of a ride, but I felt it was time to get off the horse.

I blew the girls a kiss and off we went down the hall.

"Oh, there was another message from your wife," announced Page. "She still won't be able to meet you at the airport. Something about a drapery install, whatever that is."

"Shows you how I rate."

"Don't worry," she added, "Little Miss Napoleon will rescue you."

"On her trusty steed?"

"No doubt," Page chuckled, "although she may have to enlist the help of the local cavalry to get all your belongings home."

I was still disappointed, but not surprised. Jayne had

started a little interior decorating business, which was going surprisingly well. I pictured her in a development meeting the same as she must have pictured me over the years. Although she had a number of wealthy clients and was working diligently on expanding her base, I was pretty confident that once I got home she'd put it all aside.

Jayne also had a partner named Reed Hargate that I assumed would take over once Jayne 'retired'. At first I was concerned about my wife being in business with some guy I'd never met before; but, according to Penny, he wasn't much of a threat. Though "All-Star handsome" by some accounts, it was rumoured he batted for the other team. Still, when someone of the opposite sex spends more time with your wife than you do, you get a little edgy.

Page and I headed for the Junior office, passing a row of photos I'd taken of the firm's most impressive buildings and residences. A small plastic name plate was tacked to the wall beside each one: *Photography by Stephen M. Sheridan, Senior Architect*. "Funny, I'm known more for my hobby than my real job," I said to Page, waving a thumb at a stark looking vocational college.

"It's your hobby that's made an awful lot of people – including yourself - look awfully good at times."

"Oh, come now, Page," I said slyly, "what's not to love about the tech school?"

"Ghastly…" she sighed, hiding her smirk behind her curled fist.

It's true. In my mind, it was a hideous building. But, it was exactly what the client had in mind: "a sleek, utilitarian structure whose simplicity didn't detract from the quality education inside." Frankly, it was about as inviting as a maximum security prison. All that was missing was the

11

concertina wire.

"By the way, I set up those hundred or so snapshots you've had plastered all over your office in some scrapbooks," said Page. "Wiggy's putting them in the post for you as we speak."

"You know how I love my women," I sighed.

"The images speak volumes…"

When I was home I'd take hundreds of photos of Jayne and my girls so I could always have their smiling faces around me when I was away. Their portraits lined my office walls from end to end and peppered my desktop. To my daughters, it was embarrassing. To me, it was therapeutic.

I paused to look in on the Junior Architects.

"Davey, be good. Call if you need anything."

"Wiw do, Mr. Sheridan," said Davey. "You'w come back ome day to pho'ograph my biuwding when it's dome, righ'?"

"You bet," I waved.

I had a hell of a time understanding Davey when he first came on board. On top of his thick Cockney accent, he had a speech impediment that made him sound as if he had peanut butter permanently stuck to the roof of his mouth. He was easier to understand if he was a little drunk, so if we ever had to discuss anything pertinent to the business I always made sure we did it at the pub.

"Did I forget anyone?" I asked Page as we headed down the hall to the elevator.

"Are you kidding," she smirked. "You're like the office flu. You've managed to get to us all whether we like it or not."

Page tried to hide a smile, failing miserably, and I failed right alongside her. With that, we stepped into the elevator for the last time. The doors closed smoothly and quietly, as if they'd just been oiled, while the piped in music played, "*I'll be seeing you…*" How apropos.

"You know, I'm going to miss this place," I sighed.

"Well, truth be told, it might actually miss you, too, Stephen. But you didn't hear it from me."

Page gave me a long somber gaze, a rarity for her. I was going to miss her the most and I liked to think she might even miss me. I'd been a pain in the ass at times, and she let me know it in no uncertain terms. Still, we'd bonded from the get go - and during an air raid no less. How I was going to function without her was beyond me.

When the elevator stopped, I turned and looked Page square in the eye. "I'm going to be lost you know."

"Yes, I know," she said, straightening my tie. "But, you have my number so if you do get lost just give a ring and I'll tell you where to go."

I laughed to myself. I guess I deserved that - and needed it, too. I gave Page a big hug and a kiss on the cheek which she returned in earnest. We both had a little tear in our eye which we each tried to hide - failing again in misery.

"Please don't say goodbye," I urged, as we walked arm in arm to the awaiting limo. "It makes it sound so final."

"Good riddance, then," said Page, wiping the corner of her eye with her lace kerchief. "How's that for you?"

We laughed and hugged again, trying to keep our dignity intact. "Thank you, Page," I whispered. "For everything."

"Love to the women," she quivered, and took off without looking back.

Heather Trefethen

2

"Ladies and gentlemen, we'll be arriving at our destination in approximately twenty minutes. It's a beautiful day in Boston. Skies are clear and the current temperature is around eighty-five degrees.

As usual, I slept most of the way. The trip home had become so routine that I didn't even need someone to wake me before landing. The pilot's announcement would set off my internal alarm clock and I'd be up.

"Mr. Sheridan, would you please return your seat to its upright position?" smiled the stewardess. She was among the regulars, one of many I'd become acquainted with over the years. As a Pan Am hostess, she'd been trained in every aspect of proper etiquette, all while concealing her Liverpool accent. She'd slip now and then, though, which I always found a treat. I was definitely going to miss all those dialects.

"You wouldn't happen to have a cup of coffee left, would you?" I asked, hopeful. "I missed the cart earlier."

15

"We *are* just about on approach, sir," she replied, "but I'll see what I can do."

"I'd appreciate it."

I slid into my old brogues, which I'd stored under the seat in front of me along with my briefcase. They were the first pair of Florsheim's I'd ever owned, a high school graduation gift from my parents, and I perished the thought of ever giving them up. According to my father, an unofficial spokesman for the company, Florsheim brogues were the very best shoes made. It was said they could last a man a lifetime and I had been working on proving them right. I'd had them resoled at least a dozen times and was just about on my twentieth pair of laces, nursing the current which were about to give way at any moment.

The stewardess returned promptly with a piping hot cup of coffee. "Might be a little strong, sir," she frowned, dropping the formality ever so slightly. "We're down to the dregs, I'm afraid."

"No worries, Daphne," I smiled. "Any port in a storm."

"Right you are, sir," she winked.

As I stared out the window, Boston Harbor coming into view on our left, thoughts of Jayne and the girls filled my heart. I'd been dreaming of this day forever, it seemed. So many years had come and gone, some slow, some fast.

I missed my family terribly when I was away - Jayne especially. My loins ached every time I got off the phone with her. I kept telling myself I was doing all this for her and the girls: the big house, the nice car, the fancy gifts. I wondered sometimes in the back of my mind if we'd have been better off poor. Still, every day of it was another day closer to this, the day I'd be able to spend the rest of my life with my women.

I was hoping Penny wouldn't stand me up at the airport as the pilot announced our final approach. She'd always been very reliable, even during lobster season, which was practically year round for her and her lifelong fishing buddy.

Penny and her beau, Billy Monaghan, had been joined at the hip since he was six and she was four. The day they officially noticed each other Billy, his brother, Bobby, and father, Skip, were over to help put up a fence around the front and sides of our property. Jayne always wanted one of those white picket displays like she saw in the home and garden magazines and I was more than willing to provide it.

To keep little Billy from underfoot, Skip set him up with a makeshift workbench and had him cut up a bucket of summer-ripened bait for his lobster traps. Donna, about nine at the time, was always eager to stick her nose in everyone's business and Ruthie was never far behind. Just as they approached Billy's bench, the wind turned and sent the full aroma of his stock right up their nostrils. Donna immediately threw up, prompting Ruthie to scream in horror and faint. Penny casually appeared on the scene just afterward to see what all the panic was about.

"I suppose you're gonna puke and keel over, too," sneered Billy.

"It's just an old dead fish," Penny replied, picking one up to inspect it. "The man at the hardware store said the racks make good fertilizer."

Billy must have stared at her for a good solid minute. He was in love.

We had to circle a few times before landing, which made me all the more anxious. Apparently, an overzealous luggage handler turned quick and spilled his motorized cart right at our assigned gate and crews were scrambling to clear the baggage off the tarmac. I eyed Daphne, tapping my watch as if she could actually do something about it. She just shrugged, not even allowed to get up from her jump seat.

When we finally taxied up to our gate, another equally adept handler delayed our exit even further by failing to properly park the stairs at the plane's door. It was like watching a teenager repeatedly fail the parallel parking portion of his driving test - backing and filling, backing and filling, trying desperately to get it just right. After a good fifteen minutes of stair-jockeying, the door was finally opened and we were allowed to deplane. What a fiasco.

I feared the worst at customs, after all that, and I was right. Even though Page had prepared all the proper documentation necessary for my camera equipment, I still had to pay a boatload in duties and taxes. Plus, I didn't have enough U.S. currency on me since I failed to exchange what I had in Sterling before I left. Serves me right for not buying American. I thought I'd never get out of there.

"Stephen Sheridan, please pick up the nearest red courtesy telephone. Stephen Sheridan, please pick up the nearest red courtesy telephone."

"Great," I sighed. I'd just sat down next to my giant cart of luggage and cracked open a magazine when the page sounded. I'd hoped it wasn't Penny telling me she'd lost track of the time. If she was out fishing and they were biting, she may have.

"Stephen Maxwell Sheridan..."

"I know, I know..."

Just as I got up to go to the phone, my shoe lace broke. *What next*, I thought.

I was trying not to think of this whole experience as a bad omen, but it was hard to dismiss it. Sure I'd been accused of abandoning my family on more than one occasion. After all, I'd missed nearly every major event from births to graduations. In my own defense, all I wanted to do was provide.

"Stephen Sheridan, please pick up the nearest red courtesy telephone. Stephen Sheridan…"

"Yes, I know!" I said, tying my shoe as best I could with my knotted up leather lace.

As I got up to go to the red phone, not thirty feet from where I was sitting, a mob of people came clamouring out of nowhere and descended on the lobby just off the baggage claim area. It was like kicking an anthill, the mass of humanity multiplying by the second, scurrying this way and that. Suddenly, the red phone looked a mile away and not a promising soul in sight to watch my stuff, everyone in a mad dash to find their relatives, their luggage, or just the way out. I dreaded the thought of dragging the cart with me, but I just couldn't take a chance leaving it unattended.

"Stephen Sheridan. Paging, Mr. Sheridan."

"Yes, yes, yes," I mumbled, eyeing the overhead speaker as if the robotic voice on the other end could hear me. "I'm coming."

I grabbed hold of my cart and started weaving it through the crowd, the soles of my shoes slipping on the industrial carpet. It was all I could do to gain any sort of momentum, praying my other lace wouldn't give way – or worse, that some little kid wouldn't dart out on front of me. I finally skidded to a stop at the red phone as my name was again being paged.

"Stephen Sheridan, please pick up the nearest *white* courtesy telephone."

"What?!" I thought for sure she said red.

19

"Stephen Sheridan, please pick up the nearest *blue* courtesy telephone."

Suddenly, the scene playing out began to appear awfully suspicious. I scanned the lobby looking for the PA announcer's accomplice, who was likely to be wearing bell-bottom jeans and a *My Dad went to London and all he brought me back was this lousy t-shirt* t-shirt. I caught her out of the corner of my eye just as she was about to grab me from behind.

"Stephen Sheridan…"

"Damn you, Peanut. Was that you paging me all over creation?"

"You're not the only one with connections, you know," she smiled.

I hugged her tighter than ever and kissed her on the forehead. "I missed you, you little poop."

"Same here," she said, hugging me back with equal zeal.

When Penny was born, she was the smallest human being I'd ever seen, let alone held. At five weeks premature, she weighed in at a mere three pounds, seven ounces soaking wet. She was so tiny, and red as a little beet. They didn't even want us to see her at first and actually had the audacity to tell us, "Don't get too attached. She might not make it."

"She's a Sheridan," I said. "She'll pull through."

I can still see Donna peering through the big picture window, squinting and turning her nose up as only she could. "Is she a Martian?" she asked.

"No, honey," I replied.

"Then why is she in that little space ship?"

"That's an incubator," I explained, in terms I thought she would understand. "It keeps her warm and cozy so she can grow. Like a baby chick."

"Outlandish…" she sighed.

Grandma Clara, Jayne's mother, had assumed the dubious honor of teaching Donna, her *parvenu protégé*, a new adult word every week. It was usually some lofty, dignified-sounding adjective to help affirm her repugnance of the declining social norms. *Facetious, uncouth,* and *pedestrian* topped her hit-parade list. Though barely five, Donna was being groomed for something along the lines of Queen-Of-All-She-Surveys, and Clara was doing an *illustrious* job.

"She looks like a peanut," said Ruthie, her little nose pressed against the reinforced glass.

Though outlandish in itself, she was absolutely right. All three and a half pounds of baby lay there relaxed as can be nestled in a little shell of blankets. I took pictures of her that day, one of which still hangs in the neo-natal ward.

"So, how's your mother and sisters?" I asked.

"Oh, fine. Mom had some curtains to hang up or something and Donna's busy being Donna. Not sure about Ruth Anne. I hope you're not disappointed."

"No. Not much, anyway. I'd have only been disappointed if you'd all asked me to take a cab."

"We were thinking about it," joked Penny, jabbing me in the belly. "Hey, you're all skinny," she added, noting my trim physique and jabbing me again. "What happened to you?"

"Oh, you know. *Somebody* mentioned I was getting fat last time I was home so I thought I'd better do something about it before your mother started to complain."

"Are you kidding? She'll probably want to jump you right there in the kitchen the minute you walk in - gut or no gut."

That was the plan, although I really didn't want my daughter picking up on it. I'd been working out for the past

21

two months trying to rid myself of a nagging spare tire and apparently all my hard work paid off. If Penny noticed, Jayne surely would. Talk about wanting to provide!

"Did you go fishing today?" I said, knowing the answer but asking anyway.

"Naturally," she smiled. "I have a pulse, don't I?"

"Guess that's all it takes," I snuffed. "How'd you do?"

"Great. You should have seen this one we caught. It was enormous, the biggest one we've ever seen."

"Did you bring it home for dinner?" I asked, salivating at the mere thought of a fresh lobster and drawn butter.

"Naw," she sighed. "I threw him back. He'd have been tough anyway."

"What?!" I cried.

"Besides, it probably would have been bad Karma to harvest him. It would be like stealing away an old monk from the monastery."

"I'll bet that went over big with Billy."

"Oh, he was burnt to no end," she replied. "*We coulda gut ah' name in the paypa and ev'rything for bringin' in a lawbstah like that one, Pen,*" she giggled, over-exaggerating Billy's thick Downeast accent, "*with a pikcha to boot!*"

Billy had a thing about getting his name in the paper, as if it were some sort of right of passage. "He'll get over it," I said. "Maybe."

"I told him to save you a chick, though. He and his dad are still out so we'll see if he remembers."

A *chick* was what they called a small lobster, short for *chicken*, I believe. Penny and Billy usually didn't save them unless they were having a short haul. Though legal, they always felt they should give them a chance to get bigger so they'd fetch a better price. I didn't care either way. To me, lobster was lobster and I loved every mouthwatering bite.

Together we wrestled the luggage cart across the parking lot to Penny's little pink and pearl Nash Metropolitan. How we were going to get everything into that matchbox of a car was beyond me. "Good thing I installed that roof rack last summer," she said, not even batting an eye.

Had I a little forethought, I would have brought some spare stuff with me back in June when I was home for Penny's graduation. Hers was the only one I managed to attend, and only by the skin of my teeth. I wouldn't have been able to come at all, had it not been for a last minute cancellation by a new client. I was only home for six days then and it seemed a moot point at the time to bring anything extra.

Although it would have been far more practical, I was actually glad Penny hadn't brought Billy's smelly old fishing truck. Being mid-August, it would have been pretty ripe, not to mention the fact that every square inch of it was covered in rust. Every time he pulled into the driveway I felt I should go and get a tetanus shot.

There was so much I wanted to talk about and I hadn't a clue where to start. I yanked a couple of times on Penny's Class of '65 tassel dangling from the rear view thinking that might get the ball rolling, but she just looked at me and smiled, knowing I was in agony. "No, we haven't," she finally said as she paid the parking attendant.

"Who's 'we' and what haven't you done?" I replied, knowing full well what she meant. Penny was far from shy.

"Me and Billy, of course. I'm eighteen now - almost nineteen. I know it's killing you."

"Great." I couldn't believe my ears. I knew she'd hit the

legal age limit for just about everything, but she didn't have to wave it in my face. She was about as subtle as a freight train. "I thought you two were going to see other people," I added, the paternal panic setting in as I silently prayed for mercy.

"We did. Didn't you get my letters?" she insisted.

"Hail Mary full of Grace..." I muttered under my breath.

When Billy turned eighteen, Penny was only sixteen and it was rather obvious the two of them were pretty serious about one another. One evening before a big prom date, Skip and I both gave our young lovers "the Dad speech", assuring them both that they'd be in some serious hot water if they were caught being a little more *adult* than was allowed. Even though free love was the order of the day, we made it clear that the order did not apply to them.

"So how's Eddie doing these days?" I asked. He'd been the first guy Penny'd dated beyond Billy. As I recall, she liked him a lot and found him fairly interesting – so long as he stood at least 6 feet away. Apparently, Eddie had hygiene issues and had an aversion to toothpaste, claiming it gave him the dry-heaves. It lasted all of three dates before Penny broke it off.

"Okay, I'd say," she replied. "He and some girl from St. Xavier's are getting married in January."

"You're kidding. What, did he finally wise up and start using mouth wash?"

"No, but apparently it didn't matter," explained Penny. "Rex Greene told me the girl took a spill on the ice back when she was a junior and smacked her head just right so now she can't smell anything. They say it's reversible, but I hope for her sake it's not."

"Well, good for Eddie."

"Yeah. He's a nice guy."

"Unlike Palmer…"

"Please!" cried Penny. "Stupid bastard's still limping, by the way. Serves him right."

Palmer Winestock, Penny's fourth suitor, was a real charmer. He'd chased Donna back when she was a varsity cheerleader and he was a Pop Warner quarterback, but she gave him the cold shoulder. He tried his luck with Ruthie, too, and was in hot pursuit of *her* his entire sophomore year. She never caved either. Word on the street was Palmer wanted a piece of "Sheridan ass" and he wasn't going to stop until he got some. He'd felt he'd finally scored when, after some two-hundred phone calls, Penny finally agreed to a date.

On that fateful Saturday afternoon, the eager Winestock picked Penny up in his father's late-model convertible and headed up the street. They weren't a stone's throw down the road when the car suddenly skidded back and forth across the dirt lane and landed in the marsh just this side of Stinky Creek Bridge.

Penny was tiny, but you'd swear she had the strength of ten men, especially if she was pissed off. She'd grabbed Palmer's forearm and practically broke his wrist shoving his fist into his own face. Then she punched him with all her might where no man wants to be punched.

Jayne tore down the street to the accident scene, as did Dorothy Rand and a few other neighbors. Penny jumped out of the car and was tromping for home faster than an Olympic speed walker when Jayne called out in a panic. "Penny, honey, are you hurt?" she cried, as the two passed each other on the road.

"Son of a bitch put his hand up my skirt," yelled Penny on her way by, "and I won't tell you where it went from there!"

Jayne was mortified.

"So what about Billy's exploits?" I added. "You never told me how he fared."

Penny laughed to herself, her posture changing as she shifted her weight around in the pink leather seat.

"Well, I guess he went out with a couple of girls," she reported, "but none as nice as yours truly."

"You're a tough act to follow."

"True enough," she said, primping her hair and holding back a snicker as she buffed her close-trimmed nails on her make-believe lapel. "Of course there was that one girl. What was her name? Mary Ellen something?" Her gaze wandered, eyes everywhere except on the road, as if she were searching the air for the girl's name. "He said she was beautiful. Tall, curvy, huge boobs," she pantomimed. "It's all about the boobs, ya know."

"Not true, sweetheart," I argued. "Sometimes it's about the brains. Are you watching the road?"

Penny could tell a story better than any Technicolor cinematic presentation and I couldn't wait to hear how this one was going to end. All that was missing was the popcorn. Still, with all her animation, it amazed me how she could keep the car between the lines, let alone on the highway at all.

"Anyway, she gets him to take her to their family camp someplace way out of town. So you know she's got to have a little more in mind than just rowing around the lake."

"Go on," I urged.

"He said they got there and he wasn't really paying

attention to the signs and stuff while he was driving because she had her hands all over him, down his pants and everything, if you can imagine. He said it was a long drive into the woods and it was all he could do to keep it between the trees."

"And I'm sure young William was also doing all he could to fend her off," I glared.

"Yeah, you think?"

"Road!"

Penny also tended to talk with her hands when she got riled up and she was beginning to look like a semaphore signaler during rush hour.

"Anyway, they get out of the truck and he said you could hear some kind of party going on down by the lake. You know, lots of laughing and stuff. So she says to him, *why don't you go down to the dock while I get out of these clothes…* Well, he's thinking she's going to change into something else, right?"

"Okay…"

"Wrong!" she cried, laughing as she strangled the steering wheel. "Turns out the girl and her family were nudists."

"No! Get out!" Dear god. My eyes must have been as big around as saucers. It was an image I certainly didn't want to conjure, but I couldn't help but picture it and laugh. I pointed to the road, unable to actually give warning.

"I'm not kidding!" Penny crooned. "Billy gets down by the lake and here's the girl's Mom and Dad and a bunch of other people, all ages mind you, stark ravin' naked."

"Her parents!?" I cried, slapping myself squarely in the forehead.

"Right there in front of God and everybody!" she

shrieked.

I knew Billy wasn't exactly a prude, but he did still have a certain sense of innocence about him. The poor kid must have been terrified and I thought I would bust a gut.

"Billy said he ran like hell for the truck just as Mary Ellen, melons and all, comes waltzing out of the cabin in her birthday suit."

I didn't want to envision it, but oh, to have been a fly on the wall. "Road!" I managed between guffaws.

"He did admit to staring at her for a couple seconds and then realized what the hell he'd gotten himself into. I mean, any guy would kill to get a look at a naked girl in a magazine, but when it hits you right in the face like that…"

"Yeah. I guess that would be a little disarming," I agreed.

"Disarming? Something like that could knock a guy's whole artillery out of whack."

We laughed like fools for a good half hour. Poor Billy.

We must have been a sight heading down the highway with luggage and camera cases strapped to every square inch of vacillating vehicle. It's a wonder the car could even move under the sheer weight of it all. I nearly panicked, though, when a police officer stopped us about a mile before our exit. We'd been so engrossed in conversation we hadn't even given a thought to checking the cargo and I suddenly envisioned a trail of socks and underwear behind us.

Penny rolled down the window and checked her mirror. "Oh, good. It's Johnnie."

"You know this guy?"

I don't know why I was surprised. It seemed like Penny and Billy knew just about everyone from Maine to Maryland.

"Shouldn't you be heading north?" the officer began,

resting his hand on the roof as he peeked in the car.

"North?" Penny replied with eye-batting innocence.

"Yeah. You and Billy are both going to Salem State, right? I heard he found you guys a nice apartment."

"Ummm…"

"You *guys*!?" I spat. As in: the two of them? My stomach instantly flew into my throat. Talk about being blindsided. I could see Penny trying to flag Johnnie down before he said anything more.

"Dad's home," she announced, waving a thumb at me buried alive underneath duffles.

"Oh, shoot. I didn't see you there, sir. How ya' doin'? John Reagan. I went to school with Bill's brother, Bobby."

"Hi," I said making a poor attempt to wave.

"That's an awful lot of stuff for a quick summer vacation. You must be staying for *three* weeks this time," he chortled.

I swallowed hard, trying to get my stomach a little further south of my tonsils.

"He's actually home for good," Penny intervened. "He was nervous we might forget who he was so he retired early."

I'd gained more than a reputation over the years for not being around much and it hurt like hell to hear someone I didn't even know rub it in. Forget the fact that he'd just let the cat out of the bag regarding my daughter's future living arrangements. It made me wonder what else I didn't know.

"I hope I can do the same one of these days," said the friendly Officer Reagan. "Seems like every time I turn around my son's another foot taller. It gets so I'm afraid to blink."

"I know what you mean," I managed, glaring a hole in

the back of Penny's head.

"Okay if we head out?" she asked, a hint of nervous reservation in her voice.

"Sure. Just take it slow. I don't want to see your Dad's PJ's blowin' all over town later on."

"Thanks, Johnnie," Penny waved, and fired up the Nash.

No we haven't my ass.

3

The tomblike hush, accompanied by my death glare, didn't last long, although it seemed like an eternity. My daughter's performance was over and I was long out of virtual popcorn. I knew she was growing up, but I still felt somehow betrayed.

Penny, having nearly rubbed the high-density plastic completely off the steering wheel, finally gave in. "I know what you're thinking."

"Oh…"

"I'm eighteen now, you know. Almost nineteen."

"You do keep mentioning it," I pointed out, trying to shave away my five o'clock shadow with the palm of my hand.

"Look, here's the deal," she confessed.

"The *deal* was you were going to go to college," I pleaded. "*Then* we would talk about you getting married."

"And that's exactly what I'm going to do," she

31

explained. "We weren't even thinking about getting married until I at least got my degree."

"Have you thought about kids?"

"Yes. We have. We've got it all mapped out."

Good Lord. If I'd have had a rosary with me it would have gotten quite a workout. Frankly, I'd expected as much from Donna. She'd practically moved in with her now-fiancé, Brian, her junior year of college just to aggravate me. At least I didn't think I'd have to worry about kids right away with her, though. She found the whole idea of poopy diapers and formula *repugnant*, not to mention the *abhorrent* maternity fashions she'd be sentenced to wear.

Their sister, Ruthie, on the other hand, was another story. It was no mystery that her boyfriend was the sort of fellow you'd like to wait on the porch for with a loaded shotgun and it was said he liked to play the field now and then, no matter who he was going steady with. But, even though I constantly worried about her "getting into trouble", it was the abuse that alarmed me the most.

On more than one occasion, Jayne would call with a sugar-coated update: "Ruthie ran into another door". She hated hearing the truth. Rocking the suburban boat was not her style and she did everything she could to keep the Sheridan vessel well-polished and afloat. Still, I waited on pins and needles for the day the updates would change to: "Ruthie's pregnant." Or worse yet, "Ruthie's gone."

Penny nearly got herself arrested last summer after Chuck, the boyfriend, dumped Ruth off at the emergency room with a concussion, a broken rib and a bruised spleen. Mad as a hornet, Penny tore around town until she finally found the shithead, as she referred to him, drunk as a skunk in a Roxbury pub with another girl. As Penny put it: "I gave him a few words of wisdom then promptly dragged his sorry ass outside by the scruff of the neck and stuffed him headfirst into a garbage can right in front of a fucking cop!"

Enter Officer Reagan.

The complete story, including Ruthie's hospitalization, made it to page thirteen of the local paper - with a picture of Penny to boot. Billy had always hoped his girl would become famous for something a little more auspicious than a bar fight and threatened to boycott fishing for a week unless she promised to cool her jets. Jayne, too, was livid with both her daughters, always so worried what the neighbors would think. It was an embarrassment never to be outlived.

"So you're going to live in sin for the next four years, is *that* the deal?" It was hard to cool *my* jets at the thought of my youngest, barely of age, shacking up with some guy. Sure, it was Billy. Sure he was decent enough. Sure they were in love. And in a way that wasn't the problem - but in a way, it was. I simply wasn't ready for her to leave the nest.

Penny drove in silence, the steering wheel practically bending like a spoon under some psychokinetic spell.

"Well?" I reiterated.

"Awe, Jesus, Daddy," she cursed, smacking the steering wheel. "Please don't tell me you're going to start beating *that* dead Catholic horse. We *are* adults, for chrissakes."

Penny was not unlike Page in her mastery of the English language. She could put you in your place and leave you sitting there just long enough to realize she was right. My baby wasn't a baby anymore and I found myself beating my own dead soul trying to turn back the hands of time.

After an endless mile of almost unbearable silence, Penny pulled over onto one of the scenic turnouts en route to Quincy. Without a word, she got out, leaned on the signpost and gazed at the fishermen out in Dorchester Bay busy hauling in their traps. I joined her, quietly embracing the little girl who once fit in the crook of my arm, and kissed her on top of the head. Where had the time gone?

"I'm sorry," whispered Penny.

"Me, too."

"We're being smart about it," she quietly explained. "And careful. We have plans, you know."

"Yeah?"

"We're making a life together, Daddy. One step at a time."

"I hope you'll include me in that life - now and then," I said, hoping I hadn't lost her completely.

Penny turned, looked me square in the eye and smiled that little impish smile of hers. "We will," she grinned. "If you're in town."

We stood there for the longest time, just holding one another. She hugged me so tight around the middle I thought I'd pop a kidney. I know a father isn't supposed to play favourites but, secretly, I would always be partial to my Peanut.

"Let's go get something to eat," she said.

"Fish and Chips?" I drooled.

"I know just the place."

I couldn't help but smile. *Of course you do.*

We hopped in the car, cranked up the radio and headed off like two bats out of hell. The music was great, the company spectacular. I couldn't wait to see Jayne and the rest of my family.

"Say, you never did tell me how you got to be so trim," said Penny, trying to get things moving again.

I followed her lead agreeably. It was like penance seeing

any of my women sad, hurt, or anything other than fully content, even for the briefest of moments. Admittedly, we *had* beaten the dead horse enough for one day and it was time to get back to the business of goofing off.

"I've been playing football," I bragged. "You know, soccer. With the guys after work."

"No. You?" she grinned. "Out tearing around on a soccer field?" I thought Penny's eyes were going to bug right out of her head.

"Yes! Me! And they call it a pitch."

"Were they easy on you? I mean, really. I didn't think you had an athletic bone in your body," she squealed, trying not to laugh.

"Not a bit," I groaned. "In fact, I just healed up from a big bruise on the top of my thigh where a guy kicked me. Just missed my jewels."

"Boy, that would have pissed Mom off," she burst.

"How do you think *I* felt?" I howled. "I caught a cleat in the face once, too. Took five stitches right over my left eye. See?" I boasted, pointing out the battle scar that ran almost invisibly along my brow. "Five!"

"You animal!"

"Do you think your mother will notice it?" I asked, trying to comb my eyebrow back over the scar.

Penny laughed to herself. "Don't worry. She doesn't say so, but she still notices everything."

I missed Jaynie so much. I couldn't wait to see her again and hold her close to me. It had been too long this time. I'd only been able to stay home for two weeks this past Christmas instead of my usual four and those few days in June were nothing short of a blur. I thought it would kill me, but I knew I'd be back for good this time.

"You'll be happy to know you two will have the house to yourselves tonight."

"Oh?"

Penny said it like she was some Good Samaritan prison warden granting me a conjugal furlough. But, did I really want to know why?

"Donna and Brian are going to the Cape with some friends," she continued. "And Ruthie will be on the road singing, as usual. The shithead got her some gig on the weekends at Hampton Beach. I don't know where they stay, really. It's probably best that way."

"I see. And do I want to know where you'll be?"

"Probably not. But just in case you do, we're going up to campus to look at a couple of apartments. Billy's got one picked out, which I guess you already know, plus a backup in case I don't like it. We're staying over at a friend's."

She was right. I didn't want to know.

4

It was close to four in the afternoon when we finally arrived at the house. I could see Jayne's green Jag parked in the barn as we pulled up and my heart began to race.

"You're in luck," said Penny. "Mom's home."

We parked next to the house and started taking a quick inventory of the luggage to see if we'd lost anything along the way. Thankfully, everything had arrived in good order, thanks to Penny's luggage rack and fine knot work.

"I'll get the stuff unloaded if you want to go in and see her," she offered.

"You sure?"

"I know you're dying." Penny winked. She knew way too much for a girl her age.

I grabbed what I could carry and headed in the side door. Not seeing - or hearing - a living soul, I dropped my bags in the empty kitchen and rushed straight for the bedroom, more than eager to be reunited for good with my wife.

"Honey!? I'm home!"

I spotted Jayne dressed in a black petticoat sitting at her dressing table brushing her radiant auburn hair. Her black party dress hung on the closet door, matching shoes on the floor below. Pearls were laid out next to the jewelry box on top of the bureau. I captured a mental photo of the scene, wanting to etch it permanently in my brain. She was beauty personified.

"Should I get out my tux?"

Jayne stopped brushing her hair and slowly turned. It was like a movie, her gaze finally meeting mine. I walked slowly over to her as she rose from her seat. She was surely something to behold. We stopped, silent, our bodies barely apart. "God, I've missed you," I whispered, and pulled her close.

"Damn you, Steve Sheridan," she whispered back. "Why did you have to be so good looking?"

"It's my curse," I replied.

"It makes it so much harder to be mad at you," she said as I buried my nose in the nape of her neck.

Each time I came home, it felt like a honeymoon, a virgin discovery of each other all over again. Every curve of my Jayne was like a dream, my hands wanting to run along every inch of her. In my eyes, she hadn't aged a minute since the day we met.

"Don't be mad this time, Jaynie," I quietly begged, kissing her full, ruby lips. "I love you so much. God, I've missed you."

I eased her onto the bed and began kissing her everywhere, thanking God above that all she'd managed to don so far was that wonderful silky black slip. Jayne slowly loosened my tie and just started on my shirt when all of a sudden a crash reverberated through the kitchen and down the hall.

"Dad? Dad!? Where do you want this trunk?"

"Damn kids," I chuckled. Jayne smiled and ran her hand along my bristled cheek. "You think she'll go away," I continued, all the while kissing her, touching her, wanting for all the world to make love to her that very moment.

"Not a chance," sighed Jayne, defeated.

"Dad!? Hello!?"

Penny had quickly and silently deposited every scrap of cargo into the kitchen; saving the steamer trunk for last since crashing it onto the hardwood floor would make the loudest, most *interruptive* explosion on record. An atomic bomb would have paled in comparison. In fear of the floor, I quickly responded, buttoning up my shirt as I flew down the hall leaving poor Jayne behind, aroused and yes, abandoned.

"Boy, you guys don't waste any time," Penny chided.

"Did you have to put a hole in your mother's kitchen floor?" I scolded, pointing out the steamer.

"I just didn't want you to get *too* involved before Billy got here. He wanted to say 'hi'."

"He could have left a note."

As if on cue, two quick knocks signaled Billy's arrival. He was such a familiar face around the house that he didn't even wait for someone to answer the door. He just knocked and walked right in.

"There he is," he shouted, giving me a good, firm handshake.

"Hi, Billy. Nice to see you."

"Same here. Say, you're lookin' pretty good."

"He's a soccer player now," teased Penny. "Can you

believe that? Took a cleat to the eye, even. Show him, Dad."

Embarrassed, I pointed out my scar just as Jayne, now wearing her black party dress and clasping on her pearls, entered the kitchen. "What happened?" she asked, sounding alarmed. She looked stunning, but I sure wished she'd have waited for me in just the slip.

"Nothing much," I assured. "I'll tell you about it later."

"Wow, Mom. Nice dress," said Penny.

"You look wicked nice, Mrs. Sheridan. Night on the town?" asked Billy.

"Something like that," she replied, a hint of none-of-your-business in her voice.

A pregnant pause overtook the room. Finally, Penny took the hint. "We should probably get going. Don't you think, hon?" she said, taking Billy by the arm.

"Yeah, right. That lady was going to be there to show us the place at around five."

"Don't forget. I can get you any fabric you like for curtains and bedspreads," added Jayne as she headed back down the hall for the bedroom.

Apparently, I *was* the very last to know.

Penny gave me a big hug and a kiss and headed out the door. She hated saying goodbye, no matter how long I was home for, and always just left it at that.

Billy shook my hand again. It could have just been a case of parental paranoia, but it seemed to me he was trying extra hard to get on my good side. "Have a good time tonight, sir," he smiled.

"We will. And by the way," I added, trying my best to inflict pain with my firmest, most unrelenting Dad-grip, "I know you two are thick as thieves, but I'd appreciate it if you kept your fly zipped when it comes to my daughter."

Billy looked me square in the eye, his grip equal to mine. In fact, I knew he could have easily dropped me to my knees. I just wanted to see if he had enough respect for me not to.

"She wouldn't have it any other way, sir," he replied.

He smiled and gave me an assuring nod. If he was looking for my blessing, he wasn't going to get it. Not tonight. I knew I was being hard on the both of them, but I just wanted to hang onto the thought of my daughter being young for just a little while longer.

No sooner had the door closed behind them when Jayne was back in the kitchen. She set her matching handbag and wrap down on the counter, avoiding my gaze. It felt almost awkward and I had no idea why. We usually fought for the first five minutes I was home on holiday and spent the rest of the time making up. I still didn't get it, but something told me this wasn't going to be a pretend kind of fight.

"I realize I've only been home for a couple of minutes, but have I done something wrong?"

"Oh, Steve," she began as she fiddled with her earrings. "I've been dreading this moment."

"You're dreading having me home?"

"It's just bad timing. That's all."

"But we've been planning this forever," I replied, taking her hand in mine, hoping she was just setting me up for a good make-up session later.

"I know. It's not that. It's…" Jayne sighed, a great deal of hesitation in her voice.

"It's what?"

"I have to ask you not to come tonight."

"What do you mean? Where are you going?" Now I

41

was beginning to panic. I was already losing my baby. Now Jayne? I have to confess, I liked our old fights better. They were simple, meant to make me feel bad for being away so long. This, however, had complicated written all over it.

"Reed and I have a function. They call it networking," she explained. "It's for the business."

"Why didn't you tell me before? Hell, Penny didn't even say anything."

"Penny didn't know," she claimed. "I just didn't want you jumping to conclusions about Reed. Besides, I thought you'd be upset as it is with me continuing the business. We're gaining strength, but it's still a man's world."

Good heavens. At some point my wife had become a feminist and I hadn't even noticed. I was pretty sure my daughters had joined the movement, but not Jayne. She'd been the proverbial church-going, PTA-attending, June Cleaver wannabe right down to her apron and sensible pumps. I'd thought the decorating business was meant to be a hobby for her, something to keep her busy while I was away. I knew she was doing well, but frankly I thought she'd let it go after I got home. Never before had I felt so out of touch.

"So you don't want me to be around, is that what you're saying?"

"It's not that I don't want you to be around," she assured. "It's just that all my attention is going to be focused on building my client base. If you're there, it will take all the attention away from my objective."

It was a classic text-book answer, so much so that I started wondering if I should be checking for wires in the back of her head. Had she been abducted by aliens? Because this certainly wasn't the Jayne I knew. I knew I shouldn't have read all those sci-fi comics as a kid.

"Honey, please don't be offended," she urged as I began pacing around the kitchen hoping our five minute fight was coming to a close. "It's just business."

"Oh, I'm not offended," I said, trying to act as if it were all pretend. "Maybe a little slighted. Definitely confused."

"I'm sorry…"

"I mean, here I am, finally able to spend the rest of my life with my loving wife, only to find that she'd rather be with another man."

"Reed is my business partner, Steve. That's all. There's nothing between us beyond that."

I sidled up next to her and kissed her on the ear. "Should I go put on a turtleneck?"

"Steve, he's married," she sighed, easing away from me so she could put on her other earring. "They don't exactly call it that, but they might as well."

"So are you, Jaynie. And they *do* call it that."

"His wife's name is Bob."

"I beg your pardon."

"You heard me."

It was as if I'd been struck by lightening. Bob? Penny had mentioned he was a little light in the loafers, but…

"Steve, this is important to me. Please understand."

Bob… I just stared at her, paralyzed. A moment ago, I was picturing my wife in the arms of a young stud, his well-toned arms busting out of his shirtsleeves, face buried in her bosom. The image was nothing short of racy. Now, I didn't know what to picture. Bob…

Jayne walked slowly over and put her arms round me. When it came to arguing with her, it didn't take much to calm me down. All she had to do was look at me a certain way and I'd melt right into the floor, forgetting what all the fuss was about.

"Please don't tell me I've lost you," I whispered, putting a hand on each soft hip.

She looked me in the eye, her face devoid of emotion. "I hope you're going to be okay with this."

"It doesn't sound like I really have a choice."

She kissed me softly on the cheek, not giving in completely, as if teasing me and letting me know in her own special way there'd be more where that came from later. I didn't want to let go of her.

"I have to go," she said finally, before I messed up her hair and make-up. "I'll be back around ten."

"I'll be waiting."

She smiled, her gaze dissolving me into the parquet, and slowly walked out the door. She, too, hated to say goodbye.

5

While Jayne was at her soirée with Reed, I began the monumental task of putting away my plethora of belongings. I considered saving the camera equipment for last, especially since I didn't as yet have a dedicated room for it. I'd often thought of turning the attic into a studio and considered it still. I was sure Jayne wouldn't mind, so long as I left plenty of room for the Christmas decorations and the girl's baby furniture and Clara's antique rocking chair and the trio of tricycles and what ever else we couldn't possibly part with.

My back was still a little out of whack from the flight, but nonetheless I thought I'd start on the steamer trunk. I knew my turtlenecks were in there and, even though it was mid-August, I wanted to be sure to have one on when Jayne returned.

Each time I came home on holiday, Jayne would play hard to get. She'd pretend to be mad at me, giving me that "you're in the doghouse, mister" look along with the silent treatment. It would all end when I walked back in the room wearing a turtleneck. I don't know what it is, but that woman has a thing about a guy in a turtleneck, especially if that guy is me. I own one in every colour.

Jayne asked for a laundry list of my clothes before I left London so she could map out the closets and bureaus. Usually, all I had was a single suitcase that I lived out of during my entire two to four week stay. This, however, was going to be different and she wanted to be prepared right down to my skivvies.

Jayne had placed a little map inside each dresser drawer noting just what went where and how it should be folded, not unlike the little maps you get in candy boxes to help you tell the varieties of the chocolates. I found it a bit ridiculous at first, since it looked like I had ten pounds of crap and only a five pound dresser drawer to hold it all. But once I got going, following her instructions to the letter, I could see that my wife had far more talent than I'd given her credit for. She was good.

After about an hour and a half of unpacking and refolding, I was due for a cold drink. True to form, Jayne had a six pack of my favourite lager chilling in the fridge and I popped one open just as Skip came by, rapping on the door to announce himself.

"Hey, neighbor," I smiled, waving him in as I grabbed another beer. "Care to join me for a cold one?"

"Don't mind if I do," he replied, pulling the cap off with his bare hand. Talk about tough as nails.

"I hear the kids are planning on sharing an apartment up at school."

"Ayuh," he nodded, his Downeast accent twice as thick as Billy's. "Next thing you know, they'll be pickin' out china patt'ns."

"God save us," we toasted.

I could tell Skip wasn't looking forward to Billy moving out on a permanent basis any more than I wanted Penny to. It was bad enough having them gone during the school year, but for good was really going to smart.

"At least I know your girl will be keepin' an eye on my boy," sighed Skip, drawing a hefty mouthful of lager.

"And he, her," I added.

With the exception of his boat, Billy was all Skip had left in the world. Grace, his wife, had been stricken with cancer and died about 12 years ago when little Billy was only eight. His son, Bobby, much older and in the Navy at the time, was discharged from duty and sent home to help his father take care of Billy and the house.

A year after they lost Grace, tragedy again struck the Monaghan's when Bobby, just nineteen at the time, was tossed overboard by a rogue wave while pulling traps. He was rescued by the Coast Guard and died not ten minutes after arriving at the hospital. Skip cried for a month and Billy hardly spoke for a year, not even to Penny. At Christmas time, Billy asked Santa for nothing more than to have his mother and brother back. He hasn't believed in Santa since.

Skip forever feared losing young Billy, too, since he'd been born with a common, yet sometimes fatal congenital heart defect. When he was two years old, the doctors recommended a delicate ground-breaking surgery, but Gracie flat-out refused, citing his chances of survival without it far outweighed the risks. "If he's going to die young, let him go out living," she contested. She was always sending him out to play.

It was nice having some neighborly company, but I

knew I needed to get the place cleaned up before Jaynie got home. So did Skip. Knowing Jayne's passion for a well-kept kitchen as well as I did, he polished off his beer and politely excused himself, reminding me that I always had an open invitation to go fishing whenever I felt the urge. I assured him I'd be taking him up on the offer very soon.

After Skip left, I grabbed another beer and headed upstairs to see what sort of trouble I could get myself into. I'd nested what I could of my luggage so it wouldn't take up so much room once I hauled it up there - tomorrow - and mentally planned for the darkroom. I was hoping that Jayne had made little maps for my equipment, too, like she had for my clothes. At least I didn't bring back any furniture.

As I stepped into the attic, a thousand memories came sailing back to me. It was like *This Is Your Life* with all the trimmings. Although it was less crowded than I had envisioned, there was still so much to take in.

The crib, bassinet and playpen lined the far wall, their rails gathering cobwebs and dust. I could picture each one of my girls in them, their little smiling faces, and their laughs. God, I loved their laughs. I remember being so grateful I was able to be there with each one of them when they took their first steps. It was like they were saving the moment just for me.

The big boxes of Christmas ornaments, all two dozen of them, were tucked neatly underneath and around and on top of the baby furniture. I remember when the girls were little they couldn't wait for the Christmas tree vendors to roll into town. The five of us would go out for fish-n-chips and then head over to pick out the best tree on the lot. We'd all stay up until midnight drinking hot chocolate and stringing popcorn and decorating until we passed out. It was wondrous.

The tricycles, also gathering dust, were parked in a neat row between the two dormer windows that overlooked the beach. Donna's was princess pink, with sparkly pink streamers stuck on the ends of the handle grips and a shiny chrome bell. The seat was real pink leather, the tires white-walled. She asked me to wax it every weekend, just like the car. It looked like new.

Ruthie's trike was purple metallic with silver streamers and a silver glitter seat. It had a silver basket for her dolly and a little toy license plate on the back with her name on it. Ruthie took her dolly everywhere in her basket until the day Donna told her she looked *absurd*. Ruthie, knowing that most of Donna's big-people words meant something bad, retired the tricycle that same day and asked for a proper pram instead.

Penny had your basic run-of-the-mill red Radio Flyer. No streamers or baskets for her, though. She wanted something built for speed. Unlike Donna and Ruthie's cycles, Penny's looked like it had been through the war. She and Billy, by then on a two wheeler, would race like bandits down the lane and try and make the corner into the driveway at top speed, wiping out most of the time. They'd usually land in the grass and laugh like crazy, having absolutely no sense of their mortality. Thank goodness for double-knee dungarees and Band-Aids.

Beneath one of the dormer windows that faced the ocean was a large cedar chest that housed our afghans and quilts. When Penny was little, she used to sneak up to the attic at night and sleep on top of the chest under the open window, claiming the salt air was good for her *constitution*, a word she learned from Donna. She'd shared a room with

Ruthie on the second floor that faced the road and even though you could smell the ocean from a good half mile in *any* direction, it just wasn't the same as getting a direct hit. Plus, she claimed Ruthie snored.

Jayne didn't realize at first that Penny was leaving her room to sleep elsewhere, taking it for granted that once the lights went out that was it. One night, after hearing a strange noise upstairs, Jayne went to check on the girls, thinking one of them had gotten up to use the bathroom. Donna and Ruthie were accounted for, but Penny was no where to be found and poor Jayne about had a fit.

She called the Monaghan's, called the police, even called me in London. A grueling hour and a half later, they found the Peanut in the attic sound asleep in a cocoon of blankets on top of the cedar chest.

"Weren't you afraid of bats?" I later asked her.

"Oh, no," she replied. "Bats are good. They eat the mosquitoes."

The next day, Jayne got to work moving Penny to the spare bedroom that faced the ocean. She still slept with the window open but, as Jayne put it, "at least she won't be rooming with the bats." To this day, she has the best constitution of all.

The kitchen door slammed, signaling another arrival. I hoped it was my wife, home early from her party. "Jaynie?" I cried as I flew down the attic stairs.

"No," Donna replied, pounding up to her room.

"Oh, hi, honey," I said, practically chasing her down the hall. "I didn't expect you."

"What a day," she managed, pissed off as usual. She threw a large duffle onto her bed and sighed heavily, jabbing her fists onto her hips as she finally acknowledged me. It was as if I'd never been gone. "I'm telling you. Some people," she spat. So much for hello.

"I thought Penny said you and Brian were going to the Cape this weekend."

"We were!"

She threw open the closet doors and grabbed out a pair of dressy jeans, a fresh blouse, some fashionable shoes and a garment bag. Exasperated to the max, she threw the lot on the bed and began packing. I wasn't quite sure why whatever she already had in her duffle wasn't good enough, but I learned pretty early on never to question Donna when it came to clothes. It was just too touchy a subject.

"So what happened?" I asked, lounging on the bed next to the duffle.

"A group of us were supposed to go over and stay at Nick's family cottage. You know Nick, right?"

"No, but go on." I didn't know any of Donna's friends, except Brian. She hardly wrote or phoned and when she did it was always to ask for money. Most of the time I could manage to figure out some sort of connection as to who was who by way of the conversation, but I could tell this wasn't going to be one of those times.

"We arrive there and the kitchen is nothing more than a camp stove and some poor excuse for a refrigerator not even fit for a dormitory room."

"No!" I gasped, trying not to laugh.

"Honestly, how on earth did they expect us to cook a decent meal for eight people with that kind of accommodation?"

"You cook?" I chided, desperately wiping the grin off my face.

"Oh, and it gets better," she continued, completely missing the sarcasm. "On top of all that, it's a one bedroom – ONE! - with pull-out couches and fold-up cots. I mean really. Have these people no decency?"

"How barbaric," I teased.

"I'm not even going to mention the lavatory."

"So you came home immediately, I see."

"What else could I do? I certainly couldn't stay. Not under those conditions," she argued, tossing some hosiery in her bag. "Outdoor shower. Really!"

"So, do you want to go do something? Go to the movies maybe?" I asked. I knew I was pushing it, especially since she was already packing her bags for other parts unknown.

"I can't. We're going clubbing," she said, punctuating her sentence with a zip of the garment bag as a car horn blared.

"When will you be back? Should I wait up?" I asked, following her down the stairs to the kitchen.

"I'm afraid you'd be waiting a long time. I'm staying at Brian's most of the time now. I just keep some of my clothes here because the closets at the apartment are absolutely appalling. In fact, I need to speak to you about that, but not right now. I've got to run." A quick kiss on the cheek and she was out the door. No formal goodbye, though. At least she spoke to me - for quite a while, too - and it wasn't about money. Not directly, anyway.

I looked around the kitchen at all the camera cases and boxes marked "Darkroom". If I'd been smart, I'd have had Penny leave everything in the garage, but my mind was clouded with thoughts of Jayne. I checked my watch for the hundredth time thinking it must be getting late by now, but it was all for naught. Only 8pm and a hundred hours to go until I'd see my love again.

My stomach began to growl and I realized I hadn't eaten much that day except for a small fish and chips basket earlier in the afternoon. Soup was my staple and Jayne always kept at least a case-worth stocked in the pantry for me. I opened the pantry door and found a note attached to a can of tomato:

> *There's a surprise for you in the garage.*
> *Love, Penny and Billy.*

When it came to Penny and Billy, a "surprise" could mean anything from a bushel of apples to a herd of zebra. In any event, I was anxious to see just what it was so I got my soup going on the stove and headed for the barn.

I'd noticed before that the side door, just off the kitchen porch, had been replaced, but I hoped that wasn't it. It was a welcome sight, though, since the other had been in a state of disrepair for a good two years. I was pretty handy around the house, but I couldn't hang a door to save my life. Skip, on the other hand, could hang one in his sleep and had completed the job about a month ago in exchange for the use of our lawnmower. I kicked myself for forgetting to thank him.

As I cautiously entered the barn, I saw to my delight that a small, narrow room had been cleverly built under the extra-wide staircase that led to the loft. I was so fixated on seeing Jayne, that I hadn't even noticed it when Penny and I had arrived home earlier. Upon closer inspection, I found a handsome brass plaque was affixed to the raised panel entry door: "Sheridan Photographic Studios – Chicago, Seattle,

Montreal, London, Quincy". Above the door was a big red light.

I walked into what was apparently my new, permanent darkroom and was immediately struck by a poster-sized blow-up of yours truly in front of the London bomb shelter I hid in when I first crossed the pond back in 1945. The cardboard box with the gas mask that Page had given me that day hung beside it. She was Penny's confidant, too, and I could see the two had been long-conspiring.

Inside the well-lit room, shelves had been built and racks for equipment set up. In the corner sat a small refrigerator for film and a little stereo. Next to it, a comfortable director's chair with "Steve" embroidered on the canvas back. It was like I'd dreamed it.

A lengthy counter, with room for my enlarger and plenty of developing trays, had been built as well with storage for chemicals underneath. There was even a working sink. A low-wattage red bulb hung above with an extra switch on the wall marked: "Outside Light". I switched it on and walked back out the door. Sure enough, they'd thought of everything.

Back inside my little haven, I really began taking it all in. I was so happy I could have cried. I must have done something right to have deserved all this, although I couldn't have imagined what. I could tell I'd be spending a lot of time in here.

I opened the little refrigerator door and found another six pack of my favourite beer and an envelope. Inside was a generous gift certificate to the local photography store and a note:

Get lost! Love, Page.

This was definitely a conspiracy.

Page had always been very benevolent when it came to gift giving, especially around the holidays, but went about it in a very quiet almost mysterious way. Somehow she always knew what everyone secretly wanted but was afraid to ask for - like the macho doorman that wanted a *Ladies' Home Journal* cookbook, or the cleaning woman that wanted a Mrs. Beasley doll. On Christmas Eve, packages would magically appear on people's desks, at their work stations or in their mail slots, all simply marked, "Merry Christmas." Whenever questioned, Page always disavowed any knowledge of how they got there.

Each year, I gave Page and her husband, Cedric, a little gift from Jayne and me. It was often something like theatre tickets to a popular show or a gift certificate to a fancy restaurant. We didn't want to be too generous for fear it would embarrass Page, but we did want them to have a good time since they rarely spent money on themselves.

Embarrassed or not, I'd decided before I left London that I would be a Santa to Page and make it a "Christmas in August". I knew she had a secret wish that she rarely shared with others and I wanted more than anything to be able to grant it.

Page had always spoken tongue-in-cheek about "basking bare-breasted on the beaches of Barcelona", but I could tell in a way she meant it for real. So, with Jayne's blessing, I booked a two week holiday for she and Cedric at a five star Spanish resort - airline tickets, hotel room, meals, everything included. I'd heard the place was top notch in every way. Cedric could go golfing, his favourite past time, and Page could bask bare-breasted if she felt the urge. It would be a trip well-deserved for both of them.

Fearing that Page would refuse the gift, I put the tickets, vouchers and itineraries in a lock box at Heathrow and mailed her the key on the way to my gate. She'd been so good to me and my family over the years, even keeping me stocked with Campbell's soup.

"Shit, my soup," I gasped, making a mad dash for the house.

6

I rushed in the kitchen door, the smell of burnt tomato hitting me squarely. My soup had boiled over, but thankfully not much. I thought I could at least salvage a bowlful for my dinner. I switched off the stove, put the pan on a trivet, and grabbed some bread and cheese.

I'd done such a swell job simmering my soup I figured I'd better not even try to grill a sandwich for fear the fire department might have to get involved. Besides, Jayne had bought some good sourdough and an extra-sharp cheddar. I knew it would be delicious no matter what.

I dipped the corner of my sandwich into the pan of soup, letting it sit there just long enough to soften the cheese. Boy, it tasted good. The food in England wasn't bad, but it just wasn't the same as home. The phone rang just as I was about to savour another bite.

"Hello?" I impolitely chewed. It was Jaynie.

It was so good to hear her voice. I was hoping she'd

called to say she'd be right home, but it was not to be the case.

"I just wanted to make sure you found something to eat," she said, the noise of the party practically drowning her out.

"I'm having some soup and a half a sandwich right now, as a matter of fact. How's the party?"

"It's really going well, Steve," she touted. "The Groverton's are here. I think we're going to win the bid for their remodel. You remember the Groverton's, don't you?"

"Rich bastards that live out on the point? Yes, I remember them."

The Groverton's, poster-people for Busy Body Syndrome, had tried to talk Jayne and me out of buying our house when we were first looking to move to Quincy. They'd hinted, and not very subtly, that we weren't quite right for their developing seaside neighborhood. It seems, in fact, nobody was. "The suburbs outside Roxbury might be more to your liking," I believe is how they put it. We loved the house, the view, the location. It was perfect. One look from Jayne and I knew that she was never going to back down. Neither was I. They could hate us all they wanted, but we were staying.

"They make me so nervous, though," Jayne said in a loud whisper. "He's always saying 'super'."

The Groverton's especially detested the Monaghan's, since they'd come from a long line of fishermen instead of bankers and lived mostly off the land and sea instead of trust funds. They weren't discrete about their distaste either and made the mistake of trying to embarrass Grace one afternoon in the grocery store when she needed to buy some staples on credit. Grace, never one to mince words, let them have it with a monologue that would have made a pirate blush. It was super!

Even though I wanted Jayne home instead of pressing the flesh at some "networking" party, I felt I should be as supportive as possible, especially since this might very well be her swan song. The Groverton's played hardball and I thought she should know from me she had the go-ahead signal to steal.

"So charge them double for your trouble," I said. "They won't know the difference and they'll be too proud to back out."

"It's just that they can be so condescending," she added.

Poor Jaynie. She could do anything and just needed someone to remind her of it now and again. As I tried to think of exactly the right thing to say, Page leapt to mind. She'd given a brief, yet powerful message to our first and only female architect the day she was asked to design an office building and I always kept it in the back of my mind for just such an occasion.

"Don't let them get to you, sweetheart," I began. "Just relax and be confident knowing that more often than not the best man for the job is very often a woman. And that woman is you."

"Thank you, Steve," she sighed. "You always know just what to say."

"No I don't. I just got lucky this time." We both laughed a little to ourselves. I missed her so. "What time will you be home?" I asked, hoping it would be sooner rather than later.

"I'm not sure. I know you must be exhausted. Do you mind waiting up?"

"Oh, I'll be up. If I have to sit on a bed of nails with toothpicks in my eyelids, I'll be up." I couldn't wait to see her and hold her in my arms.

As soon as I finished my soup, I took a quick shower and changed into my jeans and a black turtleneck, Jayne's favourite. I now knew for sure that Donna wouldn't be back to surprise us later on and Ruthie was away all night on a singing gig. Penny, though she ought to be home, wouldn't dare pop in. She was an imp to the *nth* degree, but she would never spoil a night for Jayne and me. As Donna would say, it would simply be *gauche*.

I decided to pass the time by moving my camera equipment from the kitchen to my new darkroom out in the barn. I was grateful I wouldn't have to lug the lot up two flights of stairs to the attic, and doubly grateful I wouldn't have to deal with the occasional bat. We'd still get them once in a while and Jayne would have to call on Skip and Billy if I wasn't home to chase the little buggers out. I hated bats.

Thankfully, it was cool for a summer night so I knew I wouldn't sweat much in my turtleneck, if at all. The long sleeves would come in handy for keeping the mosquitoes at bay, too. I hated them almost as much as I hated bats.

Mosquitoes were notorious in this area and legend had it that two of them could carry a grown man away by the shoulders and drain him dry within minutes. Legend not withstanding, you learned quite quickly not to dawdle with the door open at night because if you did one of those little bastards would wait until you just about fell asleep and then buzz your ear all night until you nearly went insane. I hated mosquitoes.

Surprisingly enough, it only took me an hour or so to get all my cases into the barn and somewhat organized for placement in the darkroom. It was good to get everything out of the house so it wouldn't be in the way when Jayne came home. She was pretty particular about her kitchen. Plus, we had free reign of the house for the evening and I didn't want anything standing in our way.

I cracked open another cold one and began unpacking my equipment, arranging the shelves as best I could by format. I had a couple of 35mm setups; plus several large format cameras, antiques I'd collected over the years. They were my favourites for photographing architectural subjects. Doing everything "old school" was what made it an art form for me. I had a fairly outdated enlarger, too, that was set up to accommodate any sized negative and included a variety of filters to adjust contrast. Nothing was high-tech, but it was all reliable.

Billie Holiday whispered in the background while I sorted through film canisters and file boxes of catalogued negatives. It seemed kind of odd having the modern stereo in my little studio full of antiquities, but I enjoyed it just the same. It helped pass the time which, by now, was fast approaching eleven. Just then, I heard the garage door magically open, one of Penny's inventions, followed by the sound of an entering vehicle - Jaynie's Jag.

I shut off the stereo and made a quick exit out of the darkroom, shutting off the lights on my way out. Jayne cut the engine and got out of the car slowly, her eyes locked on mine - or should I say my turtleneck. I sidled up next to her, running my hand along the small of her back, and pulled her close.

"Hi," I whispered.

"Hi," she whispered back, running her hand along my chest, then up and around my neck. "Nice turtleneck."

"Thanks. How was your evening?"

"Productive. Yours?"

"Productive. I've been setting up the darkroom. Would you like to see?"

"How about tomorrow," she said, resting her tired head on my shoulder. "I could really use a glass of wine."

"It's chilling as we speak."

We sauntered into the kitchen, both too tired at this point to do much of anything, but we tried. I poured a couple of healthy glasses of Chardonnay while Jayne explored my turtleneck. I raised a toast to her and her successful evening, holding her close to me.

"To Mrs. Sheridan," I announced, "Interior decorator to the gods."

"To Mr. Sheridan," she countered, "retired at last."

The wine was perfect. It had a smooth finish and I envisioned the evening having an equally elegant ending.

I found the hidden zipper in the back of Jayne's dress and eased it down over her spine while she found her way into my button-fly jeans. Her dress came off easy, flowing onto the floor around her ankles like a silky shadow. We both kicked off our shoes and headed for the living room, dropping a shirt here, a stocking there. The couch was calling.

7

I stirred to the sound of what I thought was the kitchen door closing. No other sound followed. Jayne and I lay spooned together on the living room floor in front of the fireplace. She felt so good, so warm, so close. I could feel her heart beating. The throw blanket from the couch barely covered us and we were wearing nothing but a couple of smiles. It had certainly been a while since we'd had a night like that.

I was just about to fall back asleep, gently cupping my hand over Jaynie's breast, when I heard the unexpected sound of a truck clutch-starting and heading down the lane. Suddenly, a horrifying thought raced through my mind. It was one of those *oh shit* moments you get when you're not really sure if something actually happened, but you know if it did you'll really wish it hadn't.

"Good morning," whispered Jayne, breaking me out of my panic.

"Hi," I whispered back, calming. "Did you hear that? Before, I mean."

"Hear what?" she asked, rolling over to face me.

"I thought I heard the door."

"It was probably just the newspaper."

Of course that didn't explain the truck, which had an awfully familiar engine growl.

"Last night was nice," continued Jayne, running her fingers through my thinning hair.

"It certainly was," I smiled, and forgot all about the truck.

Jayne and I made love again in front of the dormant fireplace for an entire blissful hour completely undisturbed by children, phones, or nosy neighbors. It was beautiful. However, we did know to quit while we were ahead and decided that since Penny was such an early riser and would probably be crashing in the kitchen door at any moment, we'd better get our blissfully naked selves out of the living room and into some clothes.

We quickly showered and dressed and fooled around for a little while longer before actually facing the day. You'd have thought we were a couple of newlyweds. We were usually pretty intimate the first few days I was home on holiday, but somehow this was different. I was going to be home for good and it really was cause for celebration.

Jayne made a pot of fresh coffee while I picked up the living room and kitchen, making sure we hadn't left behind any evidence of our little tryst. We didn't think we had to worry about Donna or Ruthie giving us hell. If they were to find a sock stuffed in the couch cushions they'd just say I was a *typically undomesticated male*. Penny, on the other hand, could be the devil-incarnate.

"We didn't really talk much about your party last night," I mentioned, grabbing up Jayne's slip draped over the coffee table.

"It was a nice turnout," she replied. "I think we may have at least three new clients."

"Did Reed behave himself?"

"Oh, Stephen, of course he did," as if it were a completely absurd question.

"Just checking," I defended. "I don't want some guy muscling in on my woman, you know. I don't care who he is."

"Not to worry, dear," she said, kissing me on her way to the coffee mug tree. "Reed doesn't have much muscle. Not really."

"Good thing. Was Mike there?"

Jaynie didn't answer.

I grabbed up our shoes from the kitchen floor and carted everything into the bedroom. I took a quick inventory as I tossed our clothes into the hamper, making sure I'd gathered the lot. My boxers seemed to have gone missing but, since they all looked alike, I figured I must have just put the same pair back on by mistake.

"I say, was Mike there?"

"Who?" Jayne replied, strangely aloof.

"Mike Conners. From the bank."

"Why would he be there?"

Something about Jayne's response felt very weird, like she was being almost evasive, although I couldn't imagine why. Mike Conners and his then-wife were among the first couples we'd met here in Quincy. They'd divorced a few years back when the Mrs. decided to take up with an airline pilot she met at the grocery store. Mike wasn't very upset about the whole thing, which seemed odd at the time. We later found out the marriage had been on the rocks for years. The two of them were just biding their time, waiting for something better to come along.

"I don't know," I continued. "I just thought you might have invited him. He did give you that personal line of credit."

"Oh, right. No. He wasn't. I picked up some fresh cream," said Jayne, as she poured us both a cup of coffee. So much for that conversation.

"Oh, I forgot to tell you," I said. "I take it black now. Less calories."

"No wonder you're so slim," she commented as I rejoined her in the kitchen.

"I will have some of that fruit salad, though. You want some?"

"No thank you. I'm watching my figure, too."

"I see that," I grinned, patting her on the rear on my way to the fridge.

Jayne had made a delicious salad of watermelon, strawberries, blueberries and all the other summer fruits that I so often craved. I'd had a bowl last night between trips to the barn and it tasted incredibly refreshing. Having also recently learned a little bit about nutrition, I was sure the potassium would do me good after last night's "workout".

I reached in the fridge for the bowl and spotted a lobster - with a little life still left in him - half-wrapped in newspaper. I knew it hadn't been there the night before. After all, he was right next to what was left of my six pack of beer.

"Where did this come from?" I asked, showing the lobster to Jayne.

"Penny must have left it for you. I meant to tell you, she wants to have a cook-off tomorrow."

"She must have left it for me when?" I asked.

"Didn't she and Billy stop by last night before the two of them left for campus?"

"They left from here yesterday afternoon." Suddenly, the sound of the kitchen door and the clutch-starting truck made terrible, horrifying sense. "Oh, my god," I mumbled as my pulse quickened.

"What?" said Jayne, her coffee cup suspended mid-sip.

"I must have been in that refrigerator a half dozen times last night," I explained, still holding the wobbly chick. "I'd have noticed a live lobster."

Jayne paused in thought. "Do you think she could have...?"

"I did hear the door this morning. I'm sure of it now. And then there was a truck."

"What kind of truck?"

"The old rickety, rusty kind."

Jayne put two and two together just as quickly as I had. "Oh, my god," she whispered, resting her weight against the counter as she all but dropped her coffee.

"She wouldn't have..."

"Were we...?"

"Oh, god," we both gasp in unified horror.

"Oh, my god, Stephen," panted Jayne. "What if she saw something? She'll end up in therapy, I'm sure of it."

"No she won't. But we might."

"Lord above. Do you think she would have seen us? She may not have. I hope not. Was anything exposed?" Jayne was truly horrified.

"We were pretty liberated," I said, "but I think the

important parts were covered. Although I do think half my ass might have been in the breeze."

"Oh, dear god. She *will* end up in therapy now. What will the neighbors think?" Jayne was practically hyperventilating.

"Oh, come on, Jaynie. My ass isn't *that* bad looking. Is it?"

"No. You have a very nice ass. But *she* doesn't need to know that."

"Okay, let's just calm down," I said, trying to reassure us both. Just as I realized I was still waving the lobster around, Penny burst in the kitchen door.

"Morning!" she announced, all bright-eyed and bushy-tailed and scaring the absolute shit out of us. Jayne shrieked and I must have jumped a foot in the air, juggling the lobster as if it were about the get the best of me. "Didn't mean to startle you," she grinned.

"Where did you come from?" I asked, finally gaining a hold on the dizzying sea creature. "I didn't hear you pull in."

"I walked over from Billy's. He's changing the oil in the truck. I see that chick's still alive and kicking."

I took a good look at the lobster that, at this point, appeared to be suffering from vertigo. "When did you drop it off?"

"This morning. I thought you might like it for lunch."

"This morning?"

If I wasn't sweating bullets before, I was sure sweating them now and I prayed to God this wasn't going to go where I thought it was going to go.

"Uh, huh. You guys were… hmmm, how shall I put this?" she purred, finger tapping her chin. "Asleep? Yes. That sounds right. Asleep."

That little shit smiled that little impish smile of hers and trotted up to her room like the cat that just caught the canary. It was true. We were as busted as busted gets and I thought Jayne was going to faint right there in the kitchen.

"Okay, so we know she saw us," I argued in a low voice, still waving around the lobster as if it had become an extra appendage. "That doesn't mean she's going to advertise it around town. She knows better than that."

"No, but she *will* hang it over our heads for the rest of our lives. You know that, Steve. You know that."

"She'll only hang it over *my* head because she'll think she can get away with it. She wouldn't dare do that to you."

"So what do we do now?" asked Jayne, her palm glued to her forehead.

"Nothing, Jaynie. We do nothing. We pretend it didn't happen and leave it at that."

"I need a pill."

Penny came flying back down the stairs wearing a fresh blouse and shorts. "I'm going back to Billy's," she announced, taking the last three steps in one long leap. "Chowder Cook-off tomorrow?" she asked, pausing all cheery-faced at the kitchen door.

"Okay," I nervously replied.

"Great. I'll tell Mr. Monaghan." And with that, she was gone.

I watched out the window until Penny was a safe distance away, then turned to Jayne. "See, honey? She's forgotten already. No big deal."

Jayne finally, although reluctantly, exhaled. I walked slowly over to her, held her close and kissed her. "See?" I whispered.

"Stephen?"

"Yes, sweetheart."

"Would you please put that lobster back in the refrigerator?"

8

I put the poor lobster out of its final misery early in the afternoon. It was a typically unceremonious steaming followed by the usual drawing of butter and cold, calculated dismembering.

Although it has become quite a delicacy, it always seems so barbaric eating a lobster. Local restaurants even have special paper placemats illustrated with detailed instructions on how to properly dissect the defenseless creature using cast-metal nutcrackers and little wooden hammers; although I don't know how much use the mats are being the platter the beast is served on usually covers them completely.

The waitresses love draping their patrons in those classy logo-emblazoned plastic bibs, too, like you don't have a choice in the matter. They come at you from behind, all stealth-like, and whip the thing around your neck like some sort of Navy Seal with a garrote. "You'll thank me later," they always smile, patting you on the shoulder, knowing more often than not that at some point in the evening a bit of claw meat is bound to be catapulted across the dining room and onto an unsuspecting seafood combo plate.

Nonetheless, and despite the culinary fracas, I do enjoy a good, fresh lobster and, thanks to Penny and Billy, you can't get any fresher than straight from the ocean. I do, however, draw the line at the bib, which is why I always indulge at home.

I just finished licking the last of the melted butter off my fingers when the phone rang. It was Ruth.

"Oh, hi, honey? Are you on your way home? I'd love to see you."

"Is Mom there?"

I guessed that was a "no", unless of course it meant she needed a ride. That would actually be a plus for Ruth, in light of the shithead's penchant for "driving to endanger" no matter who was in the passenger seat. It was widely understood that he rarely discriminated.

I hollered for Jayne, but there was no answer.

"She might be in the shower," I said. "Can I help?"

There was a long pause, followed by the blaring of a car horn in the background.

"I'm coming!" Ruthie screamed.

It was so alarming to hear my daughter so rageful, and yet so helpless. I felt even more helpless - useless, in fact. There just hadn't been anything I - or we, or she - could do to make it better. No matter how many times Jayne and I talked to her about the situation, no matter how many run-in's they had with the police, no matter how many times the neighbors called the next morning to complain about Chuck's reckless driving, none of it ever took.

"I need some money," was all she finally replied.

It was a quiet request, full of guilt, shame, and anger. I knew it wasn't to go out and buy pizza or burgers. It wouldn't even be for beer. It would be for drugs.

Ruth started smoking marijuana her sophomore year of high school. I blame myself, really. It was the same year she landed a major part in a musical at the local theatre. I missed opening night because of a big meeting in Manhattan of all places. A horrible ice storm that seemed to never end kept me from coming home during the run and, by closing, it was time for me to get back to London. Shamefully, I never got north of New York at all that trip.

"How hard would it have been, Daddy?" she cried that night. "You were practically right here. Right here!" She was so disappointed.

Later that spring, Ruth Anne received her first-ever detention for skipping classes. A month later, a two-week suspension for smoking pot in the girl's bathroom. It didn't get much better from there.

Poor Jayne had to start taking Valium to cope with the stress of it all and put Donna, the Drill Sergeant, in charge of the basic household duties. Penny all but ran away during that time, not really sure what to make of it all. She fished and farmed and camped upstairs in the barn just to stay away. Jayne didn't know what to do with either of them.

When I was finally able to talk to her, Ruth swore on a stack of bibles it would be the last time we would ever speak. She was just so angry with me for not being there, and not just for the play. She held her ground for an eternity.

"Are you hungry? I can take you two out to eat, if you like," I offered, trying desperately not to give in to her request.

"Is Mom there?"

Jayne emerged from the bedroom, her hair wrapped in a towel. "Who is it?" she asked.

Before I could even get the "uthie" out in "Ruthie", Jayne grabbed the phone from me like I was a naive twelve year old being suckered in by a salesman. It caught me rather off guard.

"Are you in trouble?" she snapped.

I listened to the short one-sided conversation in complete silence as Jayne dictated and argued and reprimanded. It was as if she didn't even give Ruth a chance to explain. "This is the last time, young lady. Do you hear me? The last time," she repeated impatiently and slammed the phone down on the receiver.

"Is she okay?" I asked.

"It's disgraceful, Stephen. The whole thing. Just disgraceful."

"Maybe she can't help it, Jaynie," I argued. "Maybe it's all the guy."

"I don't care. I'm just tired of feeling responsible for it all."

"Then tell me what to do. I can take care of it."

I wanted to lighten her burden in the worst way. I knew how much it pained her to hear Ruthie so lost.

"Fine. Meet her downtown in front of the drug store. Give her ten dollars, but no more than that," she reluctantly ordered as she hustled back to the bedroom towel-drying her hair. "I have an appointment."

I felt so lost myself. Half their argument had been about what the neighbors were going to think. The other half was about whether or not we were funding Chuck's drug habit. Jayne, at this point, didn't really want to know. She just needed to vent.

While Jayne readied for her appointment with the Groverton's, I headed to town to meet Ruth and, with any ill-luck, the shithead. I knew it was going to be difficult to be civil to a guy who caused such misery for my daughter, not to mention Jayne, but I was determined to put up a good front.

I pulled into the parking lot a grueling ten minutes later and spotted none other than Mike Conners from the bank coming out of the adjacent hardware store.

"Hey, Mike," I called out, trying to be friendly. He seemed startled and practically dove for his car. "It's me. Sheridan."

"Oh, hey, Steve. I didn't expect you," he replied, looking around as if he thought he was going to be ambushed.

"Yeah, well. Home for good now," I said.

He fiddled around with his little paper sack, rolling it closed tighter and tighter. "Jayne mentioned. A while ago, I mean. When she was in the bank. She mentioned something about you coming home."

Mike tended to be a little high strung at times, but it was mostly nervous energy. That afternoon, however, it was more like the nervous energy a teenager has when he's just been caught shoplifting and is trying to make a getaway. Jayne often mentioned he drank too much coffee. Apparently, he'd just had a gallon.

"How are things at the bank?"

"Good. You know. Good." He was shifting his weight from side to side, trying to look composed, but he wasn't pulling it off.

"Great," I added. "Everything okay?"

"Oh, yeah. Everything's great," he said, kneading his

little paper sack full of hardware like it was a wet chamois. "Well, I gotta go. Kitchen faucet's leaking. Don't want to come home to a flood."

"Didn't you shut off the valve under the sink?" I asked as he jumped in his car.

"Oh, yeah," he waved, and fired up his Spitfire. "Thanks."

Even I knew that.

As I walked around the corner of the parking lot to the entrance of Wilkin's Variety and Drug, a beat-up El Camino screeched to a halt and jumped the curb, its stereo blaring some god-awful acid rock. A young woman, probably about 29 or so, jumped out and swore at the driver – "Asshole!" – then slammed the door. The car took off, nearly side-swiping a Cadillac parked along the sidewalk in front of him.

The woman, dressed all in black with metal studded belts wrapping themselves all round her and down one leg, tossed her black leather bag over her shoulder then flicked her green-streaked hair away from her face. She stopped dead in her tracks as her eyes met mine and my heart held its breath.

"Dad...?"

"Ruthie...?"

All we could do was look at each other. It had only been since June that I'd seen her, yet she seemed to have aged a decade. Her posture was bent, her eyes faraway and dark. It looked like she hadn't slept for days.

Ruthie quickly gazed over her shoulder, as if to check if Chuck was anywhere in sight.

"Is that you?" I continued.

"Where's Mom?" she said as she quietly, cautiously approached.

"She had an appointment. Are you on your way to a gig?"

"No." She looked all around, but not at me. Not at first. I danced around her, trying to make eye contact and was finally successful. "Did she tell you?" she asked, letting out a big sigh.

"She said you needed money. You want to go get a burger or a pizza or something? My treat?"

"I'm not hungry."

"How about an ice cream? I'm dying for some Rum Raisin." She looked so empty, so tired. She turned her eyes away again and bit her thumbnail, avoiding me almost completely.

"I just need some money," she finally said, staring at her black biker boots. "Can I just have it and go?"

"How much do you need?"

"Couple of bucks. Just to get by until Tuesday."

"What happens Tuesday?"

"Chuck gets his trust fund money for the month then."

I couldn't help but want to meet this guy. He seemed like a real piece of work. As much as I thought Penny had been exaggerating, I thought again she may actually be right. He may actually be a certifiable shithead.

"Do you think I could meet him? Chuck?"

The El Camino came barreling around the corner and jumped the curb again, nearly running over Ruthie. She jumped to the side and looked at me, frightened, her eyes wide.

"Sorry," she apologized. For what, I don't know. What a hold he had on her.

"Did you get it?" shouted Chuck from the driver's seat.

I couldn't help but shout back at him through the

passenger window. "Hi there," I smiled with as much sincerity as I could muster under the circumstance.

"Who the fuck are you?" he graciously replied.

Ruthie pulled at my shirt sleeve. "Daddy, please. Can we not do this right now? I have to go."

She looked so ashamed and frightened.

"Why don't you come home with me, honey?" I pleaded. "We can have some dinner later, go out for a movie or something."

"Hey!" shouted Chuck. "I said, who the fuck are you?"

I stepped up to the passenger door and glared at him through the open window. "I'm Ruth's father. Who the fuck are you?"

The flies would have had a field day buzzing in and out of Chuck's gaping mouth had the stench of booze not been so bad. It was like he was having a mini stroke and, for a moment there, I thought he was actually going to drool.

"I see. Like to join us for dinner tonight?" I invited, hoping he'd balk and let Ruthie off the hook for the evening.

"We got a gig tonight," he slurred as he resumed consciousness. "We gotta get going. Come on, Ruth."

Ruthie looked at me, tears welling in her sad, tired eyes. "I gotta go," she whispered.

"No you don't. You can come home with me."

"Come on, baby! We're gonna be late!"

"I really need some money," she whispered. She couldn't even look at me, only held out her hand.

I reached in my pocket, pulled out a twenty and gave it to her. I squeezed her hand as she reluctantly took it from me, holding onto her for as long as I could.

"Come home, Ruthie. Please?"

Ruthie wiped her eyes on the back of her black sleeve

and hopped in the car. Chuck, now a proven shithead, blasted off without so much as a pause. I could see Ruth watching me in the side mirror as the El Camino sped away in a cloud of dust. My women - all of my women - hated saying goodbye.

9

I awoke Sunday morning to the sound of cardinals chirping just outside our bedroom window. They were my favourite of all birds and were one of the few sights that reminded me of home while I was in London. The males sport such a brilliant shade of red they seem to vibrate against the green of the leaves while their mates, in soft tawny, dance camouflaged in the shadows.

I heard Penny leave hours, it seemed, earlier. She and Billy had planned to head out before dawn to get fresh fish for our chowder cook off. The tide would be turning at sunrise, which was supposedly the best time for fishing. I knew that was the rule of thumb for flounder, but I wasn't as certain for deep water cod and haddock. In any event, it would serve as the day's excuse.

Jayne, wearing a silky full-length nightgown, slid next to me in the bed and draped an arm over my t-shirted chest. Being a little self-conscious about our previous "display",

81

we'd both dressed in more clothes than we normally would for a warm summer night and I found myself uncomfortably strangled in pajama pants. Normally, Jayne would have worn a skimpy negligee. Me, my boxers - if that. But, even though we were behind closed doors, we just couldn't get over the thought of Penny being in the house and possibly catching us in any manner of undress.

Ruthie hadn't as yet come home, at least that we knew of. From what I understood, it was usually pretty obvious when she arrived. Chuck, *never*-considerate of others, would peel out of the driveway and honk all the way down the lane no matter what time it was, and it was usually late - or early, depending on how you wanted to look at it. Ruthie would belt out a string of expletives at him in vain, probably to vent as much frustration as she could before she came in the house. It was such an awful arrangement. Just thinking about it tore me up.

Jayne and I got up and took our time getting dressed. Before we knew it, the morning was half gone so I decided to make another pot of coffee and fix brunch. Sunday, traditionally, was my day to make what we called in England, "The Full Fry". I whipped up eggs, bacon, sausages, potatoes, grilled tomatoes, hearty toast with jam and even some porridge. It was a meal meant to last the whole day - or at least most of it.

Jayne, reminding me of her figure, had a piece of melon and some cottage cheese which meant I'd have to consume the Full Fry solo. I knew it would shoot my own diet all to hell, but, hey. It was Sunday. Still, it didn't take much arm-twisting to get me to eat a hearty plate of anything full of fat or cooked in grease, Sunday or not. It's why I no longer have a gall bladder.

After brunch, Jayne started in making a big fresh-from-the-garden salad for the cook-off while I went to the safe to get out my secret fish chowder recipe. It wasn't really worthy of being housed under such tight security, but over the years it kind of became a novel tradition. Penny, too, had her own little fireproof box that she kept her recipe in and we each teased we'd someday break into the other's vault and steal their secret formula. It didn't take much to amuse the two of us.

I got out my big stockpot and rendered the salt pork, which I'd cut up into tiny cubes. Penny used salt pork, too, but I knew she did something different with hers. I just couldn't figure out what. I'd cut up my vegetables, onion and potato, and made sure I had plenty of canned milk. That was another thing I concluded was different. I had reason to believe, and on good authority, too, that Penny used fresh, whole milk and scalded it. I just didn't know for sure, though, and it was like pulling teeth to get any information out of her. She'd have made a great spy.

Penny'd won the cook-off every year since we started the tradition five summers ago and I was determined to best her. Every year I tried something a little different. This year I was going to add fresh shucked corn.

"Do you need any more onions?" asked Jayne.

"I don't think so. What do you think?" I replied, showing her my prep bowl. "Maybe one more?"

"Maybe."

I took the pork renderings out of the pan and reluctantly drained off the fat. I threw the onions in to sweat as Penny, donning her well-ripened fishing togs, barreled into the kitchen carrying two fresh lobsters and a good-sized gutted cod. "Hey!" she shouted, dropping the bounty into the sink for a bath.

"Hey, Peanut. Getting ready to give up the crown today?"

"Not on your life, fella," she replied, rinsing the fish.

Just then, the aroma of Penny's morning fishing jaunt caught up with her. Jayne and I both winced. It was like being hit in the face with a fly swatter.

"Oh, Penny!" cried Jayne, trying to stave off the stench.

"What?" she said, all innocent-like.

"She's right. When was the last time you washed that sweatshirt?" I gagged, cranking open the window.

"Oh, I don't wash it," she replied, trying to hold back a smile. "I just hang it on the line and let Mother Nature do the rest."

Jayne couldn't take it anymore and left the room, holding the back of her hand over her mouth and nose. By all accounts, it was pretty intense.

"You're enough to gag a maggot," I said.

"You should smell Billy," she laughed. "Thank God he's home taking a shower."

"Penny, honey, I hope you dressed that fish at the dock," Jayne shouted from down the hall. "You know the garbage man doesn't come until Friday."

"I did," she replied, wrapping the fish in some newspaper and tossing it in the fridge.

"That's not the Sports section is it?" I asked, leafing through the rest of the Herald.

"Please. That would be cruel and unusual punishment."

"To me or the fish?"

"You know who."

Penny took a look in the stock pot and stirred my onions as I dove for my recipe card laying out on the counter in broad daylight. "Do you mind!?" I crooned, taking the wooden spoon away from her.

"So you caramelize yours?"

"Not intentionally."

"What kind of potatoes are you using?"

"Get outta there, cheater," I said, lightly whacking the back of her hand with my spoon.

"It makes a difference, you know. Same with the onions."

"What kind do you use?"

"I'll never tell," she smiled.

"I'm adding corn this year, by the way," I boasted, trying to get her to spill the beans.

"Fresh or canned?"

"None of your bee's wax."

Jayne came back out still holding her hand over her face. "Penny, would you please go upstairs and get in the shower? That smell is going to permeate the whole house."

"Sorry."

"And put your boots outside, *away* from the back door!"

"I hosed them off."

"I don't care. They still smell."

"They do not," she mumbled.

Penny tromped outside, feigning disdain. She kicked her yellow rubber boots off and set them at the far corner of the barn then hung her sweatshirt up by what was left of the cut-off sleeves, clamping the smelly thing on the line with a half dozen clothes pins.

"Think that'll hold it?" I teased out the window.

"Don't want the flies to carry it away. By the way, fish only, you know," she ordered on her way back in, her worn out t-shirt far less aromatic. "That means no lobster. No clams. No shrimp."

"Then what are these for?" I asked, pointing to the two chicks staggering around in the sink.

"I'm sure you'll figure something out. Oh, and save the rack for the garden."

"Penny! Please!" shouted Jayne.

"Alright already. I'm going."

While Penny did her best to scrub away the smell of bait, Jayne readied the tureens for the final show down. She had two of them, big stoneware crocks: one with a wide blue band, the other with a wide red band. We never knew whose was going to be in which.

Penny always cooked in the Monaghan's kitchen to lessen the chances of me finding out how she made such a damn good chowder. She'd have Billy sit on the porch with a toy Tommie gun in case I had a notion to come over and spy, which I always did. Billy would then holler, "Red alert! Enemy approaching!" prompting Penny to chase me back across the salt marsh with her ladle. We'd have a ball.

The routine was that when our chowders were done we were to leave them in our kitchen to be secretly portioned out into the official Sheridan Family Chowder Cook-Off tureens by a completely impartial overseer – Jayne. She would then present the gourmet concoctions to the esteemed, yet sparse panel of judges which these days consisted of Donna and Ruthie, Brian and Billy, and Skip – the swing vote.

My sister, Catherine, and her husband, Peter, used to come all the way from Milwaukee just to join in, but had since ventured off to Paris where Catherine opened an art studio. I missed them terribly. Herb and Clara used to be active members of the committee, too. But, staying true to their not-so-idle threats, they'd moved to sunny Florida just in time for my retirement. Thank God.

According to the rules that Penny and I made up as we went along, everyone had to take a solemn vow to vote with their palates, not with their hearts, which was a complete load of rubbish and we all knew it. Nonetheless, even Skip found himself going along with the charade and standing, hand over heart, during the opening ceremonies. It bordered on the ridiculous.

No more than fifteen minutes had gone by and Penny came flying downstairs, fresh as a daisy and wearing a pretty summer dress. Even though she usually completed her outfit with her best "Sunday Keds", she was always as comfortable dressing up as she was dressing down. She wouldn't completely abandon her tomboy persona, though, but she would keep her manners in check and usually replaced most profanities with more socially acceptable commentary. She'd even put her generally unruly curls up in a bow.

"Hey, Mom, do we still have those long tongs for the barbeque?" Penny asked as she rummaged through the utensil drawer.

"What do you need those for?" I inquired.

"I'm sorry, that's classified," she glared. "If I tell you, I have to kill you."

"Will you two stop? Honestly." Jayne bored easily of our annual theatrical production. She'd play along with it like a good sport, but only for a very short while. She took life much too seriously. "They're probably in the garage."

"Thanks. We're eating at three?" asked Penny.

"*Around* three. Donna and Brian should be here around two-thirty. Ruthie, who knows."

"Skip and Billy are coming, right?" I asked. "I need their votes."

"You'll need more than that, hot shot."

"Penny..." jabbed Jayne.

"Mr. Monaghan's anxious to see you, by the way. Some magazine called last night. They're doing a story about him and his father and Billy. Like a three generation thing. I know the elder passed away a long time ago, but they still want to do it just the same. He was hoping you would take the pictures."

"I'll bet Billy's excited about that," I said.

"Are you kidding? He's practically glowing in the dark."

Jayne let out a huge sigh, her tolerance metre pegged. "Penny, don't you have to get your soup started? I have one nerve left at the moment and you're beginning to grate on it."

"Fine. I'll see you later," Penny scowled. "And it's chowder. Not soup."

I gave her a wink and she smiled and stuck her tongue out at me in return as she dashed out the door.

"Cheater!" I yelled out the window.

"Lightweight!" she yelled back.

Soon, an uncomfortable, chilly silence overtook the kitchen. Jayne quietly continued on her salad while I added my potatoes and stock to the pot. She never even looked up and seemed to be pouting like a little child who didn't get invited to a birthday party. I thought I was going to have to shut the window and light the fire it got so cold.

"What is it between you two?" I finally asked.

"What do you mean?"

"You and Penny. We were just having fun."

"She's just so cheery all the time," Jayne said, drilling a

handful of chopped peppers into the salad bowl.

"What's wrong with that?"

"It's not *all* fun and games you know. Not always."

"I know," I whispered. "I'm sorry."

A huge lump formed in my throat. I'd done my absolute best to provide for my wife and daughters and I thought I'd done a pretty good job. But now, as I'd often done in the past, I began to completely doubt everything.

"Still, aren't you happy?" I asked.

"Oh, Steve. Of course I'm happy. It's my job to be happy. Happy and stoic."

"Jaynie, please don't say that. It was hard raising the girls alone, I know. But, it was hard for me, too. I wanted to be here with you. I did. But, I couldn't do both."

"I know."

"I'm home now, honey. For good," I continued. "And there won't be any more traveling without you by my side. No more jobs. No more meetings. No more seminars. Just you and I and the girls."

Jayne stared at the kitchen counter. We must have had this conversation a hundred times. But, now that I was retired, I never thought we'd have to have it again.

I took her in my arms as she began to weep. It was so unexpected in light of our first few intimate days together, not to mention the months of eager planning to get me home. I knew menopause was partly to blame for her mood swings. I was guilty of the rest. It took the wind right out of my sails.

"I'm sorry," cried Jayne. "It's just so overwhelming sometimes."

"I know. And I'm sorry for that."

"Now there's the wedding to think about, which is

costing a small fortune, in case you hadn't noticed. Ruthie's a mess again and I don't know what to do about that. Penny, our little ray of sunshine, is going off to college with that boy. And on top of it all, I'm trying to run a business."

"And you're doing a great job, honey," I said, holding her tight. "You amaze me."

"What must the neighbors think?"

Jayne rested her weight on my chest as she wept quietly. We went through this every time I came home and every time it hurt worse than the last. I hated to see my wife cry.

A car screeched into the driveway, followed by the sound of a slamming door and, "Asshole!"

Jayne wiped away her tears and composed herself. "I wish she wouldn't curse so loud."

The car screeched back out of the driveway and sped down the lane, horn blaring. Ruthie ripped the kitchen door open and stomped in, muttering under her breath. "Stupid jerk."

"Hi, honey," I cheerfully greeted.

Ruthie, still dressed in her Gothic garb, stopped in her tracks, surprised, teetering as if she'd just lost her bearings slightly. She glared at Jayne and I for the briefest of seconds, then calmed. "Oh…"

"We're eating around three," announced Jayne, as if nothing at all had happened. "And please don't wear black today. It makes you look so maudlin."

Ruthie, who still looked as if she hadn't slept, quickly gathered her senses and trudged upstairs without another word.

Jayne straightened her hair and smoothed her apron. "I think I need a pill."

10

Donna and Brian arrived on schedule at around two-thirty that afternoon. Donna, wearing a pretty summer dress that seemed an exact match to Penny's, brought a box of expensive gourmet chowder crackers that could only be found at specialty shops in Greater Boston. Brian brought imported beer. I'm sure the bill will arrive soon.

"Hi, honey," I smiled as she walked in the kitchen.

"Hi, Daddy." She gave me a quick "air kiss" so as not to smudge her make-up. "Do you think you could have the limit raised on the credit card? Brian and I are booking the reception hall next week."

"Boy, you cut right to the chase. Don't you."

"I've just got so much to think about," she gasped, "and I just can't bare the thought of missing out on this place."

"Hey, Mr. S.," said Brian, extending his hand in greeting.

Donna's fiancé, Brian Webster, had been an all-star football jock and received a very liberal, Liberal Arts degree. He had aspirations to go pro, but wracked up his knee during a pre-season scrimmage his senior year. That plan all shot to hell, Donna decided he should become a sportscaster instead and hinted daily that he should hire a talent agent. I could tell this marriage was going to cost me a fortune.

"How's everything going, Brian?" I replied. "Heard from any scouts?"

"No, I haven't. I wish I would, though. We're all out of Chocolate Mints already."

The sad thing was he wasn't kidding. That poor guy was as dumb as a stump. He was proof positive that there needed to be some substantial improvements made to football helmet integrity. He'd simply, and quite obviously, been drilled in the head one too many times.

Donna slumped and sighed loud enough to wake the dead. "He means talent scouts, Brian. Not Girl Scouts."

"Oh? Oh! Yeah." The light bulb, all struggling twenty-five watts of it, finally turned on. "No. I haven't."

"You still might," I said, trying to be reassuring.

Jayne, dressed in a floral sundress, joined us in the kitchen. She looked like a million bucks and I could feel myself staring.

"Hi, honey," she said to Donna as they gave each other air kisses.

"Hi, Mom. Nice dress. Is it new?"

Despite being conspicuously passed over, Brian forced his way in to give his future mother-in-law a hug just the same. "Hey, Mrs. S."

"Please, Brian," Jayne corrected. "It's Mrs. Sheridan. Not Mrs. S. The same goes for Mr. Sheridan."

"Oh, yeah. Sorry."

Donna zapped Brian with her laser beam death glare. In another rare moment of lucidity, he got the message, grabbed a beer and headed for the patio deck just off the kitchen.

"Honestly, I don't know what you see in him," said Jayne.

"Mother! He's gorgeous. And his Daddy's loaded."

"Well, there you go," I added. "What more could a girl ask for." How a guy with virtually no neck could be considered gorgeous was beyond me, but there you have it.

Just then, Penny piled into the kitchen carrying an empty bowl. Donna immediately spotted her matching dress and gasped as if she'd just seen Medusa. "You did not!" she cried.

Penny laughed like mischievous. "Nice dress, Sarg."

"You do this on purpose. Don't you."

My girls had a terrible coincidental habit of showing up at family functions wearing the same, or remarkably similar, dresses. It dated back to when they were little and Jayne would outfit them in matching ensembles with all the trimmings right down to their white lace anklets and patent leather shoes.

Donna always found dressing alike to be *revolting*, not to mention *supercilious*, and announced on her thirteenth birthday that she would commence choosing her fashions independently from her sisters. Invariably, one or the other sister would end up with a dress far too similar to Donna's, sending her into a decline so overtly severe she was often moved to run screaming upstairs to change before the neighbors could find out. Ruthie would usually cry and want to go change, too. Penny couldn't give two shits, but did prefer her Keds to the patent leathers.

"Girls!" Jayne shouted. "Please. Not today."

"Mother, make her go change."

"I will not!" Penny shouted, crossing her arms, stamping her foot and trying not to laugh. "So there!"

While Penny took her bowl and began to load it full of fruit salad from the fridge, I buried myself as deep into the corner of the kitchen cabinets as I could, trying desperately to blend into the countertop. I knew, from sporadic years of experience, that it was a fatal mistake to get in the middle of any verbal skirmish that involved my women. What was even more fatal was to laugh at the pure levity of it all.

"Girls, I will not have this. Penny, go change."

"No," she insisted. "Besides it's not the same dress anyway. Hers has a bow in the back."

While it was true that Penny's dress lacked that little tie in the back, it made little difference to Donna who was, at that point, about to blow a gasket.

"She probably cut hers off," said Donna as Penny fled out the kitchen door with her salad.

"Gotta go!" she shouted on her way out.

"Oh, Donna, just go put something else on if you can't bear it," Jayne implored.

"Like what? All my good dresses are at the apartment. There's nothing left up there but a bunch of rags."

"You look fine, honey," I bravely commented. "I doubt anyone will even notice."

Donna let out an exasperated burst and pounded upstairs, no doubt in search of some safe *haut monde* haven.

Two quick knocks at the kitchen door announced an entering Billy with Brian in tow. "Hey, folks. Thought you might need a hand with the picnic tables," he said. "You want me and Brian to bring them down to the beach?"

"Thank you, Billy. That would be nice," said Jayne, relieved that at least *that* wasn't going to cause any chaos. "Just make sure you sweep them off first, please."

"Yes, Ma'am..."

Brian grabbed another beer from the cooler on the patio deck and they were off.

Curious, I took out the fruit salad from the fridge and stared at it. "You don't think she's going to put this in her chowder, do you?"

"Oh, Stephen, don't be ridiculous. She's probably bringing it over for Skip."

"Oh, right. I guess that does make better sense."

As I added the canned milk to my chowder, Donna reemerged from her upstairs bedroom in record breaking time wearing a fresh seersucker dress with spanking new white sandals. I was in awe that she was back so soon, thinking she must have been zipped through a fashion teleport or something. It usually took her an hour just to put a bobby pin in her hair.

"Thank God I at least had this in the closet," she sighed.

"You look lovely, dear," said Jayne. "But, aren't those Ruthie's sandals?"

"No. They're mine. I bought them last week."

"Well, they look lovely."

Jayne gave me a look that said, *Oh, my, this could get ugly and I really can't take it,* and went on to get some fresh rolls out of the bread box.

Ruthie, wearing an all-too-familiar seersucker dress and spanking new white sandals, joined us, but just long enough to get a cold ginger ale from the fridge. Thankfully, Donna was looking out the kitchen window and didn't notice until Ruthie let the cat out of the bag on her way back up the stairs. "I'm not changing," she blurted, and casually sauntered up to her room.

Donna spun round and let out a bellow. "That's it. I'm going home."

"You *are* home, dear," said Jayne. "Besides, you know Ruth Anne. She probably won't even come out of her room for the rest of the afternoon, so just let it go."

"Mother!"

I always seemed to forget how volatile my girls could get when they got their Irish up. I guess it was part of the whole state of denial I'd lived in over the years, always wanting to believe that everything was perfect. I could see why Jayne would get so worked up sometimes. It was easy for me to make light of it in an afternoon. She had to handle it year round.

"Mr. Sheridan? Penny wants to know if you're ready," said Billy sticking his head in the door.

"Give me five more minutes," I replied. "And tell her she better bring her 'A' game this time. I'm out for blood, you know."

Billy smiled and gave me a nod. He knew Penny as well as I did, if not better. She dueled to the death.

"Do you think she puts the whole thing in?" I asked Jayne, holding up a stick of salted butter.

"I said, I'm going!" shouted Donna, still standing just off the kitchen, wanting our complete and undivided attention.

"No you're not," Jayne shouted back. "For heaven's sake, put the other one back on."

Donna let out another exasperated grunt and thundered

back upstairs with such ferocity that I couldn't help but feel bad for the oak risers. "Is there just no end to this insufferable indignity?" she screamed. I made a mental note to check the foundation for cracks later on.

"I'm sure she puts some in, don't you think?" I said, returning to my chowder pot. "You can see it floating on the top."

"I haven't any idea."

"I'll start with half."

I took a glance out the window and spotted Penny and Billy making their way up to the house with her vat of chowder while Skip headed for the beach. I was happy to see her coming. Even though I didn't take things as seriously as Jayne, I could sure use a break from the tension.

"Maybe three quarters," I said, more to myself than anyone, and added another chunk of butter to the pot.

I took a taste as soon as my butter had melted and added a pinch of salt, a dash of pepper, and a handful of fresh chopped parsley. It sure tasted good, as good as any I'd ever made, and I felt confident that I might actually have a snowball's chance this year.

"I hope you're good and ready," proclaimed Penny as she and Billy clamoured into the kitchen. For a little girl, she could sure make a lot of noise.

"Must you be so hard on that door?" asked Jayne. "You girls are all worse than boys - no offense Bill."

"None taken, Mrs. Sheridan."

"You're the one who'd better be good and ready, young lady," I touted, waving my wooden spoon at her. "This stuff's gonna knock your socks off."

"Oh, yeah. Let me see."

"Oh, no you don't," I shouted, defending my territory

like a knight guarding the queen, my spoon my sword.

"That's enough you two," yelled Jayne. "Stephen, are you ready?"

"One more taste." I took a tiny sip and let it mull. It was really quite spectacular, which made me kind of nervous. "No. Another minute. Maybe two. Maybe not."

Poor Jayne sighed. "All right then." She grabbed my spoon away, knowing I was just stalling. "You're done. Out. Penny? Out."

"But, I have to go change," I lied. I was really having fun, but at Jayne's expense. She could get so worked up over the littlest thing and it took her forever to let it go. Penny and I tended to take the whole chowder cook-off thing to the extreme and, despite the wardrobe wars, we were really pushing the envelope this time.

"Then go change," sighed Jayne. "Penny? Out!"

"Why do I have to get out? He doesn't have to get out."

Jayne gave Penny the lethal Mom-glare and that was it. Even she knew to back down when Jaynie brought out the big guns. Anything less than a full and immediate retreat was suicide.

"Fine. Billy," ordered Penny, "if my father so much as reaches for that lid, you're to shoot him on sight. You got that?"

"Yes, ma'am," he saluted.

Donna came back downstairs, again in record time, wearing white clam diggers and a pink blouse over her polka dot bikini top. She stood face to face with Penny and pointed a finger right under her nose. "I don't want to hear one word!"

"How about two," Penny challenged.

"Penny Jayne Sheridan, would you please," cried Jayne. "And don't slam the door!"

"Going…"

Penny dashed out the door, Donna right behind her.

"You, too, Billy. I'll call you when I need you."

Billy gave another salute and another, "Yes, ma'am." He knew when to get, too, and made a hasty exit, carefully closing the door quietly behind him.

"Honest to God," said Jayne, "I don't know where that child gets it."

"Which one?" I asked.

Jayne blew the hair out of her face a leaned on the edge of the counter. I could tell she'd had enough and we hadn't even begun. She looked exhausted, and over what. "I need a pill," she sighed.

"I thought you took one already," I said.

"I did. I need another."

I walked over and held her close, kissing her on the temple, smoothing back her hair. "We were just having fun," I whispered. She leaned against me, weary to the bone it seemed, and sighed. Of all the things I wanted to give her, the weariness was the one thing I wanted to take away.

"It's nearly three," she finally said. "Why don't you go upstairs and get Ruth while I dish these up."

I looked her in the eye, wiping away the one tear that managed to escape. "I'm here now," I whispered. "I'm here."

Jayne rubbed her hand along my chest then quietly began the task of filling the crocks and giving a final toss to the salads. As I stared at her in the silence, I had to ask myself: Is this what it meant to provide?

I went in the bedroom to hunt down my Hawaiian shirt, then headed upstairs to fetch Ruthie. I heard Jayne call for Billy, so I knew we'd be eating soon.

"Ruthie, honey. Can I come in?" I said, quietly tapping on the door.

"Just a minute."

I heard a lot of rummaging around, like she was tidying up or something. The girls all kept their rooms fairly neat, so I didn't really know what all the fuss was about. After all, it was just me. A drawer closed hard, followed by some coughing and sniffling. I guess it should have been obvious. I just didn't want it to be.

"Come in."

Ruthie was seated on the edge of her bed, hands folded. She didn't look at me at first - just at the floor and the ceiling and the floor and her feet and the floor - like a kid who thought she was going to be scolded. She'd changed out of her dress and into white clam diggers and a pink – well you know the rest.

"Hi, honey. We're just about ready. Are you coming down?"

"I don't think so," she replied, sniffing and wiping her nose. "I'm not really hungry."

"You don't have to eat, really. Just take a taste so you can vote. I think I'm going to win this year. You don't want to miss that, do you?"

"I don't know why you make such a big deal out of it."

"It's just fun. You know? Your boyfriend's coming over isn't he?" I asked. "What's his name? Chuck?"

"He's not into family stuff."

"I see." I gently pulled the hair away from her face and over her shoulder. "He's really not that nice to you is he," I said, still seeing the remains of her blackened eye concealed under her make-up.

"I can take care of myself. Shouldn't you get down there?"

"Probably. But, I want you to come, too."

"I really don't want any milk stuff right now. I kind of have a hangover."

I was trying so hard. I was surprised she hadn't kicked me out of the room yet. If nothing else she'd be able to see her sister have a fit and fall in it because the two of them were wearing the same outfit - again. It was a last resort to even mention it, I know, but I had to think of something.

Ruthie cracked a smile, which she hid behind the back of her hand. She turned her head away, allowing her hair to fall back off her shoulder and over the side of her face. She may have even laughed.

"Okay?" I pleaded.

Ruthie composed herself. She turned back to me, flicking her hair back over her shoulder. "I should probably change."

"You're fine."

"Mom will be mad."

"No she won't. It's fine, honey."

"She always gets mad."

"She's just a little uptight."

Ruthie chuckled to herself. "A little?"

I wrapped my arms around her shoulders and kissed her on the temple. To see her smile was a huge victory for me, like winning the lottery, and I felt like the richest man in the world. It had been such a long time since we'd spoken and to have her laugh on top of it all absolutely made my day, if not my week, if not my everything.

"Dad?" she quietly asked.

"Yes, sweetheart?"

"I'm sorry about yesterday."

"It's okay."

"I'm sorry about a lot of stuff."

"It's okay, honey. I am, too. I was just a little worried about you. I'm always a little worried about you. Actually, I'm a lot worried about you. I want to make sure you're safe."

"I'm kind of glad it was you. In a way, I mean. But not really. In a way. Mom always makes such a scene. She pretends not to, but it ends up a scene anyway."

"She's got a lot on her mind."

"Yeah. I guess. I'm sorry."

Ruth and I sat together in silence another long while. I waited for more to come from her, but there was just silence. It was a good silence, though, like the kind you get when you just want to sit and take something in rather than talk about it.

Ruthie rested her head on my shoulder and exhaled a breath that she seemed to be holding forever. "Daddy?" she whispered.

"Yes…"

"Is it true?"

"Is what true?"

"That you're staying - for good now, I mean?"

"Yes. I'm staying - for good."

Ruthie took in another deep breath then rested her head on my shoulder. "Good," was all she whispered. "Good…"

11

The tiny crowd mingled around the picnic tables, all waiting for Jayne and Billy to bring the official Chowder Cook-off entries down to the beach. Brian took another beer inventory while Penny and I kept Skip company.

"I hear there's going to be an article written about you and your father," I said to Skip.

"Ayup," he replied. "They're throwin' Billy in there, too, only 'cause he's good lookin'."

Skip grew up in Jonesport, Maine, and worked on his father's lobster boat from the time he was old enough to pull his rubber boots on. His mother, also a Jonesport native, ran the local greasy spoon where it was said she made the best steak and eggs on the planet.

Skip's father, Brud, was also a part-time naval architect and built some of the fastest lobster boats running. A life-long admirer of famous builder Will Frost, Brud fashioned his stealthiest boat after Frost's *Red Wing*, canvas spray hood and low-profile wheel house included. He and Skip, a born speed demon in his own right, raced the old girl against anyone and everyone that dared. It seemed no one could touch her.

One fourth of July in 1955, the elder Monaghan, manning the helm while Skip rode stern, took on the entire fleet of Jonesport in what would later officially become the annual *World's Fastest Lobster Boat Races*. Ironically, the team was disqualified for having spray rails, even though hardly anyone even knew what they were. Although a legitimate argument according to the unofficial rule book, the disqualification was a petty technicality according to Brud, who vowed never to race again and subsequently burned all his blueprints. Skip, 45 years old and even more bullheaded than his father, still threatened to compete every year. Gracie, her spirit ever with him, would have had a fit.

Skip met Grace way back in the summer of '28 when she and her family were visiting relatives at their camp in the nearby town of Kennebec. It was love at first sight and the two of them eventually married and settled in a little fishing village just north of Revere where Grace had been raised as a girl. When little Bobbie came along they made the short move south to a bigger spread and promising schools. We were blessed to have them as neighbors.

"You weren't so bad yourself at his age," commented Penny. "Or so I hear."

"I expect Gracie, for one, must have thought I was alright," smiled Skip, toasting the air to his late wife. "'Course the boy's a little soft around the edges."

"Who are you callin' soft, old man?" chimed Billy, giving his Dad a big bear hug round the neck. He'd just brought down the blue crock and Jayne wasn't far behind with the red. "I'll show you who's soft."

Suddenly, Donna was heard shouting in the background.

"Every time! This happens every time!"

"Better get over there and break it up, Dad," moaned Penny. "Otherwise the world will probably come to an end."

Donna was busy accosting Ruthie for once again picking a matching outfit - on purpose, of course. Ruthie mostly ignored her, paying more attention to the cheese and crackers at the food table than anything, which really pissed Donna off. However, Ruth, like her mother, had a breaking point. Matter and anti-matter were about to collide and it was obvious I'd have to break away to prevent world-wide calamity.

I was having a good time and hated to step away just to break up a cat fight. But, truth be told, Donna happened to like my chowder and I couldn't risk losing her vote. It was usually the only one I got so I knew I had to do something to appease her.

"Problem girls?" I bravely asked as I stepped between the two of them.

"Did you tell her what I was wearing?" glared Donna, the tails of her blouse tucked behind the clenched fists on her hips. Although she was only about a half inch taller than I was, she always postured herself as if she had at least a two foot advantage. Between that and the command of her Drill Sergeant voice, she could disarm just about anyone. It was the only time I sympathized with Brian.

"*My* blouse is buttoned," Ruthie argued.

"It makes a big difference," I agreed.

"It does NOT make a difference!" Donna growled, insisting that the fact that she was flashing her bikini top was no different than not flashing it. The blouse was still the same.

"Greetings, beachcombers," came a cheery voice from the dune.

I looked over my shoulder and spotted a well-dressed, virile-looking man emerged from the path carrying a decorative baking dish in one hand a bottle of Bordeaux in the other. He was followed by an equally handsome fellow, about the same age, carrying a lined picnic basket with baguettes peeking out the red checked liner.

"Oh, great," sighed Donna.

"Here come the twins," muttered Ruth.

Enter Reed and wife - Bob. They were good-looking in their own right, although I'd never met anyone who came to a beach party dressed in pressed khaki's and starched button-down shirts. Reed's was pink.

Their matching haircuts were like something out of a style magazine. It seemed incredible that even in a stiff wind not a single hair blew out of place.

Donna put on her best party smile and forced her way over to greet them. "What a surprise!" she lied, and gave them both air kisses. That girl could turn her attitude on a dime.

Reed dashed right over, embracing me like some long lost brother - or lover. "Oh, my god!" he squealed. "Jaynie said you were handsome, but really. I had no idea. Bob? Isn't he just gorgeous?"

I could clearly see that "a little light in the loafers" had been an understatement. I met a guy at a pub once who moonlighted as a drag queen. He had nothing on Reed. At least I knew I'd sleep well tonight knowing that if this guy was the only threat to my marriage, I needn't worry.

Bob heartily agreed I was "gorgeous" and took my hand in greeting. He was so delicate about it, though. It was like shaking hands with a handkerchief.

"Nice to meet you," I said, being careful not to wrinkle him.

"All right everyone," piped Jayne. "Let's get started. We'll go by colour as always. Just put your vote in the basket and we'll tally them when everyone's had a taste."

I sauntered over to the table and stirred the chowder in the blue crock. I was actually glad to have the extra guests on hand, delicate or not. Every vote counted and I always needed as many as I could get. "Gosh, this one with the corn looks good," I said to anyone who'd listen.

"It sure does," said Penny, stirring the red. It had corn, too.

At last the game was afoot.

"Off to the side you two," said Jayne, smiling and calmly taking us both by the arm. Her pill - or pills - had obviously kicked in.

Penny and I reluctantly gathered at the empty picnic table while Billy tuned in the portable radio and the others sampled our wares.

"You turd," I mocked.

"What," Penny laughed. "You said the gloves were off."

"Aren't you ever going to tell me?"

"Tell you what?"

"Your secret," I urged. "We obviously use the same ingredients. How come yours is always so much better?"

"Sometimes it's not what you do, but what you *don't* do that makes the difference." She smiled that little impish smile of hers and I couldn't help but smile back.

"Thanks, Buddha," I said. "I'll remember that."

What a turd.

I spotted Reed getting awfully cozy with Jayne. He pulled her close, his arm round her waist, and kissed her on the cheek chummier than me on a morning after we'd made love. For an effeminate guy, he sure was manly.

"There he goes," said Penny, noting Reed, "puttin' the moves on Mom."

That bastard, I thought. It made me wonder what else he was going to do.

I didn't have to wonder long, though. Within seconds, he'd cast his ballot and started dancing cheek to cheek with my wife, and ignoring his own by the way, to whatever tune was on a radio. As far as Jayne went, it was like she wasn't even bothered that I was sitting right there with a bird's eye view of the whole thing. That must have been some pill.

Apparently, Bob didn't care in the least either. He was too busy chatting up Brian, who was too stupid to realize he was being flirted with. Donna finally intervened just as Bob, in harmless admiration, was about to squeeze Brian's bicep. It was no mystery that she was the jealous type, no matter who was after her man. Still, Brian, though a little slow on the up-take, couldn't stand it when a guy like Bob got too close. He'd have nailed him once he caught on. Then, of course, he would have felt bad afterward because he really was a gentle, innocent sort underneath all those muscles. So was Bob.

"Kind of touchy-feely, aren't they?" I half joked.

"Bob's alright," said Penny. "He's just trying to be friendly. Reed, on the other hand, is a lech."

"He's not like that with you girls, is he?"

"Oh, no," she scowled. "I made it pretty clear that we

didn't tolerate that kind of crap. Besides, he's gay. Gay guys like Mom for some reason. I guess it's the whole decorating thing."

"Right." I hated to picture decking a guy in a pink shirt for fondling one of my daughters. Forget the fact that he was getting way too friendly with my wife.

Donna, having given up on the wardrobe battle, walked up to us with two bowls and her coloured voting cards. "Alright, Daddy. Which one's yours?" she said, more than asked.

Penny and I each took a look into the bowls. There was very little difference and frankly we couldn't really tell one from the other at first glance. Could it be possible that I'd bested my rival?

"I think you took two of the same," thought Penny aloud.

"No, I didn't," barked Donna. "I'm not stupid, you know."

Penny and I looked at each other and shrugged. Then, we each took a taste from the red rimmed bowl. Good flavour with a hint of smoke. Could she have grilled the fish? We each took a taste from the blue. Good flavour with a hint of Worcestershire. Could I have discovered a new angle? I could tell it was going to be a close race.

"Not a word," glared Penny.

I glared back. "How about two."

"Donna, honey. We need your vote," shouted Jayne.

"Okay, fine," muttered Donna. And with that, she swaggered off to cast her ballot.

My heart started to race. I might have a shot this year. I really might have a shot. Penny knew it, too, and she stared at me, desperately suppressing all emotion, as I beamed.

"Cheater," she mumbled, holding back a grin.

"Lightweight," I replied, in simulated earnest.

I saw Ruthie heading up to the house and gave chase. I suddenly realized I'd been neglecting her and wanted to make sure she'd stay at least until Jayne announced the winner, which could be any second - which could be ME.

"Has everyone cast their ballots?" shouted Jayne, finally enjoying herself - a little.

I caught up to Ruthie while Jayne tallied the cards. "Honey, wait," I called out.

Ruthie stopped and turned. She was looking a little green around the gills and I could tell she was in no mood to stay.

"Everything okay?"

"I think I need to throw up," she replied, rubbing her stomach.

"I hope it wasn't from my chowder."

"I kind of have a hangover. I think I need to throw up."

"I'll go with you," I said, taking her gently by the arm for support.

"I'm fine. You don't have to. Besides, Mom will be mad if she finds out."

"No she won't. I'll go with you."

"Stephen?" shouted Jayne. "We're ready. Where are you going?"

"I have to use the john," I shouted. "I'll be right back."

"I'm not going to make it. She's going to be mad," cried Ruthie, her pace quickening.

"You'll be fine."

Ruthie and I headed for the house in silence. I could tell she really didn't feel well as she held one hand on her stomach, the other over her mouth. I felt bad for her, remembering hangovers from my own youth. They were never pleasant.

The second we hit the patio, Ruthie cut loose and vomited all over the deck. "Oh, no," she cried.

"It's okay, honey. Let's get you to the bathroom."

"Oh, no," and with that, she heaved again.

She seemed so frightened and ashamed. She kept saying how her mother was going to be so angry. "Not the patio." The way I designed it, no one, including Jayne, could even see the deck from the beach. It was also built out of nearly indestructible cedar. The hose was right nearby, too, so all evidence could be washed away immediately. It was unfortunate, however, that her mother's chief concern above all else would be that the neighbors might find out – again. The fact that Ruthie had been sick due to an overindulgence of alcohol and narcotics was simply an afterthought.

"Whew!" came a voice from behind. "That's wicked." Billy hopped up on the deck as Ruthie rushed inside. "Everything okay?" he asked.

"Yeah, fine. Just watch your step," I replied, pointing out the spill.

"She partying again?"

I think "still" was the more appropriate term, but I didn't want to get into it with young Bill. He probably knew more than I did about the situation, but to me he was still the kid next door.

"Don't say anything to her mother, will you? She'll pitch a fit."

"No problem. You want me to take care of it?"

"Thanks, but I'll do it. Did you need something?"

"Forgot the cheese for the burgers."

"Oh, right. Help yourself."

Billy dashed inside while I got the hose. It was an awful stench and I could tell a little bleach was in order. Billy was way ahead of me and brought out the gallon jug of Clorox from the laundry room along with the package of cheddar.

"Deck brush is just inside the garage," he said, as if this were part of a routine.

"Thanks," I replied. "Cover for me?"

"I'll say you got a phone call."

"Good man."

Man... It was the first time I'd ever said it, like that anyway. He'd grown up right before my eyes and I hadn't even noticed until just now. It meant my girls had grown into women, too, and even though I'd referred to them as such, tongue in cheek, it never really dawned on me that they'd actually *become* women.

Donna was getting married and it didn't seem real then. Ruthie was having her run-ins with twenty-five year-old Chuck and it didn't seem real then either. Penny was heading off to college in the fall and shacking up with Billy - the good man - and it still didn't seem real. Jayne had changed, too, so much so that at times I didn't even recognize her and she seemed too often not to recognize me.

Where had the time gone? Where had my wife and girls gone? Where had I gone? I guess it was all part of the denial.

"Dad!? Dad!!!"

Penny came flying up onto the patio like a scout dashing to warn the troops of impending - and immediate - doom. I thought for sure someone had had a heart attack and frankly I was about to as I splashed down some bleach and frantically scrubbed the deck.

"Don't tell your mother!"

"You're never going to believe this!"

112

"What?" I paused.

"You're never going to believe this," she bellowed, out of breath. "We tied! WE TIED!!!"

And with that, I fainted.

12

It turns out my fainting spell was caused by a common, yet sometimes fatal, chemical reaction. I was lucky to have come out of it without so much as a proverbial scratch.

Jayne had mopped the bathroom floors with ammonia the night before and tossed the water out the kitchen door just over the patio deck. Some of the bleach I used to clean up Ruthie's mess mixed with a minute puddle that hadn't yet evaporated and the noxious fumes got to me before I even knew what was happening. Thankfully, between the fresh air and a spray with the hose, I was revived quite quickly without any aftereffects. It was equally fortunate, according to Jayne, that the mishap didn't make the papers – although, our now famous "Chowder Cook-off of 1965" did.

It was a decent sized article on the back page of the local section with a big picture to boot. Billy, holding the winning crock, was featured in the photo alongside Penny and I - "...'cause he's good lookin'", they said. It had been two solid weeks since the article hit the newsstands and I have reason to believe that Billy's still strutting like a rooster and signing autographs all around town. Finally, his rite of passage had come.

Much to everyone's surprise, especially mine, the cook-off was indeed a tie - initially, that is. Bob, who would have been the swing vote, was allergic to fish and sat out during the vote, rendering the judges to an even stand. We couldn't just leave it at that, though, so Penny and Billy, with all of us in tow, took both crocks down to the fishing docks and had several "impartial" judges make the final decision.

Dorothy Rand's dockside diner, known as "Hot Dot's", was a buzz of excitement as a gang of local lobstermen sampled our best. In the end it was yours truly who out-chowdered the champ and I thought everyone, including Penny, would have hysterics.

Penny was definitely a good sport about it all, which didn't surprise me. In fact, it was she who called the local paper, making sure they brought a photographer along and extra film. Much to the media's surprise, however, neither one of us gave away a single hint about our recipes and vowed to take the secret formulas to our graves, which actually made pretty good press. It's hard to go shopping now and not have someone stop one of us to try and get us to confess. We're practically famous.

Penny also made sure they put a plug in for Jayne's decorating business, which prompted a plethora of calls from new, prospective clients. She's even thinking of hiring a secretary. Cod and salt pork sales have risen as well, as locals try to outdo each other with their best concoctions. It's said one of the restaurants plans to organize its own contest with generous prize packages, including a year's supply of fish.

Dot's had to double her coffee bean order, too, just to keep up with the flow of customers. Who knew a bowl of chowder could spawn such widespread economic growth.

Reed stopped by earlier to pick up Jayne for another design meeting and practically gave her a hickey right there in the kitchen. Honestly. Why can't the guy just say good morning like everybody else?

He and Jayne had won the bid and were going to be doing a complete remodel of the Groverton's beach house. According to Reed, they were very particular about the details, which wasn't exactly a shock. I was surprised, though, when Jaynie hired a young buck architect from Stamford to do the renderings instead of me. She truly wanted to be independent and if hiring someone else to do her drawings was what it meant then so be it. At least I was asked to do the before and after photos.

Ruthie was off again with the shithead and Penny was down at the harbour with her beau. I never realized how lonely it could feel when everyone was out. I actually missed the chaos.

I decided to head down to the docks to see if I could get myself into trouble when Donna popped in unexpectedly.

"Oh, good," she said as she dropped her spanking new designer handbag on the counter. "You're home."

"Hi, honey. What's going on?"

"Did you call the credit card company? Brian and I are going to be booking the honeymoon this week and they'll want a deposit. It'll be very embarrassing if it declines."

"Why would I have to call the credit card company? And why would it decline anyway?" I asked, a bit taken aback by her almost insolent attitude.

"These things have limits, you know," she continued, talking to me as if our roles as parent and child had been reversed. "It's very embarrassing when it declines because you've exceeded the limit."

"I hope 'you' doesn't mean 'me', because I haven't bought a thing," I informed her.

"You know what I mean," she sighed.

She went upstairs to do god knows what, leaving me in the kitchen - alone. The clock ticked loud, like a metronome, and I was left to wonder to the beat of what drummer she marched. She sure had a lot of gall.

Donna came back downstairs a few minutes later with a sweater and a yellow shoe box. It was likely she was going to try and return the pair of white sandals she'd worn to the cook-off since they matched Ruthie's almost to a tee. She was always returning things. It got so the store clerks hated to see her coming.

"Well?" she demanded.

"Well what?" I asked.

"Did you call?"

"Just now? No."

"Well, our appointment with the travel agent is in a couple of hours. You might want to get on that. I have to go."

I was so stunned I couldn't even wave goodbye. Was this *my* daughter? It couldn't be. Suddenly the term "Drill Sergeant" no longer seemed appropriate. I'm sure Penny could come up with something far more colourful than that. I, for one, didn't even want to attempt it for fear I'd go overboard.

I finished my coffee, grabbed my camera and headed

down to the harbour to try and find some solace. Even if Billy and Penny weren't there, I knew the salt air would at least do me good.

I took the short way round, walking the beach instead of the lane, and spotted my girl and her guy tuning up the *Bobby Grace*. They worked so perfectly together, like a well-oiled machine, and I wanted to get some candids of them on the boat. I pulled my cap down low and meandered onto the dock, pretending to be a tourist reading a charter boat pamphlet.

Billy had the engine hood pulled off and was changing a spark plug while Penny worked on a hydraulic pump. "How's that winch workin' this mornin', babe?" asked Billy. "Do you feel it slippin' at all?"

"Not really," she replied, running a length of line through it. "I think it might hold now."

"Toss a trap over and give her a go."

Penny grabbed a trap off the deck and tossed it onto the gunnel like it was a box of crackers. While some had switched to using lightweight metal traps, she and Billy used old wooden traps with hand knit heads made of sisal dipped in tar and buoys fashioned from old cedar telephone poles. Soaking wet, they must have weighed a good hundred pounds a piece. When I asked her why they didn't spring for the techno-traps, she said it was because they were purists. I said it was because they were tightwads. Frankly, I think it was a toss up.

Penny slid the trap along the gunnel, positioning it next to her hauling rig, and shoved it over the side. Billy sidled up next to her and fired up the engine while she hauled in the trap to test the winch. He revved the beefy inboard a few times then shut her down and grabbed his girl round the waist as she swung the dangling pot back onto the gunnel.

"Works fine, lasts a long time," she sang, smiling from ear to ear.

"Same go for you?" he said, drawing her in and gnawing on her neck.

Penny smiled and looked up just as I snapped a photo of her and Billy.

"Damn it, Dad," she laughed, knocking the trap back over the side as she shoved herself off of Billy's hip.

"Whoa! Mr. Sheridan. I didn't see you there, sir."

Billy kind of laughed nervously, adjusting the front of his jeans and grabbing at his t-shirt. I laughed along with the two of them. You had to admit. They sure were a pair.

"What are you doing down here?" asked Penny, playfully slapping Billy in the gut while trying to wipe the smile off her face.

"The Drill Sergeant was hitting me up for honeymoon money so I thought I'd duck away before she booked a trip to the moon."

"Good call."

"Hey, we're goin' out for a short run in a few minutes," said Billy. "You wanna tag along?"

"Oh, I don't know. I'd just be in the way, wouldn't I?" I replied. It sure sounded inviting, though. Plus the bait was fresh and didn't stink in the least.

"Don't worry about it," said Penny. "If you get under foot, we'll just toss you overboard with the shorts."

Billy laughed and nudged her in the ribs. "We got some extra oil skins if you want," he offered. "We were just gonna go out to check a string we set yesterday," he continued.

I had a small hope that they'd ride past the shoal islands on the way to wherever they were going. I loved going out by the shoals. They had a dock out at Lovell and I'd often thought of camping out there so I could do some photography, although I wouldn't know the first thing about how to pitch a tent and I couldn't park a boat to save my life. It did always sound like a good idea, though.

"Okay," I replied. "I just want to run into Dot's and grab a donut or something. You two want anything?"

"I'll take a cruller if there's any left," piped Penny.

"Nothin' for me, thanks," added Billy. "I'll be in to get some coffee in a minute, though, and then we'll go."

"Sounds great."

I stepped up the dock and into the little diner just as Dorothy was putting up a fresh pot of coffee. She was a pleasant woman about my age, round as a melon through the middle, rough as a cob around the edges. She had a giant heart made of pure gold and cursed worse than a pirate. She was quite the character.

"Well, I'll be goddamned. Look what the cat dragged in," she said with a big welcoming smile. I noticed the newspaper article from our chowder cook-off pinned on the board above the cash register with a small, hand-scribbled sign – *Mention this article and get a free small coffee refill!* – which was kind of funny, since she always gave free small refills anyway.

Dorothy had had a roaming eye on me since the second I stepped foot in Quincy and she wasn't shy about mentioning it. The feeling was never mutual, but I always tried to be nice about it. Besides, her harbour master husband, Walter, could probably crush me between his two fingers so it was best to kind of stay on her good side, which wasn't hard. She was a sweetheart.

Walter and Dot had six kids and had been married since

121

they were teenagers. Neither one finished high school, but you'd have thought they were both college graduates. Walt, a fourth generation lobsterman, dabbled in the stock market and it was said he was worth millions. Dorothy was an avid reader with a photographic memory and could recall just about anything from Elizabethan poetry to encyclopedia entries on the vaguest of subjects. Their kids were no lightweights either, five of which finished high school before their fifteenth birthdays. The other isn't far behind.

"Hi, Dot. Got any crullers left?" I asked.

"Are you shittin' me? It's damn near nine-thirty for chrissakes. Where the hell have you been?"

She did have a way with words.

"Oh, you know. Around."

"I got fresh coffee comin' up, though, and a couple of old dead cakes I squirreled away from first thing. You want those?"

"You know I do."

Dot made the best donuts I'd ever tasted, and I've tasted my share. She must have sensed I was coming because the cake variety was my all time favourite – as well as everyone else's – and there was never any left after about 7am. Her coffee rivaled that of the best restaurants in town, too, and folks came from far and wide just to get a cup to go.

"Those two ever gonna get married?" she asked, nodding toward Penny and Billy coming up the ramp.

"Eventually, I would imagine. I hope they wait a little while, though. My oldest is running me into the poor house with her own wedding as we speak," I noted.

"Yeah, I heard. No holds barred, eh?"

"You said it."

"Hey, Mrs. Rand!" shouted Billy on his way in. "Think you could spare some of that coffee for us late comers?"

Dot grabbed his thermal flask and sloshed it full of hot coffee while the filter continued to drip into her own, well-brewed mug. "The hell I can," she spat. "Shit, I harvested the beans myself and roasted them over an open pit all goddamn morning just waiting for your sorry butt to arrive."

Billy stood at the counter laughing and juggling his thermos lid while Penny fished around in the cooler for an OJ. Dot slammed the loaded flask down sending a stream of steaming coffee into the air that miraculously landed straight back into the thermos bottle. It was like watching a physics lesson on The Mr. Science Show.

"Thanks, dear," said Billy, tightening the lid and giving her a wink. "You ready, Mr. Sheridan?"

"Just need to settle up with Dot."

"Yours and Penny's are on the house," she smiled, "but Monaghan, here, has to pay double, bein' that he's a fuckin' celebrity and all now."

Dot winked at Billy, too, as he handed her a dollar just in case she wasn't kidding. She threw it back at him and we were on our way.

13

Penny ducked below as we chugged past the mile buoy and brought out a fresh oilskin slicker wrapped in a clean plastic bag. "It's pretty smooth out here today, but you still might want this," she said, handing it to me.

"Don't you want it?" I asked, noticing their well-worn jackets hanging next to the bulkhead door.

"Nah. We're tough guys, right Billy?"

"Like a couple o' nails," he growled, throwing an arm around her shoulder, and I quick snapped a picture of the two of them as he kissed her on the cheek.

It was still pretty warm for August, but the air turned quickly cooler the further out we got. I could tell the jacket was going to come in handy.

Penny and Billy owned their boat together since their early teens. It was a good-sized, twenty-seven footer that had been salvaged from a storm and they christened her the *Bobby Grace* after Billy's late mother and brother. It was pretty beat up and needed a new inboard, but over the course of a summer they had her running like a champ and ready to haul lobsters. Although they didn't haul as many traps as some, they remained true to their goal of earning enough money to see them both through college. As the years went by, though, those plans extended even further to include buying a house and raising a family. They had been building a life together before they even realized what it meant.

"So what are you going to do with the boat while you're up at school?" I asked.

"We're going to be home to fish on the weekends," replied Penny, "so, we'll keep her moored in the harbour. Billy's Dad will keep an eye on her."

"What about your studies?"

"We'll do that at night."

"I've had a whole routine worked out since freshman year, sir," added Billy. "Works pretty good, except around midterms and finals. Then we'll only fish on Saturdays."

"Guess that doesn't leave much room for hanky panky, huh," I teased, hoping I was at least partly right.

"That's what Spring Break is for," Penny grinned, poking Billy in the ribs on her way to the bulkhead.

"Don't worry, sir," blushed Billy. "She's just tryin' to get me in trouble."

"Uh, huh," I sneered, trying to hold back a smile. I was sure going to miss them.

Penny pulled on her oilskin pants and threw on her old, ripened sweatshirt as we motored around to the far side of the shoals' big island. The entire area had been fished out for years, but they took a chance that the lobsters might be returning. Penny soon spotted their short string of about a half dozen traps set along a narrow ridge about a hundred yards from shore.

"Right where we left 'em, hon," she cried.

Billy, an expert helmsman, drove while Penny hauled, a routine they'd had down pat since forever. I snapped a few more photos as we idled up to the first buoy.

Billy coasted alongside the red and white bobber just as slick as you please, while Penny reached overboard with the gaff and hooked the warp. She slung it over the snatch block and around the winch and up it came, water from the drenched hemp flying like a rooster tail.

"Hold on to your hats, boys," cautioned Penny as she gazed over the side. "You're gonna flip when you see this one."

Penny dropped the swollen trap onto the gunnel. It was teaming with lobsters, some still hanging onto the side looking for a way in to what they called the kitchen and Billy about went nuts.

"Son of a bitch, Pen," he shouted. "I was right. I was right!"

"They look a little small," she noted.

"Doesn't matter. I was right!" he cried, jumping for joy. Billy grabbed a pencil and marked a circle on his chart where the string had been set. The oceanographic survey was a spray of coloured markings: stars in red, squares in blue, triangles in green, purple lines this way and that. They all meant something and only Billy had the key tucked away in his head.

Penny whipped out her gauge and checked each lobster as she pulled them out - and off - of the trap. Most were shorts, but the few that were within the legal limit were tossed back overboard to mature a little while longer. "No sense taking them while they're young," she said. "They need to keep growing up and making families."

"The more the merrier," cheered Billy.

Each trap was the same, full of shorts, and they decided to pull in the string and set it elsewhere to allow the herd to multiply. They only yielded two decent keepers, but the thought that there'd be more to come in a year or so made it far worth their while. As long as no one else caught on, they'd make money hand over fist next summer - just in time for the tuition bills.

"Let's go pull a couple from the five mile string," said Penny. "We'll have a clam bake to celebrate before we head up to school."

"You got it, babe," said Billy and we were off again.

Billy was elated that he'd found the pot of gold at the end of the rainbow and couldn't wait to tell his father. I, however, had to swear an oath of secrecy not to breathe a word of it to anyone, for fear the entire fleet would pounce on their new found bounty.

"How did you know they'd be there?" I asked. "I thought that area had been barren for years."

"It has to do with a type of vegetation they feed on," Billy explained. "A kind of algae. The scientists aren't quite sure why, but the stuff kinda died off around this island about a decade ago. Apparently the conditions have been right for it to start growing again. I've actually been trackin' it myself for about three years, gatherin' samples and takin' pictures with these rigs Penny built. It's taken a while, but the lobsters and the other marine life are finally findin' it again."

"See, Dad," joked Penny. "He's not only good lookin'. He's smart, too."

"You're no slouch either," Billy grinned.

Penny was all geared up to study engineering at Salem State with an eye to developing research equipment for oceanographers and marine biologists. Billy's shoals study was her first concerted effort in development and the two worked together for two summers getting the equipment just right.

Since neither she nor Billy were avid scuba divers, Penny had built a special waterproof box that housed a Polaroid camera and flash that Billy could use to quickly check the appearance of the terrain out at the shoals. In addition, she developed another device that used a tiny mechanical claw to gather samples of the vegetation that he suspected had been growing there. She said she got the idea from a pickle retriever they bought at L.L. Bean.

It was obvious that college was already paying off for young Bill. He was studying to be a marine biologist, also at Salem State, and had submitted an application for a coveted internship at the Marine Biological Laboratory in Woods Hole. It was highly competitive and you really had to be on the ball just to be considered. According to Skip and Penny, Billy was a shoe-in for the position, but he'd have to wait until mid to late fall to find out for sure.

I was certainly happy to be able to spend a little time with the two of them before they left for orientation the following day. Although I wasn't thrilled about the idea of them sharing an apartment, and likely a bed, I was comfortable with the notion that Billy was half of the equation and not just some jock, or worse - a shithead.

It was a short ride to what Penny and Billy called "the five mile string" and we all sipped coffee and nibbled donuts during the journey. A small pod of whales greeted us as we paused to cut bait and I got a couple of good shots of their flukes as they rolled along silently.

Billy pulled up to the first trap in the string and Penny snatched up the line and started to haul. The trap must have been seated in the mud because it took several revolutions before the winch took hold and started the trap's ascent. "Come on, Bessie," said Penny, encouraging the winch. "Keep on truckin'."

"She slippin' again?" asked Billy.

"Yep. I think we're going to have to bite the bullet and get a new one, though."

"Something wrong with your rig?" I asked.

"Maybe. We salvaged it from a wreck in the spring," Penny replied. "I was lucky to get it running at all."

"Your daughter's awful handy with the hydraulics, though," said Billy. "That stuff's a total mystery to me."

"I thought by now you'd have invented something better," I said to Penny, pointing to their make-shift hauling apparatus. "That thing looks like a death trap."

"Are you kidding? We can haul twenty times more than we used to with this so-called death trap," she smiled. "We're raking in the dough, now."

Point taken.

Billy popped the boat into gear and roared to the next trap in the string. As he dropped her back into idle, the sound of an equally beefy inboard was heard revving up in the near distance. Billy quickly spotted the competition and sprung into action.

"Better strap your father down, Pen," he warned. "There's a boat load o' trouble headed right this way." He grabbed the jackets and gaff and anything else that wasn't nailed down and threw the lot in the bulkhead while Penny organized the traps on deck, stuffing three and four into each corner of the stern.

I was a bit alarmed, not knowing what sort of unlawfulness had been brewing that season. A few years back, an out-of-towner, who fished no more than nine or ten traps, was caught poaching. One fateful day, he went out to check his string and found he was down to one with a knife stuck in the buoy and a shark's head stuffed in the pot. The guy got the picture and was never seen or heard of again.

Billy switched on his radio as the competitor slowly approached. Nervous, I zoomed in with my telephoto and was relieved to see it was the infamous *Rum Runner* with the equally infamous Skip at the wheel.

"This could get interesting," Penny squealed, although we both knew it could also get ugly.

"You lookin' for trouble, old timer?" Billy barked into the mic.

"It's my middle name," was the reply over the raspy speaker.

Penny took my hand and led me to the stern where we each took a seat and prayed. "You're going to want to hang on," she said, both eyebrows raised and grinning.

The *Bobby Grace* was known as one of the fastest lobster boats for its size in the area. No one could match her. The hull had been designed by another famous builder, Royal Lowell, and Billy made sure she was restored with his fullest intentions for unmatched stealth in mind. It made Skip all the more bent on making his own boat faster.

As somber and sober as he appeared on the outside, Skip did possess a wild streak that was clearly on display that afternoon. In fact, he was worse than a kid at times, and was up to his usual no good. He'd just finished hauling his string for the day when he spotted the *Bobby Grace*. Talk about the game being afoot.

Skip, captaining one of the last Monaghan designs still afloat, moved to within 15 yards of Billy and dropped the engine to an idle.

"Think you can take me, old man," shouted Billy, clipping his radio handset back into the holder.

The two were stock still, even up with each other, neither one daring to look away for fear the other would get a jump. The *Rum Runner* dwarfed the *Bobby Grace*, but it didn't matter in the least. A race was a race and they were about to have one.

Billy, his hand poised on the throttle, chided his father again. "I got five bucks says you can't!"

He and Skip were like two teenagers in Corvettes waiting for a stop light to change. Suddenly, Skip slammed his thirty-six footer into gear, stuffing the throttle into the corner, and Billy wasn't far behind.

Penny and I must have pulled three G's as we hung on for dear life, white-knuckled all the way while Billy tried his best to outrun his father. Just as Skip would gain a yard, Billy was right there to gain it back. It was cat and mouse all the way and it was all I could do to hang on.

"Come on, Billy! Come on!" Penny shouted, hooting and hollering.

"Give it up, old man!" he shouted to his father.

Skip, still even up with Billy, gave a little salute and punched an additional secret throttle on his dash, cranking open the second of two four-barrel carburetors. His boat seemed to fly into overdrive and he sped away like we were standing stock still. He had to have been doing 70 knots.

"Son of a bitch!" shouted Billy, finally easing off. "Son

of a bitch!" He slammed his cap on the deck and turned to
Penny as the boat continued to slip effortlessly through the
water at a steady clip. "That old fart's gone nitro on me! Did
you see that?! He's gone nitro!"

14

We had a great send off for Penny and Billy, some three Sunday's ago now. We partied on the beach until close to midnight and ended up with a bonfire large enough to be visible from space. Even Skip was out with us until "last call". He didn't want to let go any more than we did.

Jayne and I, a bit bleary-eyed, got up around six the next morning to see Penny and Billy off and gave them one last speech about behaving themselves. I wanted to follow them up to campus in Jaynie's Jag, but they insisted on having me wait until they got the apartment set up. I humbly took that to mean I wasn't going to actually be invited - ever - but that was okay. I was willing to give them their space so long as they promised to come home every weekend.

The days certainly dragged with everyone being gone to do their own thing and me without a car. Penny tried to talk me into buying an economical Beetle, but I had my eye on the hot new Thunderbird I saw showcased down at Dixon's

Automotive. It was far from economical, but I hadn't owned a car of my very own since our old Plymouth and I felt I was about due for something sporty. I just had to wait and see if I had enough money left over after Donna's wedding before I signed the paperwork. The way things were going, though, it was looking better and better for the Beetle.

Sadly, I'd barely seen Penny during those first few promised weekends. She and Billy would go out fishing during the day and would only stop by at dinner time to grab a quick bite before heading out again to take in a movie or study at the library. Some evenings, they'd just ride around in Penny's Nash until they found a place along the shore to park. God knows what they did then. I missed her.

Donna stopped in, sometimes twice daily, to extort money from me and harangue her mother for not keeping better tabs on Ruth. You'd have thought she was the matriarch of the family the way she bossed us all around. Frankly, I was growing a little tired of it and was about ready to announce it to anyone who would listen.

Donna was right about her sister, though. I'll give her that much. Ruthie needed some sound guidance but, unfortunately, was never around to receive any. A week ago Thursday, she came home late crying with another black eye and, this time, a limp. She was so weary from her time with Chuck, she couldn't even yell at him before he sped away in his usual insane manner. It was an exercise in futility to try and get her to stay home. He'd just be there the next morning, horn blaring and shouting, coaxing her - threatening her, really - to get a move on. I wanted to kill the guy.

On top of that, Reed seemed to be having his way with my wife on a regular basis. She claimed he was harmless and there was nothing to it, but to me his business practices were way too casual for my taste. I caught him earlier in the week embracing Jayne from behind while they looked over a brochure for wide-slat blinds. His groin was buried in her rear while his hand explored the upper feminine curves of her dress. I thought I was going to scream.

I'd been developing the "before" photos of the Groverton beach house in my darkroom that Saturday afternoon when I heard Reed's car pull in the driveway. I knew how fast he worked so I had the prints under a little fan to get them to dry as soon as possible. I feared if I wasn't there to chaperone the two of them I might end up finding him and Jayne spread eagle right there on the kitchen floor.

I grabbed up the series of prints, stuffed them in an envelope and practically ran for the house. As I walked in, I caught Reed already about to kiss Jayne.

"Oh, hi, honey," said Jayne, startled and pushing Reed away.

"Stephen. Nice to see you again," he added, smiling and offering his hand in greeting. "We're off to the Groverton's."

"Super," I sneered, ignoring the handshake. I'd rather have clocked him.

"We were just heading out," added Jayne. "Did you get a chance to print the photos?"

I held up the envelope, my gaze never wavering from Reed's. He backed up, still smiling as if his face were stuck, until he abruptly met the kitchen counter. I was pissed and he was sensing it. So was Jayne.

"Good," she said, visibly unnerved. "I'll just get my purse."

While Jayne went to the bedroom to grab her handbag,

Reed and I had a stand off. He just smiled that stupid smile of his, like nothing was wrong. How could there be nothing wrong? He was violating my wife right in front of me. Still, it kind of made me wonder who was the bigger idiot. Him, for being so brazen? Or me, for allowing it to get that far. Either way, it was really starting to eat at me.

"I don't know what your problem is, buddy," I said, poking him in the chest good and hard, "but I sure would appreciate it if you kept your mitts off my wife."

I was so close to him I could smell his hair tonic, his cologne, his mouthwash. I envisioned a bathroom vanity full of every conceivable men's grooming product - and more I hadn't even heard of. I could even smell the heavy starch in his blue and white pinstripe shirt. He probably starched his shorts, too. There were other smells I couldn't even identify. It must have taken him hours just to get ready in the morning.

"I was just fixing her hair," he explained, his UltraBrite grin about blinding me.

"Uh, huh. And what were you doing the other day? Giving her a breast exam?"

I was really getting hot, the events of the past days culminating, then brewing, stewing like an angry soup. The last few weeks had been a real test, I admit. But this was more like "finals". Was this what it was going to be like? All the time?

"Jayne and I have a special kind of business relationship," Reed commented, trying to step away from me.

"I don't give a shit," I replied, getting right back up in his face. "If I see you lay one more hand on her, I'm going to take you out behind the barn and your jaw and my fist are going to have our own special kind of business relationship. You got that?"

For an average looking, average sized guy, I somehow must have miraculously appeared intimidating. Whether it was the five o'clock shadow or the scar over my eye - or maybe both - I'll never know. But I thought Reed was going to soil his pressed khakis right then and there, which was exactly the type of reaction I was gunning for.

"Ready to go," called Jayne, calm and smiling as she returned with her handbag and lightweight wrap. It was evident she'd just taken a pill.

Reed bolted for the door, standing behind it for safety as he held it open for Jayne, then all but ran for the car as he saw me start to follow.

"Jayne?"

"Yes, dear?"

"Don't forget these."

I handed her the manila envelope and she was off. No goodbye. Just a kiss. Then off. What an afternoon.

I called Page later on for advice. I'd always felt terrible for being away from my family and now, after only a month, all I wanted to do was get away from them. All my denial hadn't paid off in the least and now the guilt and anger was beginning to settle in like a morning fog that wouldn't lift. It was worse than penance.

"Do you need me to tell you where to go, love?" Page asked, her tongue firmly planted in her cheek.

"That would be a start," I replied. I needed her words of wisdom no matter how much they might sting.

"Well, if you haven't been already," she began, "don't bother going to hell. I've tried it myself and frankly it's not all it's cracked up to be."

There was one off the list.

The devotion I have for my family had forever been my singular mainstay, my purpose for providing, and was what kept me going during the long days, weeks, and lonely months apart from them. In a quiet moment of epiphany, I painfully realized that although I'd always held faithfully onto my love for my women, my new purpose had to be to regain their love for me. To say the task was daunting would be a shameful understatement.

By the time Page and I wrapped up our conversation, I was feeling at least human again and slightly less than completely overwhelmed. She assured me that becoming a permanent part of the family was going to take some getting used to and that all of us would have to go through the period of adjustment in our own way and at our own pace. It would be what she called "a process".

We'd talked a full hour and a half and I hesitated to think what the phone bill was going to cost. It didn't matter, though. According to reports from Penny, therapy was far more expensive - or so she'd heard.

"Love to the women," said Page, her voice ever-tranquil and comforting.

"Love to you, too," I replied.

It was never *goodbye*.

It was close to seven o'clock and still no Jayne, but then again I half-expected her to be late. The Groverton's were known for holding people hostage with bottomless cocktails and endless gloating about their doctor and lawyer sons, both of whom were widely hailed as nothing short of reckless womanizers. How they made it through Harvard without being expelled was beyond me. It's amazing what an endowment can buy you nowadays.

In spite of the chaos - and in spite of missing the girls - I was sort of getting used to my quiet evenings of soup and sandwich. Still, I secretly hoped for a little company from someone other than Walter Cronkite. He was a good conversationalist and all, but dry as toast. Even Donna would do. However, the company I really longed for was Jaynie.

Just as I flipped my Monte Christo onto the plate and was about to cry in my tomato bisque, the Peanut came crashing through the door.

"Whew! What a day!" she exclaimed as she bellied herself up to the breakfast bar.

"Good or bad?" I asked, happy to see her - happier still to see her sit for a second.

"Good. Great, in fact! We made two hundred and twenty-nine dollars at the dock today. Our biggest day ever."

She was glowing, and it wasn't all sunburn.

"That's fantastic, sweetheart," I said.

"Yeah. I'm beat, though. Is Mom home?"

"Not yet. I guess the Groverton thing is running long. You want some soup, or are you going out again?"

"I guess I could join you. I'm starved."

I was elated. Company at last! I jumped up and quick poured her a bowl of bisque before she changed her mind. "You want a sandwich, too?"

"I'll fix it," she said sidling up next to me at the stove.

"I missed you this morning."

"Yeah, well. We got a late start from campus this morning and ended up heading right to the harbour."

"Up late studying?"

"Something like that," she replied, blushing and hiding

a smile.

"Uh, huh. So where's your guy?"

"It's his mom's birthday today," she quietly explained. "He and his dad have a thing they do. It's kind of personal, so they like to be alone. It's kind of nice, really. They have a special supper, bring flowers to the cemetery, go out in the boat to her favourite spot and have a beer. That kind of thing."

"That's nice," I added. "Really nice."

"Yeah. They're good people," she smiled, placing her cheese sandwich into the cast iron skillet. "Billy might even make a half-decent son-in-law one of these days. Don't you think?" she winked.

"Don't push it, Peanut. You're still my baby and I want you to stay that way," I nudged, kissing her on the top of the head.

"Uh, huh."

"At least until you start to drive me nuts."

Donna dropped in unexpectedly, too. I thought it funny, though, that at that hour she was still wearing her sunglasses, the frames of which bore a striking resemblance to those worn by Jackie Kennedy in a recent magazine spread. As much as Donna hated someone else copying what she was wearing, she did have a unique habit of copying what other people were wearing - especially if those other people were celebrities.

Penny stood at attention and saluted: "Atten Hut!"

"Shut up, brat," replied Donna.

"Want some soup, honey?" I asked, knowing the answer would be 'no'.

"Gross," she cringed. How *pedestrian* of me. "Is there any coffee?"

"At this hour?"

Donna inspected the empty percolator then slammed it back onto the counter. "Of course not," she scoffed.

"Say, I've got a credit card statement to go over with you," I mentioned, hoping that not all the charges were legitimate. "Do you have time?"

Donna just glared at me over the top of her designer Foster Grants.

"Of course not," I sneered. "Do you think you could have your secretary pencil me in for, say, tomorrow afternoon?"

Penny sat down with her grilled sandwich and snickered into her bowl of soup while her sister scowled.

"I don't see what there is to go over," Donna snapped. "I give Jayne all the receipts."

"Jayne?!" I exclaimed.

Penny and I looked at one another, both dumbfounded.

"That's a new one," Penny mumbled.

"Is she home, by the way?"

"Since when did you start addressing your mother as 'Jayne'?" I asked, almost laughing at her pomposity. "And how come everybody always wants *her*. Doesn't *anybody* think *I* can do anything?"

"Please, Daddy. All the girls are doing it. It's just not a big deal. And yes, you *can* do something. You can raise the limit on the card like I asked you to three times."

"You know, I wish you'd get a job like everybody else and stop mooching off me for a change."

"Oh, stop it. I've already put my time in raising this family for you while you were out jet-setting with your British gang. Get a job. It's *preposterous*."

I couldn't help but laugh out loud. Was she kidding? I

so wanted for someone to let me in on the joke because I really didn't believe that what was happening was real. "Am I on Candid Camera?" I laughed. "I mean, really, Donna. Come on."

"I have to run."

"You just got here."

"I know," she replied. She barely kissed me on the cheek and left without another word.

I sat down next to Penny, rested my chin in my palm and stared at the kitchen cabinets. "Who was that?" I finally asked, feeling like I'd just come out of a weird, drug-induced coma.

"That was your daughter. Donna. Queen of all she surveys. Drill Sergeant to the masses. Ball buster to the gods."

"I was afraid of that," I hesitantly replied.

Penny slung an arm around my shoulders. "But, don't worry, Steve. You still have me."

I looked her point blank in the eye, pressed my forehead against hers and in my deepest, darkest Dad-voice ordered: "Don't you dare, little girl..."

As if she would ever take me seriously.

15

I got up early that Sunday and spent the morning in the darkroom, hoping Jayne would sleep in. She'd been working feverishly on the Groverton project and hadn't slept a wink in days. The renovations had come to a close and she wanted everything to be perfect for the official unveiling scheduled for the end of the week.

I'd taken some photos during the remodeling, as well as the "before" and "afters", so Jaynie's clients could see the process unfolding. Though they were likely to only be interested in the finished product, Jayne thought the photos would make a great addition to her portfolio and I did my best to please her.

I finished rinsing the last of the prints and hung them on the drying line. Jayne was going to have a brief meeting later that afternoon, so I wanted to make sure everything was ready. I was worried about the lighting in the photos and had to adjust the contrast a bit during the developing stages. The results were pretty spectacular if I do say so myself.

I hung the last of the prints on the line and heard the side door to the barn open and close followed by Billy's unmistakable voice - "Hey, I got an idea..." - and Penny's equally unmistakable giggle. They were getting a late start - again - and were clearly up to no good.

Two pair of unbeknownst feet quickly and quietly ascended the stairs above my head and danced around on the ceiling. Then, quite suddenly, they stopped. I didn't know whether to fly up there and scold the two of them, or just wait. I knew they worked upstairs in the barn on occasion, knitting heads for traps, repairing fishing nets for bait, that sort of thing. Maybe it was that. Yes. Maybe it was just that.

A strange sound followed, like a long zipper being undone, then two softened thuds.

"Ooh. Nice idea," crooned Penny.

Something about the way Penny swooned told me they were not about to knit heads. I wasn't exactly feeling angry. More like opportunistic. I really wanted to get even with her for catching Jayne and I that morning in the living room, although I hoped I wouldn't find she and her boyfriend in the same condition.

Billy didn't even get to the 'you' in "I love you" and I was up the stairs, taking the risers four at a time it seemed. I flew up to the loft so fast neither one had a chance to gather themselves and I about tore a ligament.

"Dad!!!"

"Shit, sir! Oh, shit!"

I quickly discovered the *zipping* was from that of an opened sleeping bag thrown over a makeshift mattress of fishing nets. Penny, her blouse undone, was as red as a radish with embarrassment while Billy, bare-chested and equally humiliated, scrambled to cover her up with his t-shirt.

"Shit, sir. We thought you were at church or somethin'."

"Damn it, Dad!"

"I thought we had this conversation, young lady? And you," I shouted, dramatically pointing at Billy and trying to look genuinely outraged. "What's the big idea? I told you to keep your fly zipped around her."

"It wasn't like that, sir," Billy claimed, struggling to find the capsule end of his Medic Alert pendant. "We were just foolin' around." The poor kid looked terrified and it was all I could do to keep from laughing.

"It wasn't what you think, Dad," Penny contended as she hid behind Billy, struggling with the buttons of her blouse.

"Uh, huh."

"We were just celebrating," she added, shoving Billy's t-shirt into his gut and coming out to face me. "That's all."

"Please don't tell me you're engaged," I begged, my heart sinking through the floorboards in instant terror.

"Oh, hell no, sir," said Billy, throwing his shirt on. "I'd have had the decency to ask you first."

"Gee thanks." As if that were reassuring.

"It's about the internship. Billy's in the running. The letter came by special delivery this morning."

"On a Sunday?"

"The courier is a buddy of mine," said Billy.

"Of course he is."

"It's true. Show him, Billy."

Billy pulled the wadded up letter out of his hip pocket

and handed it to me. "I don't want to get my hopes up or anything. There's still a few more rounds to go. They want to know more about my shoals study, though, and how Penny and I have been trackin' the lobsters over the years," he explained as I read the letter. "I guess it's a good thing I kept all my charts and stuff."

"Does your Dad know about this?" I asked. "The letter, I mean?"

"Not yet, sir."

"He called in on the radio a little while ago and said the mackerel were running," added Penny, still pink in the cheeks. "We were going to take the nets out and surprise him."

"Looks like somebody else got surprised first, huh," I smiled.

"Sorry about that, sir," Billy blushed, eyeing his Chuck Taylor's and kicking around a piece of string he spotted on the floor.

Penny stuffed her face into his bicep and giggled. "Shit," she mumbled. She knew we were even.

I couldn't help but be happy - for the two of them, really. Billy dreamed about this opportunity his whole life and there was no way I was going to steal his thunder, even if he did just have an admittedly innocent roll in the hay with my daughter. "Well, congratulations, son," I said, shaking his hand. "Your father's going to be real proud."

"Thank you, sir." He simply couldn't wipe the smile off his face. "I still have to keep my fingers crossed though."

Penny, beaming like a lighthouse, hugged him tight. "I'm crossing mine, too."

I handed Billy back his letter which he promptly folded tighter than a road map, stuffing it deep into his pocket. Had his mother still been alive, she'd have had a fit that he didn't keep it neat and clean for his scrapbook. Nonetheless, she'd have been elated, too.

"We should probably get going, huh," said Penny, practically cutting off the circulation in Billy's arm.

"Yeah, probably."

"Well, stay safe," I said, done with my mock-interrogation, and headed back down stairs for the darkroom. "By the way," I added, pausing at the landing. "Next time you want to celebrate, go get a malt or something, will ya? You about gave me a heart attack."

"Tell me about it," said Billy. "I almost had to toss a pill under my tongue."

The two just looked at me and smiled. I doubt they'll try and pull the same stunt twice.

Jayne finally got up around noon and I made her a nice brunch of poached eggs, toast, and fruit salad. It had been weeks, it seemed, since we'd made love and I was beginning to miss our moments together.

"Would you like to go out to dinner tonight after your meeting?" I asked, taking her hand gently in mine.

"I don't know," she wearily replied.

"Donna mentioned a new French Bistro in town that's supposed to be good. Very chic, she said."

Jayne barely ate a thing. She just sat, staring at her plate, fiddling with her eggs. I ran a finger through her hair and gently smoothed a stray strand over her ear.

"Could you pick up a prescription for me today?" she asked. "I seem to have run out of my pills."

She took an empty bottle from out of her robe pocket and placed it on the table. I picked it up and, curious, read the label – *Valium – Take 1 pill daily as needed or as directed by your physician. Not to exceed two pills per day.*

"Are they open today?" I asked.

"Noon to four, I think."

Jayne had been taking a lot of her little pills lately, far more than the maximum two per day, and I was beginning to get a little worried about her. The stress of the Groverton project, not to mention the rest of our family affairs, had been weighing heavy on her and it was the only way she knew to cope.

"Honey, why don't you try and go without them for a little while," I said, gently massaging her shoulder. "I'm here, you know. We can work through these things together."

"It's fine, Stephen. They're perfectly safe."

"Just try it, okay? For a day or so?"

Jayne sighed heavily then slowly rose from the table. "I think I'll go lay back down."

I followed her to the bedroom, where she slipped into bed and fell immediately back to sleep. It made me wonder if she'd actually been awake at all but maybe sleep-walking instead. I spooned up against her on the bed and held her close. This was not the Jayne I knew.

She slept another two hours and upon rising begged me to go to the pharmacy. She just couldn't function without her pills. She promised me she'd go to the doctor after the Groverton project was finished to see if there was something else she could take instead. I suggested a holiday.

I took a roll of colour film with me to the drug store for developing along with a short grocery list. Donna wanted me to take some portraits of she and Brian to send with the invitations that were due to be mailed within the month and she wanted to be able to pick out the best shots herself. I'd never actually heard of anyone sending photos with their invitations, but apparently it was a new thing and, if it was new, Donna was going to have it.

I never delved into colour processing myself, probably because you had to do it in total darkness. Plus, to me, there was too much of an exactness to it. Green was green was green and it had to look green or else. With black and white I can play with contrasts, bleach out areas that are dark, darken areas that are light, and so on to give it the look I want. And, if I do want colour, I can always add it by hand with special paints later. It makes me feel like an artist.

"Stephen Sheridan to the pharmacy counter, please. Mr. Sheridan to the pharmacy counter," said a pleasant voice over the intercom.

"I'll call you in a week or so," said Vera, the photo clerk. "Shouldn't be more than that."

"Any way you can put a rush on it?" I asked. "They're for Donna and you know how impatient she can be."

"No problem, Steve," she smiled. "Wouldn't want to upset *that* apple cart."

"Thanks." Everybody knew Donna.

At the pharmacy counter, Murray, who'd been the local pharmacist for as long as anyone could remember, informed me that he'd just filled Jayne's prescription two days prior.

"Did she pick it up herself?" I asked, a bit confused.

"As I recall it was your daughter, Ruth, that came by. She was with some weirdo. I almost didn't give them to her, but I knew Jaynie wouldn't send her unless she was too busy to come down herself. She probably just forgot with all she's got going on. By the way, how are the wedding plans coming along?"

A million thoughts raced through my mind. What on

151

earth was Jayne thinking? And where had Ruth been all this time? I hadn't seen her all week and envisioned her strung out on Valium, stoned on a couch somewhere - or worse.

"I say. How are the wedding plans coming along?"

"Oh, sorry, Murray," I said, snapping back into reality. "They're going great. Just great."

"Good. Well you let me know if we can do anything else for you."

"Yeah, thanks. Sorry to have troubled you."

If I'd had any inkling as to where to look, I'd have driven straight to Ruth Anne to take her away from whatever mess she was in. But as it was, I hadn't a clue even where to begin. She seemed so lost and so was I.

As I slowly drove through town, struggling to get my head wrapped around what was happening, I noticed the new French Bistro Donna mentioned. It was a quaint little place and I stopped to look over the menu posted on the window outside and to clear my head. I knew I was looking at the menu, but I couldn't even see it. All I could see was Ruth strung out and being beaten. Then, Jayne. I was so afraid to face the reality of it all, but quickly realized that I had to face it no matter what.

I got back in the car and drove straight home, hoping Ruthie would somehow be there. What I found instead was Donna. She was on the warpath again and the last thing I wanted to do was engage her in battle.

"Did you call them?" she immediately barked as I walked in the kitchen door.

"Where's your sister?" I asked.

"Three guesses."

"I mean Ruth."

"How should I know?"

"Where's your mother?"

"Sleeping. You might want to get her up, though."

"Why?"

"Reed called about ten minutes ago and said he'd meet her at the Groverton's around six. Why didn't you call?"

"Call who?"

"The credit card company. It declined this time, you know."

"And it'll probably decline again," I said, heading down the hall for the bedroom.

"Excuse me?" said Donna, her syllables drawn out in long angry tones, her blood pressure visibly rising by the second.

I paused and turned to look at her. I knew what I was about to say might send her into a murderous rage and if that were the case I wanted to see it coming.

"I closed the account," I declared, trying to ready myself for her onslaught.

"You what?!"

She was completely incensed, as I knew she would be. She was practically shaking with fury, but I didn't care. As much as I'm sure she'd disagree, there were far more important things that needed tending to and it was going to take more energy than I had to argue the fact. I loved her dearly, despite her faults. But, she'd gotten out of control, just like her sister and mother, and I had to put a stop to it.

"Are you *trying* to ruin my life?"

"Donna, you've already spent over five thousand dollars and I haven't even seen so much as an invitation, let alone a dress. What exactly have you been buying?"

"Does it really matter?"

"Honey, you're my daughter. Everything matters."

"Since when?"

"Look, I'm not going to get into it with you right now. Your mother needs me and I need to find Ruth Anne."

"Well, good luck with that."

"Thank you."

Donna spun round on her designer heels and stormed out of the house, slamming the door behind her. A hand gently rested on my shoulder.

"What's happening," said Jayne, still a little drowsy.

"That was Donna. She's not too happy with me right now. How are you feeling?"

"Did you get my prescription?" she asked, looking down the hall at no one.

"Murray said he filled it two days ago and that Ruthie picked it up. He thought perhaps you may have forgotten."

Jayne continued to stare down the hall, but I could tell her mind was wandering even further. Her brows began to crease to a sad point. Tears started forming in her tired eyes.

I knew it was getting late and that she needed to meet Reed in less than an hour. She'd slept away the better part of the day and I was sure she hadn't a clue what time it was. Still, at this moment, I felt the Groverton's could wait.

"Jaynie? We need to talk," I said quietly.

She shook her head, as if to wake herself, then looked at her wrist as if there were a watch on it. She pressed her palm to her forehead. "Is that the time? I've got to get ready." She turned and headed back down the hall as if in a trance.

"Jaynie, please," I pleaded, following her to the bedroom.

"I can't, Stephen. Not now. I can't." She wandered into the bathroom and locked herself in.

"Jaynie..." I knocked, then pounded on the door. "Jaynie?" The shower turned on and I could hear her weeping. "Jaynie, honey, please?!" There was no reply.

I leaned against the door, sliding down it onto the floor and, not knowing what else to do, prayed.

16

Penny and Billy stopped by as Jayne, running about twenty-five minutes behind, was about to leave for the Groverton's. Billy needed a Polaroid snapshot of himself to send with his "Round Two" paperwork and they came to borrow the camera before heading back to their campus apartment for the week.

"Good luck, Mom," said Penny as Jayne, not acknowledging anyone, walked trancelike out the door. I could tell Penny's feelings were hurt and so could Billy. He casually put an arm around her and kissed her on the top of the head. It was so rare to see the Peanut frown.

"She's not feeling well," I said, trying to ease Penny's wound.

"I know. It's okay."

Penny spotted some photos of London I had on the table along with a few others I'd taken of she and Billy. "Hey, who's that good lookin' couple?" she joked, forcing

157

her mood into a hundred and eighty degree turn.

"Gee, I don't know," grinned Billy, "but the girl's kind of skinny. Don't you think, Mr. Sheridan?" He poked Penny in the ribs.

"I guess that means you'll have to take me out to eat and fatten me up, huh," she smiled, tickling him in the gut.

"That camera's in the darkroom if you want to go get it, Bill. It should be in one of the cabinets above the sink. Film should be in there, too."

"Thanks, sir. I'm going to fish around upstairs while I'm out there and see if I can find my father's knittin' needle. We were using it to fix the nets a couple of weeks ago and I forgot to bring it home."

"Need some help?" asked Penny.

"No, I got it. Besides, your dad looks like he could use some company."

Billy headed out to the barn, winking on his way out, and Penny took a seat next to me at the dining table. She noticed my half eaten bowl of chowder left over from an afternoon snack and gave it a whiff.

"Still trying to figure it out, aren't you," she said.

"Someday you'll confess," I replied, slinging the sarcasm right back at her.

"Yeah, right. When I'm on my deathbed." She picked up a photo of Balliol College, one of my favourites. "Cambridge?" she asked.

"Oxford," I replied. "I loved Oxford. Very Oliver Twist looking."

"So do you miss being over there?"

"Oh, I don't know. I'd rather be here with your Mom and you girls."

"Wait until we're all having our period at the same time.

Then you'll miss it," she grinned, jabbing me in the arm with her elbow.

"I've got Page's number tattooed to the bottom of my foot just in case," I said, staring her down over the top of my reading glasses.

Penny and I looked over the photos in silence. The way Billy winked at her, I thought maybe there was something she wanted to talk about, but the words never came. Just the silence.

"Can I ask you something?" I finally said.

"It was all Billy's idea," she began, obviously harboring a guilty conscious. "A crime of opportunity, he called it."

"A crime of opportunity?" I laughed.

"We *are* talking about the sleeping bag thing, aren't we?" she asked, looking at me over the top of her own make-believe glasses.

"No. But now that you mention it…"

"Crap. Okay, we're even. Okay?" she begged, realizing she'd stuck both feet in her mouth. "Okay!?"

"Okay."

Penny shuffled through the deck of photos and came across one of Reed and Bob at the Chowder Cook-off. "I sure feel sorry for Bob," she commented. "He's an awful nice guy. It's a shame he had to pair up with *that* idiot."

"Do you think Reed's having an affair with your mother?"

I couldn't believe I'd said it. I just blurted it out like one would blurt out, *could you please pass the salt*, but I didn't know how else to broach the subject. It seemed somehow inappropriate to ask my own daughter about something so personal, but she'd always been my family confidant and I knew she'd tell me the truth if that's what I wanted to hear.

"Gross. I know Mom's a little out of it," she replied, "but I didn't think she was *that* out of it."

"I suppose you're right," I sighed.

We both sat in silence looking over the photos, Penny pulling one or two to the side that she wanted copies of. The silence seemed awkward, though, as if she wanted to talk more about it, but didn't think she should.

"I used to kind of worry about Mr. Conners from the bank having a thing for Mom," she unexpectedly added, her eyes never leaving the stack of prints.

"Oh?"

"Yeah. He was always asking her out for coffee, said he was trying to get her to invest in some land or something. It kind of blew over after a while, though. It was probably nothing."

Mike Conners. My god. The thought had crossed my mind, but I always dismissed it for lack of evidence. Looking back, though, it was no wonder he was always so jittery when I was around. There was a period about two years ago when he was especially nervous. So much so, in fact, he would have to excuse himself from the bank anytime I was in town and wanted to check on my accounts. Still, I couldn't imagine Jaynie cheating on me. I loved her dearly and she knew it. I told her - and showed her - every chance I got. My head was swimming.

Billy returned from the barn with my bulky Polaroid and a package of film.

"Is this it, sir?"

I snapped back into focus, the thought of Mike and Jayne fleeting for a short moment.

"Yeah. That's the one. And use as much of that film as you want," I offered. "It's been kicking around for a while and I'm not sure what kind of shelf life it has."

"Thanks. Might take a few tries to get a good shot of this ugly mug," he smiled, pointing to himself.

"Don't say that!" Penny jeered, both of us welcoming the distraction. "You're better looking than about ninety-nine percent of the other guys left in this town."

"So where do I stand in that crowd?" I asked.

"Oh, you're way up there, Dad," said Penny, nodding like a little dashboard bobble head. "Way up there."

I knew I'd baited my own hook, but it was good for a laugh and we needed one.

"Say, have either of you seen Ruthie?" I asked, changing the subject rather abruptly.

"I think we saw her coming out of the drug store Friday night, didn't we, babe?"

"You can't really miss her," replied Penny. "I wanted to talk to her to see if she was okay, but the shithead grabbed her and took off like a house afire. Stupid bastard. I hate that guy."

"Do you know where I might find her? She has something of your mother's."

"Shit. Did she take her necklace again?" asked Penny, quite serious, a hint of genuine concern in her voice. "She better not have. I told her to ask me if she ever needed some money."

Ruth had been known to pawn jewelry when she needed a fix and money got tight. When she'd gone through all of her own valuables and some of Donna's, she began to steal Jayne's. Penny usually managed to track it all down and buy it back before her mother and sister were the wiser. She reluctantly kept me informed, but refused to tell me what it cost her. I owed her in spades.

"It doesn't matter," I said. "I'd just like to find her."

"She's really a mess this time, isn't she," she replied, real worry washing over her.

"Yes. I think maybe."

Billy put his hand on Penny's shoulder. He knew as well as I did that if someone had so much as a fleeting thought of causing harm to either one of her sisters, it meant war. Donna may have been the Drill Sergeant, but Penny was always the Napoleon of the family.

"Well, she could be anywhere," Penny began, her thumb firmly pressed to her chin as she strategized, "but I'd check the shithead's place first. He lives in that little dive motel behind the drive in. I'd go over there myself, but I'd probably end up getting arrested again."

"Yeah, you would," Billy interjected. "We can check around at the clubs, too. Plus I got a couple of buddies who kind of follow the scene. I'll give them a buzz and see if they know where she might be singin'."

"I don't want to spoil your evening. Besides, don't you two have to get back up to school?"

"It's not that far a drive, sir. And, neither one of us has a class until around nine."

For them, nine in the morning was practically mid day. Besides, when it came to looking out for family, everything else was secondary. Including school.

Penny hung her head low. "I'm sorry, Dad. She's not usually gone this long. I should have checked up on her. I'm sorry."

"It's not your fault, Peanut. She's probably just been working."

"Yeah, well. Still. I hope she's okay," she said quietly.

"You want to head out then?" asked Billy. "We can

meet your father back here in an hour or two, if that sounds good with you, Mr. Sheridan."

"That sounds great, Billy. Thanks."

"I'd better go pee," said Penny, trotting upstairs.

I hated to get the two of them involved. But, they knew absolutely everyone and chances were in our favour that someone would have seen Ruth somewhere at some time.

I grabbed my flannel shirt and was ready to head out the door when a very familiar screeching of tires reverberated up the drive. In a split second a door slammed and the car was off again. Billy and I rushed outside to find Ruthie collapsed in the driveway, her nose bloodied, both eyes blackened.

Penny rushed out of the house not far behind us and spotted Ruth. "No!" she screamed. "No!"

Billy held her back. "It's okay, hon. It's okay."

"That bastard!"

I picked up Ruthie's lifeless body and brought her into the house, placing her gently on the couch. "Penny, call the ambulance."

"That son of a bitch!" she screamed, clenching her temples, staring at Ruthie and crying. "Damn him! That's the last time!"

Penny ran out of the house and into the barn. Billy gave chase, yelling along the way. "Penny, no! Penny!"

Ruthie moaned and coughed and began to push me away, thinking I was Chuck about to strike her again.

"Ruthie, honey. It's okay. It's me. It's Dad." I tried to calm her, to console her. I could hear Penny and Billy screaming at each other in the barn. Ruthie was terrified, confused. I didn't know whether to get on the phone or take her to the hospital myself or what. My mind was a blur. It was all happening so fast.

Suddenly, Penny's Metro fired up and peeled off down the lane. Billy, screaming, chased her as far as he could before running out of breath. He rushed back in the house. "Damn it," he cried.

"What's happening?" I shouted.

"Shit, sir. I gotta go. I gotta go after Penny. If she gets a hold of that guy, she's gonna kill him. I know she is."

"I don't know what to do," I shouted, nearly tearing my hair out. I felt so helpless. One daughter was in my arms, dying for all I knew. The other was out looking for death. "Please. I need some help."

Billy got on the phone and called for an ambulance, then called the police to try and have them intercept Penny before she got to Chuck. He hated to do it, knowing she'd be pissed at him for an eternity, but he couldn't risk having her come in contact with Chuck. Although his stature would lead you to believe he could be blown over in a light breeze, the truth remained that if Chuck were strung out on angel dust or something similar, he could literally tear just about anyone to shreds - including Penny.

Billy stayed long enough to help me stabilize Ruth while I waited for the ambulance to arrive. He called his father, too, to let him know it would be coming for her and not him. Skip often worried about losing his last remaining son, either to an accident or heart failure, and the sound of a siren could easily set him on edge.

Skip came quickly and offered to wait with me while Billy took off to try and track down Penny. I was so glad Jaynie wasn't there. She would have had a nervous breakdown and I was about to have one myself.

Within minutes the medics were at the house tending to

Ruth. They put her in a neck brace and then another brace, fearing she had a cracked skull, and transported her immediately to the hospital. Skip and I followed in his International, passing the Groverton's beach bungalow on the way. I could see Jaynie in the big bay window having cocktails as we passed by. I knew she couldn't see me, but somehow it seemed her gaze followed us. I could only imagine her thoughts.

17

It was a horribly unnerving hour and a half of pacing in the emergency room waiting to hear from the doctors about Ruthie's condition. She'd been beaten so badly. The image of her fractured body kept creeping into the forefront of my mind and it was all I could do to keep from throwing up.

"Mr. Sheridan?"

"Yes," I replied, rushing up to Dr. Brice, the jack-of-all-trades specialist on duty. I was thankful it was him. He'd been the chief surgeon in a busy medical unit during World War II and you couldn't ask for a better guy to handle your wounded, even if your wounded needed nothing more than a stitch on the chin from a tricycle accident. He'd delivered all three of my girls into this world and I prayed he wasn't going to be the one to tell me one had left.

He proceeded to give me a laundry list of Ruth's injuries which included a severe concussion, a broken nose, fractured cheekbone, two broken ribs, and a bruised spleen.

I was amazed I'd heard that much. My brain simply couldn't process it all.

"There's something else I want to talk to you about," Brice added. "Would you mind joining me in my office?"

The words took every breath in me away. You never want to hear that from a doctor. Ever. It's like being called down to the police station when your kid's done something bad, only a thousand times worse. I had a difficult time imagining there could be anything more dreadful than what was already said except perhaps that Ruth was dead. If that were the case, the rest would simply have been a moot point.

Dr. Brice motioned me into his tiny office and shut the door behind us. My heart was pounding so hard I thought the black watch plaid would vibrate right off my shirt. He wiped a hand across his tired face then rested it on his chin. He took a deep breath, shook his head, then spoke.

"She's a mess, Steve. God damn it. She's a mess."

"I know."

"Do you?"

I thought for a long moment, then another. "I don't know."

Brice kept shaking his head. He wasn't exactly blaming me for not knowing, but as her father, I certainly should have been aware.

"Forget the beating she took. It's the drugs I'm worried about. She was pretty strung out when she got here."

"Yeah. Penny said it's been getting pretty bad."

We proceeded to talk about Ruthie's sordid past and her terrible relationship with Chuck. He'd seen her in the emergency room once before when she allegedly fell off a stage and fractured her wrist. He suspected the shithead back then, but couldn't do anything about it since Ruth refused to change her story. Drugs were an issue then, too, but not as pronounced as what he was seeing now. He mentioned that based on her level of apparent dependency she was likely to have a difficult time during recovery. Getting over bruises and broken bones would be nothing compared to the DT's.

It was all terrible enough, but what came next was more than I could handle. You can ready yourself for the birth of your child, their subsequent birthdays, graduations, even their wedding. But nothing can prepare you for the death of that child or the death of the child's child.

"How long ago did she have the abortion?" Brice reluctantly asked.

I sat there, my mouth agape, a thousand thoughts rushing through my mind. My lips were moving, but no sound emerged.

"I'm sorry to put it to you that way," he continued. "Sexual assault is something we have to check for in these situations. She wasn't raped, but the signs are there that she'd terminated a pregnancy sometime recently. Doesn't look like they did a very good job either. Jesus, Steve. She's really a mess."

I just shook my head. I never wanted to be a grandfather this young, but I'd have given anything to have seen that child enter the world.

"I'm sorry you didn't know," he said quietly.

My head hung low. I felt so defeated. I thought I'd done everything I could to be a good husband and father and yet I'd done nothing. I didn't even know who my children were. I didn't even know who my wife was. I didn't know a damn thing.

Brice gave me a brochure outlining the hospital's rehab program and suggested Ruthie be enrolled in their intensive

3-week program immediately. Although I was certainly far from being of sound mind, I agreed nonetheless and signed any and all documents to admit her to the treatment centre upon her release from the recovery ward. She wouldn't even be allowed to go home in between.

I was in such a daze I had to have the nurse escort me back to the lobby. It must have been ten or eleven o'clock and Skip was still there reading a magazine and sipping coffee. You couldn't ask for a better friend.

"She gonna be alright?" he quietly asked as he gently placed his hand on my shoulder.

"Eventually," I replied, fighting back the tears.

"Can I get you somethin'? Take you home?"

"I don't know. I need to see Jayne. To tell her."

It was during times like this that I missed asking Page for advice as I'm sure Skip missed seeking the same from his amazing Grace. Their strength is what gets us through the hard times and keeps us going. They raise our children, keep our homes and offices running smoothly, reassure us when we doubt ourselves. They say that men run the country. I beg to differ. In truth, we are nothing without our women.

As I tried to think of just what to do, Billy walked into the emergency room with Penny by his side. They had a frightening amount of blood on them, Penny sporting the lion's share. She held a wadding of bloodied gauze over her eye and appeared to be crying.

"My god," I gasped, rushing up to her.

"Looks worse than it is, sir," said Billy, practically carrying her. "She'll be alright."

"Stupid bastard cuffed me to the car door," Penny cried.

"What?!"

"Some rookie cop," explained Billy. "He got to her just as they were dragging the shithead out of his apartment. I guess Penny about flipped, so the guy cuffed her to the cruiser so she wouldn't haul off and attack Chuck. I hate to say it, but in my book he should've let her have at him."

"My god."

I wiped Penny's tears away. Her wrists were torn and bleeding, sure signs of a struggle. She tried to suppress the flood of emotions running through her, but she just couldn't hold it back any longer. She turned and buried her face into Billy's chest and wept.

"Chuck spotted her and went nuts," Billy continued. "It took four guys to pull him off her. It was wicked."

"He cuffed me to the door, Daddy. I couldn't do a thing. Not a damn thing. Stupid bastard."

I pulled her close and held her tight. My little Napoleon had been to battle and lost. It was all she could do to stand.

The nurse came out with a wheelchair and took Penny back to triage where Dr. Brice, probably sick of seeing the Sheridan's file in and out of his surgery ward, would stitch her back together.

"You alright, boy?" asked Skip.

"Yeah. I'm fine," replied Billy.

"What did they do with Chuck?" I asked.

"They got him on all kinds of stuff on top of what he did to Ruth and Penny. Possession, intent to sell, probably grand theft and I don't know what else. They're gonna throw the book at him, for sure."

"I know the guy doesn't deserve to be on this earth, but I'm glad Penny didn't kill him."

"Yes, sir. Me, too. She's gonna have a scar like yours now, though," he said, pointing to my brow.

I remembered what it felt like to get kicked in the face and cringed at the thought of my baby girl experiencing the same type of blow. She was so fierce, always believing she was bigger than life – a five foot, one inch mountain. Still, I hated to think what she must be feeling. She tried so hard to protect everyone.

"Mr. Sheridan? They're moving your daughter, Ruth Anne, into recovery now," reported the pleasant night nurse. "You'll be able to see her in about fifteen minutes."

"I'll take care of Penny, sir," offered Billy. "I'll get her home and stuff."

"No, you two go," I replied, feeling guilty I'd kept them both so long. "I can call a cab."

"You should head home and get yourself cleaned up," Skip told his son. "I'll stick around."

"I can't, Dad," he sighed. "You know I can't leave her."

Billy, clearly exhausted, took a seat while Skip freshened his coffee and sat down with another magazine. I was so grateful for the two of them. I knew the fifteen minute wait was going to seem like an eternity and I took the opportunity to make a much needed phone call.

I walked down the quiet corridor to the little phone booth and locked myself inside. I must have sat there for five minutes before I picked up the receiver and began to dial, dismayed about the conversation that was about to ensue. Only two rings and she was there, but silent.

At the sound of my voice, Jaynie burst into tears, sensing the news was not good. She'd heard the sirens, seen the ambulance, seen Penny tearing down the street, Billy giving chase soon after. She couldn't speak, couldn't stop crying. I assured her Ruthie was alive and would eventually be okay. I assured her Penny was alive and would be okay, too. It would all be okay. Still, she couldn't help but feel responsible.

I left the little booth no better than when I went in and was escorted to the recovery ward where Ruthie was resting somewhat comfortably. The little monitor next to the bed emitted a glowing green line that peaked with each beat of her heart, its accompanied tone beeping a quiet, steady rhythm. She had multiple IV's pumping antibiotics and God knows what else into her veins at a fairly rapid rate. A tube was inserted in her nose for drainage and wires were taped to her chest and temples to monitor her vitals. She was bruised, bandaged, broken. I barely recognized her.

"Jesus," I whispered.

"She's going to need more than Him, by the looks."

I turned and found Donna standing in back of me, a tear running down her polished cheek. She quickly dabbed it away with a pale green tissue and sighed. "I suppose Penny's a mess, too," she added.

"They're stitching her up right now."

"Lovely."

"How did you find out?" I asked.

"Brian's friend, Ronnie York, was one of the police officers on the scene. Apparently he's got a thing for Ruth Anne. Have you called Jayne?"

"Yes. She's pretty upset. Do you think you could go over there and stay with her until I get home?"

"How long will you be?" she asked.

"Does it matter?"

"I didn't exactly pack a bag, you know."

Of all the things that were vastly more important, she was concerned about her wardrobe. I began to think that perhaps it was just a defense mechanism for her, a way of dealing with things without really dealing with them. Another tear escaped.

"Could you manage for just a little while?" I asked, offering her my handkerchief.

"I suppose," she sighed, dabbing the corner of her eye and delicately wiping her nose.

Donna stepped up close to Ruth and stared at her battered shell. She gently rubbed her sister's shoulder, desperately suppressing her own emotions. Without another word, she turned and walked out.

I stayed with Ruthie another hour or so until I suddenly realized that Skip was probably still waiting in the lobby for me. I hated to leave her side, but was assured by the night nurse that we'd be contacted if there was any change in Ruth's condition.

Skip, born with the patience of Job, must have read every magazine in the lobby and drank at least two pots of coffee. He never complained and even offered to stay longer if that's what needed to be done. However, I knew what needed to be done right then was to go to Jayne.

Billy had tended to Penny and was by now home with her. I pictured Jayne in hysterics, no pills to calm her down, panicked over what the neighbors were going to think of our family's night on the town. I perished the thought of tomorrow's Herald headlines.

Skip and I talked on the way home about our kids and the guilt we each carried regarding their upbringing. Skip felt terrible that Billy no longer had a mother, but grateful for Dorothy, Jayne and the other women of our little village, since they'd always been positive and ever-present female role models for him. He was especially grateful for Penny. As tom-boyish as she was, she did have a sensitive feminine side. In terms of guilt, I myself carried enough for an army of thousands.

When I got home, I found Donna asleep in the recliner, her hair still perfect, her dress still fresh like she'd just picked it up from the cleaners. She looked like a mannequin. The sound of the creaking kitchen door woke her and she sprang up like an alarm had gone off.

"Where's your mother?"

"Asleep," she replied, primping her hair and holding back a yawn. "I brought her some Nitol, so good luck waking her."

"Penny?"

"Upstairs with Billy. They're probably asleep, too."

"Good."

"Since you're here, I'm going."

"Thanks for staying."

No goodbye. Just gone.

I looked in on Penny. She and Billy, both cleaned up and wearing fresh clothes, were spooned together asleep in her bed. They looked so perfect together, each consoling the other. I gently put her pink throw blanket over them, turned off the bedside light and closed the door. Morning would come soon enough and I knew she needed him and he needed her.

Jayne was out of it, too. So much so, I couldn't even stir her. When I checked the bottle of sleeping pills next to the bed, I found it was almost empty. Since Donna had brought her a fresh bottle, it meant she'd taken most of them in one shot, which alarmed me to no end. I shook her again. No response. I placed the back of my hand over her mouth and could hardly detect her breathing. Her pulse was barely there.

I grabbed the phone immediately and called the ambulance, asking them to come quickly but quietly so as not to disturb the neighbors again. The medics were sure going to earn their keep tonight taking care of the Sheridan's, not to mention the fact that these little trips to the emergency room were becoming redundant.

I left a note for Penny and followed the ambulance in Jaynie's Jag, so tired it was a wonder I didn't nod off and drive straight into the bay. They brought Jayne directly into triage where Dr. Brice began the unsavory task of pumping her stomach. It would be a good hour before he got her stabilized.

I stared out the window of the emergency room lobby, reflecting on the day's events, my life in general. What a strange portrait I'd painted of my family. I'd covered up all the dysfunction, all the pain, all the anger with shades and hues of gifts and denial. I'd done such a good job of covering it up, in fact, I never in all the years saw the real picture at all.

What I wanted to see each time I came home was a Norman Rockwell image of my Jayne standing there, waiting for me, looking like a goddamn million bucks. Her hair, her nails, her dress, all perfect like she just stepped out of a Harrod's window. Every time I saw her flawless vision, I couldn't wait to carry her into the bedroom and make love to her until sunrise. She was the benchmark from which I measured all beauty.

Donna would always waltz in the house wearing some pretty new dress she didn't think anyone else in the world owned. Her make-up was always seamless, like a magazine ad, and she couldn't wait to find out what new piece of jewelry I'd gotten her. She'd even say thank you and seem to mean it.

Ruthie would fly in looking like she'd just stepped off a concert stage. She'd be smiling and singing to herself until she noticed I was there, listening. She'd laugh, half embarrassed, then ask if I'd found her some obscure jazz album she'd be searching for. Thankfully, Page could find me anything, and it got me a hug and a kiss from my starlet. At least that's how I remembered it.

Then there was the Peanut. She'd come crashing into the kitchen, baggy pants and dirt on her face, like a dead-end kid that just weeded a mud garden. I'd smile and throw her some cheap t-shirt I picked up at the airport and she'd be happy as all hell. She'd grab me and hold me tight and throw her shirt on right then and there and wear it continuously, day in and day out, until it about drew flies. We'd laugh and smile so much it made my face and gut ache with joy.

We'd all go out to eat, sing and dance, and carry on like the world was ours and we hadn't a care in the world. And at the end of the day, I truly believed that everything was perfect, everyone was happy, just like a Normal Rockwell. But now, as the days and weeks rolled on, layer upon layer of the family portrait I'd so painstakingly painted for myself was slowly fading away and what was left was an image I did not want to see.

"Steve?"

"How is she, Doc?"

"She's a bit groggy, but she'll be fine in a few days. It was good you called right away."

Dr. Brice escorted me to Jaynie's room, where she lay quietly sobbing. He left us alone, letting me know he wouldn't be far.

"Jaynie? Honey?"

She couldn't even look at me. All she could do was say, "I'm sorry. I'm so sorry." Over and over again. "I'm sorry." She'd been harbouring the secret of Ruth's abortion for months, unable to tell even a priest. She was always so worried what people would think. Within minutes, she was asleep, the tears still flowing, soaking the pillow. I placed my hand gently on her forehead and smoothed her hair away from her weary face. She carried such a burden.

18

Billy came down quietly from upstairs. "Sorry, sir. I guess I fell asleep."

"It's okay, son. How is she?"

"She's pretty upset. She wanted to go down and see Ruth, but I told her she should rest a little while. She looks like shit, if you ask me."

"Thanks for taking care of her. I appreciate it."

"Don't know what I'd do without her, sir. I really don't."

"Same here," I quietly replied.

Billy left in silence, the night catching up to him as much as me. I stood at the kitchen window and watched him walk across the salt marsh for home, the unseasonable chill in the morning air catching him by surprise. I saw him wince and stuff his hands deep into his pockets as he looked out over the black waters, the angry red sky glowing above and beyond.

I took a mug from the dish drainer and stood guard over the percolator waiting for the coffee to finish brewing. The wind was strong and steady that mid-September morning, enough to make me want to go out and split wood for a fire. I grabbed my jacket and a cup of coffee and headed out.

As I walked out back, the cold air hit me square in the face and all but took my breath away. It was unusual for it to be so chilly this early and I'd hoped it wouldn't last. I hadn't yet prepared for fall, let alone winter. There was always so much that Penny took care of.

Behind the barn was a stack of wooden traps, the first of several strings that would be brought in for the winter to hibernate until spring. In the distance, I could hear the *Rum Runner* growling out of the harbour, others following her in the hopes they'd get a string or two of their own pulled before the storm blew in.

I heard Donna pull into the driveway, her unmistakable gait pounding across the deck. I met her at the side door so she wouldn't thunder in and wake Penny.

"I see you're rushing to get back to the hospital," she sneered, standing with her arms folded as if I was supposed to open the door for her or kiss her feet or do *something* chivalrous.

"I'm going in a few minutes," I said, not really wanting to get into a pissing contest with her. It had been much too long a night. "Would you like to come with me?"

"Where's the brat?"

"Sleeping. She was hurt pretty badly."

"I'm sure Jayne was impressed."

"Please, Donna. Do you think you could put it on hold just for a little while? It's been a rough night."

"Put what on hold?"

"Oh, I don't know. How about the biting sarcasm and the *geez Dad, you're such an incompetent ass* routine. That. Do you think you could spare me that just this once?"

"I don't know what *you're* getting so upset about," she snapped. "This is all probably just a big inconvenience for you."

"What?! How dare you," I shouted. I couldn't believe her insolence. She was really pushing the envelope and I'd had it. If she were any younger I'd have turned her over my knee.

"How dare *I*?" she cried. "Who do you think took care of this family all the while you were away? Did you think it was Jayne? Well it wasn't. It was me."

"You're full of shit," I yelled. "Your mother did everything she could to make sure you girls got everything you ever wanted. Singing lessons, dance lessons, tennis lessons, cotillion. No wonder she's on her fourth car."

"And she hated every minute of it."

"She loves you and so do I, although I don't know why. You treat me like some son of a bitch who doesn't deserve the time of day." I was hotter than I'd ever been and it didn't seem like the flame was going to go out any time soon. I'd given her everything, and it had always been out of love. Why she couldn't, or wouldn't, accept that was beyond me.

"That's it," she snapped, reaching for the doorknob. "I've had enough. I'm going in."

I slammed the door shut again. "You've had enough? You've had enough?!" I was so angry I could have spit nails. "I've done everything I could to provide for this family and you know it. I'm sorry I wasn't here all the time, but that's the way it was."

Donna pushed me aside, ripped open the kitchen door and pounded down the hall. "Jayne?" she hollered.

"Keep your voice down," I said, following her to the bedroom and trying to suppress a scream. "Your sister's asleep."

Donna looked in the empty bedroom for Jayne, went further in and threw open the bathroom door. "Did she finally wise up and leave you?"

I took a deep breath. It was the last straw. I absolutely could not believe this was the same woman who had been raised to be kind and grateful and polite. This woman was nothing short of a monster. "Your mother was admitted to the hospital last night," I replied, calmly, calculatingly. "She overdosed on the sleeping pills you so graciously provided her. Thank you for that, by the way."

"I beg your pardon?"

"You heard me." The way I said it was cold, I know, but so was the wind outside and the atmosphere inside and I wanted to get out of it all. "They pumped her stomach and kept her overnight for observation. They say she'll live, thank God."

"But…"

"She could have died, you know. She took almost the whole bottle."

Welcome to the real world, Donna, I thought. That statement hit her like a ton of bricks and, for the first time in her young adult life, she had no further response.

She looked around, at what I don't know. Perhaps she was searching for something to say, something to make me feel guilty, to make me feel like it was all *my* fault. She didn't need to, really. As mad as I was, I already knew it.

"But, she was fine when I left," she said, trying to

excuse it away. "What did you do to her?"

"I didn't do anything, except call the ambulance. She was probably fine when you got here, but she was completely out of it when you left."

"My god."

Donna pressed her palm to her forehead, then her cheek, then covered her mouth to keep from making a sound. She closed her eyes so tight her eyebrows seemed to mesh with her lashes. Somehow, tears managed to escape.

"We're falling apart, aren't we," she whispered.

As difficult as it was to imagine, I thought perhaps that she may actually, finally be getting it. I stared at her for the longest time, trying to decipher her emotions. Then, it hit me. Donna, the Drill Sergeant, was crying.

"It's okay," I said, gently drawing her near, feeling sorry that I'd fought so intensely with her, sorrier still that I'd been so cruel. "You couldn't have known."

She recoiled slightly, gathered herself, and carefully wiped away her tears with the back of her finger. "Well," she began. "It's a fine mess we're in now, isn't it. So much for having an uneventful wedding."

"Honey, it's almost two months away," I assured, sensing her defense mechanism kicking into high gear. "By then everything will be back to normal."

"Normal? What would you know about normal?" She just couldn't let it go.

Trying to break through Donna's tempered exterior was like trying to break through a steel hull with a toothpick. You simply couldn't do it no matter how hard you tried. I could see it was going to be one of the tougher journeys on my road to redemption.

Donna stormed off. I could see her behind the wheel of

her car as she drove away, intercepting more tears that managed to make a break for it. She was just so angry at the world - and me.

I took several deep breaths then went upstairs to check in on Penny, sleeping peacefully with her old, ratty teddy bear tucked tight under her arm. Her swollen eye was black and blue and a red welt stuck out from her cheekbone. My little corporal looked so tiny and frail, curled up in a ball under her pindot coverlet.

I took the pink writing tablet from off her desk and jotted her a note:

Gone to get Mom - Love, Dad.

I left it on the nightstand and gave her a soft kiss on the forehead. "Bye, Peanut," I whispered, not even thinking.

I dreaded the drive to the hospital, but rushed just the same. I was anxious to see how Ruthie was doing and even more anxious to see how Jayne was. I arrived just in time to meet Dr. Brice heading home from his night shift.

"Helluva night, eh, Steve?" he said, pulling up beside me in his vehicle.

"I'll say. How are my women doing?"

"They're processing the missus as we speak. She'll be fine, but be sure to have her check in with her doctor, at least by tomorrow. He'll probably want to give her a check up and review her medications."

"Thanks. Will do."

"Ruth's going to have a time of it, though. She's got the shakes pretty bad this morning. It'll get a lot worse before it gets better. She's going to need a lot of support."

"We'll give her all we've got," I replied.

"I know you will. Take care, Steve. Let me know if I can do anything for you."

"Thanks, Doc. For everything."

Brice rolled out of the parking lot in his old military jeep, top down despite the cold. I'd hoped the next time we met it would be under better circumstances.

Inside the hospital an orderly escorted me to Jayne's room where she was dressed and waiting for me. She didn't say a word, just stared at the floor with her hands folded in her lap, her blazer draped over her arm.

"I want to see Ruthie before we leave," I said. "Would you like to go up?"

Jaynie shook her head. She looked so empty, all the life drawn out of her like a wilted flower. I took her to the cafeteria and set her up with some hot tea and toast. I promised I wouldn't be but a minute.

Upstairs, poor Ruthie was indeed having a time of it. She was quivering, quaking really, as the DT's began to set in. She said it felt like a million little pin pricks under her skin that made her want to itch and itch and itch. She complained of the cold, yet was drenched in sweat and I offered her every blanket I could get my hands on.

"I want to go home," she begged. "I don't belong here. Take me home."

"I can't, sweetheart. You need to stay. They're going to help you get better."

It was a gut-wrenching exchange of *I hate you*'s, and *I'd rather die*'s interlaced with screams and thrashing. At one point I thought Ruthie was going to throw the bedpan at me, but she decided against it at the last second. I thought I'd die myself when the nurse came in and threatened to restrain

Ruth if she didn't settle down, which we both knew was impossible. She was so tortured, and this was only the beginning.

After twenty minutes of watching my daughter go through hell, I left. The nurse strongly advised that I not come back for at least a week until her withdrawal symptoms subsided, but I wouldn't have it. I assured her I'd be back that afternoon at the latest, DT's or no DT's.

I was so disoriented after seeing Ruth I couldn't find my way back to the elevators and ended up in the Geriatrics ward where nurses and orderlies were scrambling to track down an elderly man with full blown dementia who'd gone missing. In their haste, they were kind enough to point me in the direction of the elevator and map where, with any luck, I'd be able to find my way back to Jayne.

I managed to find the lift and, as the doors slid open, low and behold standing before me was Colonel Reginald Q. Pendlewaite, the dementia patient. Had he been able to stand erect, he probably would have been the tallest man I'd ever met – and the skinniest. As it was, his posture made him look somewhat like an elongated "S", his body an amazing example of balance in motion like a mobile suspended from the floor instead of the ceiling. He was sporting the biggest smile on record and was dressed in nothing more than a pith helmet and well-worn Florsheim brogues, the finest shoes ever made.

"Dr. Livingston, I presume?" the colonel gleefully shouted.

"No. I'm Steve. But I think I know where you might find the good doctor."

I threw my jacket around Reginald's naked midsection and brought him back to the nurses' station where the entire staff seemed to sigh in collective relief.

When I finally made it back to Jayne, I found her exactly as I'd left her. She hadn't touched her toast or even had a sip of tea. In fact, the bag was still steeping in the cup, the brew dark enough to pale ink. She didn't say a word.

I tried to talk to her on the way home, but she just stared out the window in silence. Fearing she'd fly into another fit of hysterics, I warned her about Penny's appearance, but assured her just the same that she'd be fine. "Her pride took the worst of it," I said. "And she'll get over that, too."

Jaynie went right to bed when we got home. I was worried that she hadn't eaten anything, but she promised before she fell asleep that she'd maybe have something for lunch. At least she said that much.

I lay with Jaynie about a half hour before tiptoeing upstairs to check on the Peanut, who'd apparently been gone the whole time. I went upstairs in the barn, too, to see if she and Billy were working on their nets, but she was not to be found. Back in her room, I noticed that she'd tacked a note to Tally, her bear:

Gone fishing – Love, Penny.

Of all the days to go.

The house was quiet – too quiet – and I was afraid to make even the smallest sound. I looked out the kitchen window as I silently emptied the grounds from the perc and spotted a boat coming back into the harbour. The sea was rough and I watched intently as the little vessel bobbed and thrashed its way in, struggling to gain ground. I thought of Penny and Billy going out in the nasty weather and decided to take a walk to the docks to check on them and clear my head. It seemed I'd been doing a lot of that lately.

Dot whipped up a fresh pot of coffee and offered me an old dead cake, as she called it, for dunking. I never refused a donut in my life and hers were the best.

"Word has it you had quite a shindig down at Chez Memorial last night," she quipped, tossing the Herald on the counter in front of me. "Everybody make it out alive?"

"Barely," I replied.

Dot had the paper folded just right to reveal the headline on page seven: *Local Man Charged With Assault*. I was thankful there wasn't a picture to go with the quarter-page article that seemed to give a blow-by-blow of the whole incident at the motel, including the melee that ensued upon Chuck's subsequent arrest. It was bad enough that both my girls were mentioned as being the victims in the crime. I certainly didn't want it advertised any more than it already was with a photo spread. Then Dot flipped the paper over.

"Jesus Christ," I mumbled under my breath.

"Yeah? Maybe if *He* was on the scene things would have been a hell of a lot different," said Dot, freshening my coffee.

"Jaynie's going to have a fit," I mumbled.

"Can't blame her. Even I'd be pissed off at that one. Must have been a slow night at the news desk."

"I'll say."

Opposite the article about the shithead, was an even bigger spread, a "human interest story", about domestic abuse. A recent police photo of Ruthie, both eyes blackened and her lip split, accompanied the piece. She was barely recognizable.

Penny got a mention, too, although the fact that she fully intended to and would have killed the shithead had she not been cuffed to a car door was conveniently disregarded. It was probably a good thing, though, since that in itself would have led to yet another article. As far as anyone knew, she was simply there to "support" her sister.

The fierce wind blew over the trash can outside the diner, sending a pair of scavenging gulls into flight. Dot about had a fit.

"Hey, Walter!" she screamed. "Come clean that shit up off the deck. The goddamn can blew over again."

She could be so subtle at times. Like a runaway train loaded with drunken sailors.

Like many of the other fishermen that day, Walter balked at heading out in the nasty weather. Even the harbour was rough, the boats bobbing up and down at their moorings enough so it made me seasick just to watch them. The few diehards that did go out, namely my daughter and Skip's son, did so at their own risk. By all accounts, it really was bad. Even Skip, who fished everyday but Christmas, chose to come in early.

John P. Jenkins, known as Jewel-Eye, skipped fishing for the day, too, and popped in the diner for a quick cup of coffee. He was a regular here at the docks and had quite a reputation for exaggerating the current forecast.

"Christ, Jewel-Eye. Don't tell me *you've* been out in this shit," cried Dot.

"Oh, not on your life, Dottie. A fog could come rollin' in right behind that storm so thick you won't be able to see a thing. Can't be too careful when it comes to them storms and that fog."

Jenkins got his nickname due to the brilliant jewel-like

189

colour of his glass eye, which he'd had since he was twelve. Legend has it, Jenkins was playing goalie in a pickup game on a frozen pond across from Gunniford's Auto Parts when a fog bank settled in over the ice. Kids being what they are, they continued the game anyway, taking full advantage of the obstructing fog to score. No one ever fessed up to who landed the fateful blow, a slap shot from the imaginary blue line that Jenkins never saw coming, and the game ended abruptly with kids screaming and pointing fingers and blood flying everywhere.

To this day, Jewel remains terrified of fog, fearing something might again fly out from nowhere and take out his other eye. It could be a picture-perfect day, sun shining, the ocean smooth as a smelt, and he would invariably warn, "*Better keep an eye out for that weatha'...*", no pun intended.

"I see your girl's out in it, Sheridan," he said.

"Yes. She's in good hands, though. Young Bill won't let her get too carried away."

"Good man. Good man."

Jewel grabbed a cup of coffee to go and cautiously made his way back to his truck, all the while looking over his shoulder in case *that fog* rolled in. He was a trip.

Dot jested on and on about Jewel-Eye, his over-developed phobia, and his antics at sea - or lack there of. We both got to laughing, which was actually unusual for Dot. She could usually keep a pretty straight face. You never wanted to play poker with her.

As our laughter died down, she and I began to hear a familiar, yet unsettling pulse coming from the south and we both grew silent. It was the kind of sound that made you stop what you were doing, whatever it was, and take notice. The kind of sound that made you hold your breath and say a prayer. Dot blessed herself and turned on the scanner as the sound grew. I got up from the counter and looked out the window, watching silently as the Coast Guard helicopter headed out to sea.

Walter joined Dot's side and put an arm around her shoulder as she tuned into the emergency channel and grabbed a box of tissues from under the counter. Their antenna was none the worse for wear and the static proved it. Still, we were able to make out a word or two here and there.

"We read you, *Elizabeth Bailey*," came a voice. "Please repeat."

"This is the *Elizabeth Bailey*. Repeat. Man overboard the *Bobby Grace*. Man overboard. Heading is one half mile due northeast of Spectacle Isle. Repeat. Man overboard. Man overboard!"

You could hear the commotion in the background over the scanner, yelling and screaming, the static making it sound even more chaotic and my heart sank as low as it had ever gone. I couldn't even breathe. All I could think of was Skip losing his only remaining son, how empty his life would become without him. With all I'd been through the past few days, I still couldn't fathom what it would be like to suffer the kind of loss he had already suffered. It was the worst of all injustices.

Then I thought of my daughter losing the only soul mate she might ever know. The two of them had grown up together, joined at the hip, and fell in love along the way. I couldn't imagine one being able to live without the other, the two of them complimenting each other, completing each other, like earth and sky.

Skip walked into the diner, his face white as ash. Dot

191

rushed up to him and held him tight, tears streaking down her cheeks. She harboured so much love for all the men of the sea and any loss for them was a loss for her. Skip reciprocated, but only for a moment. He wasn't much for showing affection, except toward his son, who was now quite possibly gone from this world. I put a hand to his shoulder as he stared at me, tears beginning to well.

"Jesus, Skip. I'm sorry. I'm so sorry."

Skip put a hand on my shoulder in return and spoke softly... "It's not Billy."

19

For the past twenty-four hours, I'd felt like I'd been standing on a tissue paper floor. Donna had really gotten under my skin and I started to wonder if I was even going to have the strength to walk her down the aisle. On top of it all, I was worried sick about Ruthie, not to mention Jayne. But when the words came that I may have lost my Penny, that floor ripped apart from underneath me without another bottom in sight. I couldn't even catch my breath, the fall was so fast and so furious.

Dot grabbed me and held me steady, the scanner screeching in the background.

"Coast Guard One to base. Target in sight. Repeat. Target in sight."

"Switch over to 19, Walt. See if you can get Bertie," urged Skip.

Dot, having grabbed my coffee mug just as it was about to leave my grip, led me back to the stool at the counter and helped me take a seat. I still hadn't drawn a breath and I thought I was going to pass out.

Walter got on the radio. "*Hot Dot* to *Elizabeth Bailey*. You out there, Bert? Over."

There was no answer. Just static.

"Try twelve," said Skip.

Walt switched channels and tried again. "*Hot Dot* to *Elizabeth Bailey*. You out there, Bertie? Come in. Over."

The radio scratched and squealed and finally grabbed the signal from the *Elizabeth Bailey*. "We're here, Walt. Coast Guard just got here, too." I could hear Billy and some others yelling in the background, the thump of the helicopter gradually overtaking everything.

"Have they got her, Bert? Did they get little Sheridan?" cried Walter into the battered mic.

"They're working on getting her up now," he replied, the helicopter making it almost impossible to decipher his words. "Jesus, Walt. I don't know. She was down there an awful long time. I don't know."

Dot rubbed my shoulders, hugged me tight. I tried in vain to hold back the tears, but I was doing a terrible job. I was trembling like an earthquake, the ground beneath me still out of reach. Then it hit me. Earlier that morning, I'd done the unfathomable, a thing that could not be undone, and now all I could think was that I may never be able to take it back.

In all the years of coming and going, there was a singular rule, a silent pact really, that my women and I all kept true to no matter what. The one thing we all agreed never to do was to say *goodbye*.

"I never should have said it," I whispered.

"What's that, honey?" asked Dot, handing me a tissue.

"I never should have said it. Goodbye. When I left her this morning, I said goodbye. I never should have said it."

"Let's not get ahead of ourselves," said Skip, his hand firmly planted on my shoulder. "Nobody said a damn thing about goodbye."

I saw Dot give him a look, and Walter, too. It was always a pretty sure bet that once a sailor goes under for an extended period of time the assignment changes dramatically from rescue to recovery. Still, goodbye or not, I had to hold onto the one shred of hope I had left. I had to believe she might still be alive.

"Come on," said Skip. "Let's get down to the hospital. Once they get her up, they'll be there in no time."

"Good luck, honey," said Dot, kissing me on the cheek. "We'll be praying for her."

Skip led me to his International and helped me in. I felt like a zombie, unable to control any of my faculties. I still wasn't sure if I'd drawn a breath or even had a pulse at that point. I couldn't even see. Complete devastation would have been an improvement over how I was feeling at that very moment.

Before I knew it, we were driving up to the emergency room entrance. Skip had it floored the whole way and, come to think of it, I don't think he hit the brakes once, not even at the traffic lights. He shut the key off and coasted into a parking spot, jumping out as he pulled the parking brake. I managed to jump out, too, gathering my senses as best I could, and we ran for the door.

The two of us headed straight for the nurses' station. They said Penny had just arrived, but they didn't know anything beyond that, not even if she was being triaged. I still didn't even know if she was alive or dead and I begged them for more information. Something. Anything. All we could do was wait.

No sooner did we sit down when we heard Billy down the corridor, yelling at an orderly. We couldn't see him as yet, but his voice was unmistakable.

"You have to let me in there, Tommy," he screamed. "I have to see her!"

"I can't do it, Billy," the orderly shouted. "You have to let them take care of her. I'm sorry, man."

The orderly pushed Billy into the emergency room lobby where Skip and I had been waiting then pulled the door shut behind him. Billy, his hands and arms bloodied and bandaged, clawed at the locked door trying desperately to get back to Penny. Had there been a handle, he would have ripped the door clean off its hinges.

Billy, overcome with grief, slumped to the floor in front of the door and wept uncontrollably. Skip took a knee next to him and held his son's head in his arms.

I felt my legs begin to buckle beneath me and I grabbed the nearest seat, collapsing into its hard, industrial base. Billy spotted me, our eyes meeting, and he did all he could to rise from off the cold floor. I gathered all the strength I had, rose, and met him face on. I took him in my arms and held him tight as we both wept.

"I'm sorry, sir. I'm so goddamn sorry."

"Is she alive?" I asked, hopeful.

"She was gone for the longest time. I don't know how long. They almost called it, but she come out of it for a second or two so they kept working on her. I just don't know if they can keep her going. I don't know, sir. I'm so sorry."

Billy, gasping between phrases, told about the angry sea,

a widow maker's sea, and how Penny ignored – no, defied – its threat against them. She was determined to pull just one more trap - *one for Dad, for lunch* - and it proved to be one too many.

The waves were steep and many and the boat bucked as if it were a wild bronco, daring the two to ride her just a little longer. The winch was slipping, the snatch block creaking, and suddenly the whole hauling rig let go like a crack of thunder. The heavy trap plummeted to the ocean depths, the rope careening over the side so fast you couldn't get away from it and Penny got caught up in the line. She was ripped over the side, tangled in the mess of hemp and metal rigging, and Billy was unable to stop her descent. He grabbed the line, tempted to coil it round his arms and hands, and tried with all the strength God gave him to stop it from running out any further. The line tore through his palms, wrenching every bone in his upper body, until the trap - and Penny - finally lay to rest on a ledge just shy of the sandy bottom.

As Bertie brought the *Elizabeth Bailey* alongside, his son, Frankie, jumped on board the *Bobby Grace* to help Billy hold the double-weighted warp. They tossed Bertie the slack end, which he threw over his pulley and winch. The Coast Guard arrived just as Penny's body broke the surface of the water and they got to work reviving her immediately.

"I saw her goin' down," Billy lamented. "Her boots come off right away, like they were supposed to, and they just floated there under the water while she disappeared. I couldn't stop her," he cried. "I tried. I just couldn't do it. I'm sorry, sir. I'm sorry, Dad. I'm so sorry."

A nurse came out to escort Billy to the x-ray room. His arms and hands had been pretty well torn apart and they feared he may have a stress fracture or two. Skip and I sat and waited and waited and waited for news about Penny that seemed to never arrive. I thought I'd wear out the soles of my shoes pacing.

"I wonder what's taking so long," I said under my breath.

"Time's a good thing," Skip replied. "It would have been bad for them to come right back out."

"Oh?"

"I remember when I lost my Bobby. It wasn't more than ten or fifteen minutes and they was out here to tell us he was gone. Time's a good thing."

"I hope so."

I knew I needed to call Jayne, but I was afraid to leave the waiting room. Murphy's Law dictated that if I were to leave they'd have news, which made me want to bolt the scene immediately just to prove them right.

Just then, Donna came storming into the emergency room lobby, smoke practically billowing off her heals. She spotted me instantly and flew over like a witch on a broom, skidding to a halt in front of me.

"What's going on?" she blurted.

"I don't know, honey. They haven't told us anything."

"Is she alive? Do you at least know that?"

"No. I don't know. They haven't told us anything."

"Have you called Jayne?"

"Not yet."

Donna stomped over to the nurses' station and demanded answers they didn't have. It was back and forth, back and forth, *I demand to see a supervisor*, and so on and so on. She finally gave up, having exhausted all her remaining arsenal to no avail on the head nurse.

She stormed back over to me, arms folded in

abhorrence. "Their level of incompetence is incomprehensible," she gasped. "How's Ruth?"

"Not good," I replied. "She's starting to detox. She's going to have a tough time."

"Well, just so she's over it by the wedding. She's supposed to sing, you know."

"Donna, please."

"And Penny's supposed to…" She paused, mid-sentence, her emotions beginning to take hold of her. She put her hand to her mouth and clamped her eyes shut, her lashes clinging to each other in a tight weave. She took a deep breath, let it out slowly, then opened her eyes. "Well, God knows what she'll be able to do now."

I offered her a tissue from the wad Dot had stuffed in my jacket pocket. "We'll know soon," I said. "We have to be hopeful. It's all we can do."

"How's Billy?"

"He's pretty beat up, inside and out. He might have a broken arm."

"Lovely."

"Do you think you could go check on your mother for me? I'll call her to let her know you're coming."

"I'm awfully busy," she sneered, but I could tell it was all just a front. She didn't want to face this any more than I did, but she certainly wasn't going to let her guard down now, even though her tear ducts were beginning to spring leaks. "I guess I could, though," she replied, delicately dabbing the corner of her eye. "Somebody has to take care of her."

"Thank you."

Donna left in the same manner she arrived. I was thankful she was at least going to stop by the house. I didn't want to call Jaynie with news like this and have her sitting alone, wondering, worrying. Worse, I didn't want her taking any pills, of any kind, and getting behind the wheel of the car. As much as I loved my women and would do anything for them, I just couldn't take another incident.

Billy returned from x-ray, his arm in a sling and fresh bandages on his wounds. "Have you heard anything?" he asked, immediately rushing over to Skip.

"Not yet," his father replied. "How about you? What's goin' on with your arm?"

"Don't know yet. They're gonna holler when the pictures are developed. I'm pretty sure my hand's busted up, maybe my wrist, too. They're not a hundred percent sure about the rest. It's startin' to hurt like hell."

"I'll bet," said Skip. "How's your ticker. She hangin' in there?"

"So far. I lost my capsule overboard, though. Must've got caught on somethin', I guess."

Billy carried a tiny stainless steel container housing a nitro pill round his neck along with a Medic Alert badge noting his heart condition. In all his young years, he only had to break out the capsule once when an idiot gym teacher made him run flat-out two and a half miles for a physical fitness test in junior high. Skip came close to suing the school and was instrumental in having the guy fired for incompetence. Ironically, the fellow left town shortly afterward and was never heard of again.

"Do you two think you could stand guard while I make a phone call?" I asked. "I really need to call Jaynie."

"Oh, I'm not goin' anywhere, sir. You can count on that," said Billy, starting to look a little pale.

"We'll come pound on the door if we hear somethin',"

added Skip.

I headed down the public corridor to the bank of phone booths adjacent the elevators. The little light came on as I shut the bi-fold door behind me and I sat in silence wondering what I was going to say to my wife. While I was thinking, I tried to calculate the amount of time it would take Donna to reach her, the amount of time it would take for a pill to kick in if she had one, the amount of time it would take for her decide this was all too much.

The time. Where had it all gone?

I picked up the receiver, put a dime in the slot and dialed. I still didn't know what to say, since I really hadn't any news. Only two rings and she was there, but silent.

"Jaynie?"

I could hear her quietly weeping on the other end, her grief stifled only by a linen kerchief pressed tight to her lips. "Is she gone?" she finally managed, her voice so faint it almost evaporated over the wire.

"I don't know, sweetheart. We're still waiting to hear."

News traveled quickly and indiscriminately throughout our little village. Many were eager to spread the wealth of knowledge, but not all were as willing to help those left in its wake. I could hear the business end of the phone drop onto the counter, then a voice - not Jayne's. The receiver slid back across the Formica. "Steve? Is that you?"

"Dot?"

"Yeah. Hi, honey. I thought Jaynie might need a shoulder, so to speak. I figured I got two big fat ones I wasn't usin', so I thought I'd stop by."

"Thank you. She could sure use it right about now."

"No word, huh?"

"Not yet."

"Well, you keep us posted, okay, honey?" said Dot. "We might come down in a little bit if Jaynie's feeling up to it."

"Thanks," I replied. "Say, Donna's supposed to be stopping by to check on her Mom. If you could hang around until she gets there, I'd appreciate it. She left from here just a few minutes ago."

"Of course I'll hang around. Where the hell did you think I was gonna go? The nail salon?"

I couldn't help but smile to myself. "Thanks, Dot. I owe you."

"Yeah, I know."

I hung up the phone somewhat relieved that Jayne would be in good hands. Dot was like Skip's Gracie when it came to being there for you when you needed it most and right now Jaynie needed it bad. It made me wish for Page, too, and I found myself picking up the phone once again.

I'd never made a call to London from a pay phone and hadn't any idea how to go about it. I sat there with the receiver to my ear, trying to read all the instructional placards pasted to the phone and on the wall in the little booth. Finally, a voice came over the line:

"If you'd like to make a call, please deposit ten cents or dial 'O' for the operator. If you'd like to make a call, please deposit ten cents or dial 'O' for the operator."

I hung up the receiver and fished around in my pockets for a dime, two nickels, a quarter - anything. All I had were a couple of pennies, several spent tissues and a melted peppermint candy that had gone through the wash. As I sat wondering if I should even be taking the time to make another call, a middle aged couple stopped outside the booth to console one another.

"I can't believe she's gone," said the woman.

"I know," said the man.

"So young. So young."

All I could think was that could be Jayne and I and it stopped my heart mid-beat. I paused, said a prayer for the couple and their lost soul, and picked up the receiver. The operator had to jump through several hoops but, finally, after a series of double rings, she was there.

"Donovan-Davis Architectural. This is Mrs. Reynolds. How may I direct your call?"

I thought I had it all under control. I thought I could handle letting my guard down for a second. After all, this was Page. However, something about her tranquil, ever-comforting voice shot that guard all to hell and I was left sitting there, whimpering like a little puppy. I couldn't answer. Couldn't breath. Couldn't move. I knew if I spoke the ceiling would likely come crashing in and there wouldn't be a thing left of me but a melted mint and some tissues. I couldn't do anything but cry.

"Stephen? Is that you?"

"Yes," I whispered, fearing the building might collapse around me if I spoke any louder.

"Lost again, love?"

Heather Trefethen

.

204

20

Donna brought Jayne over to the hospital and immediately set out to vehemently extract information out of the nurses they *still* didn't have regarding Penny. It had been forever and had I not been as anxious as she was for some news, I'd have thought Donna was being downright rude. As it was, she had a reputation for getting results so I just let her fume.

Finally, Dr. Brice emerged from the surgery ward still dressed in scrubs and wiping his sweaty brow with a wrinkled army surplus handkerchief. We all gathered round to hear his report, Skip and Billy included.

"Steve? Jayne? Can I see you in my office?" he requested.

"We'd all like to be included, if you don't mind," spat Donna.

"It's okay, Brice," I assured. "We're all family."

I caught Donna giving Billy and Skip an insensitive look

down her nose. Skip, somewhat insulted but understanding the personal nature of it all, lowered his gaze and headed back to the coffee machine while Billy, not giving an inch, stood his ground. This was *his* Penny, too, and he was prepared to take on the lions.

"Very well," Brice began. "Your daughter hasn't fully maintained consciousness as yet, but she is stable. The water's not real cold yet, but cold enough, which is actually in her favour. She's pretty beat up, but there's still a small chance she'll come out of it and be perfectly fine."

"Which means there's a small chance she won't," noted Donna, always the pessimist.

"We'll just have to be patient," added Brice.

As much as I hated to hear Donna point out the obvious, I was hopeful to at least hear something positive. She was alive. She was stable. She had possibility.

"When can we see her, doc?" asked Billy, his arm really starting to sing. He was still looking pretty pale, but wouldn't give in.

"Soon, son. They're setting her up in ICU right now. Somebody taking care of that arm of yours?"

"Yes, sir. I'm just waiting for the pictures to develop."

Brice motioned for Jayne and me to follow him alone into his office for further briefing, which pissed Donna off to no end. Even though she quite overtly purported to have full and complete responsibility of the family, she didn't need to know everything. Not this time.

As we stepped just inside the double-doored corridor, something stopped me. Although there were probably several good reasons why Donna should be excluded from the conversation with Dr. Brice, there were a million reasons why Billy shouldn't. After all, as much as I hated to admit it,

Penny was practically his wife and I could see the torture in his face wanting to know more about how she was.

I peeked my head out and waved Billy in. "You should be in here, too, son," I said quietly.

"Thank you, sir. I appreciate it."

I never saw anyone move so fast.

Donna, suddenly realizing she was playing second fiddle to the neighbor boy, pounded on the locked hallway door, hollering for someone to let her in. It was awful, I know, to ignore her pleas, but it would have been worse to exclude young Bill. He and Penny were set to make a future together, one step at a time, and it was important that he know what that future would hold.

During the meeting, Brice gave us the lowdown on what to expect during Penny's recovery. The first few days are always the hardest to endure, he said, since that's the time when infection would most likely occur. After that, it would be a matter of assessing the damage.

The rope had done a real number on her leg, breaking it cleanly in two places and ripping her knee to shreds. The trauma from her injuries sped her into shock and was likely the reason she was unable to be revived completely at the onset. On top of that, oxygen deprivation can wreak havoc on the brain and we had to prepare ourselves for the possibility that she may not recover fully, if at all. Worst case scenario would be that she would live out the rest of her days in a vegetative state.

Neither Jayne nor I spoke the whole time and I could see Billy crumbling as Dr. Brice laid out the whole package of clear-cut, well-documented uncertainties. After an agonizing forty-five minutes of *could be*'s and *might be*'s and *possible long term effects could include*'s, Billy had had enough.

"Doctor Brice? No offense, sir, but you don't know my Penny, do you?" he began. "Not really. I mean, you might have brought her into this world, but it's gonna take a helluva lot more than a storm and a busted snatch block to take her out. She's *not* gonna be an invalid. She's *not* gonna be a vegetable, either. She's tough as nails and you can take that one to the bank, sir. No offense. Now I don't know about anybody else, but I'd sure like to see her, if you don't mind."

The three of us were overawed by Billy's bravery in the face of such indetermination. He'd seen his mother pass, and his brother, but he sure as hell wasn't going to see his girl pass, too. Not without a fight, anyway.

Brice personally led us to the ICU, where Penny was being hooked up to untold amounts of machinery. It brought me back to the days almost nineteen years ago when she lay in an incubator with tubes and IV's hooked up to her, the French fry lights keeping her warm and cozy like a baby chick and ridding her of jaundice. So tiny and frail, my little Peanut was once again struggling to survive.

Jayne couldn't bear to watch and asked that I escort her back to the waiting room. She confessed to feeling guilty about blowing Penny off the other day when she was heading out to the Groverton's for their meeting. "All I had to do was say thank you," she emoted. "How hard would it have been to say thank you. I've treated her so awful."

"You had a lot on your mind, honey," I replied. "She understood."

"She works so hard and does so much. And she never asks for anything."

"I know."

I led Jayne back to the elevators and held her close as

we journeyed down to the first floor. Billy, still waiting for the results from his x-rays, stayed behind to keep an eye on Penny. As the doors opened, we were met face on by Donna, raving mad.

"Where have you been?" she blasted. "I've been waiting for over an hour."

"I'm sorry, sweetheart," I replied, so exhausted I couldn't even get upset. "It was a long meeting."

"Would you mind taking me home, dear?" Jayne asked her. "I've got a splitting headache."

"Fine! I guess I'll have to read about my sister in the paper since nobody seems to be interested in informing me otherwise."

"We'll talk on the way home," assured Jayne.

Donna pounded off to get the car. It made me wonder if there was ever a moment during her day - any day, in fact - when she wasn't pissed off about something. She seemed to live in a constant state of wrathful indignation, the world and everyone in it owing her for the so-called painful injustices she's had to endure throughout her life. I owed her the most and I was surprised she hadn't yet taken the time to remind me of it.

Skip, on at least his twelfth pot of coffee, offered Jayne and me a cup. "It's fresh," he said. "Just brewed it myself." He'd been there so long, the nurses decided to teach him how to work the commercial-grade Bunn and he'd become a real pro. Truth be told, at this point he could probably give Hot Dot a run for her money. We gladly accepted, both needing something to keep our eyelids half open.

Donna beeped the horn as she pulled up to the entryway, obviously too exasperated to venture back inside. I gave Jayne a kiss and escorted her out, reassuring her that I'd call immediately if there was any change in Penny's condition. I found myself actually wishing she had some of her pills to help her cope with all that was happening. But then again, it was probably best that she didn't.

With all that had been happening with Penny, I nearly forgot about Ruth and felt I should check on her right away. She surely must be feeling abandoned, since I'd promised I'd come back and I hadn't. Skip was worried about Billy, too, so I conned the nurses into letting him come up with me to ICU where he could sit with his son while I checked on Ruth.

Navigating through the different wings of the hospital was like trying to navigate through a labyrinth designed by M.C. Escher. Up and down, left and right, corridors dead-ending. You wouldn't think there would be so many twists and turns in a square building, but there were. I wanted to wring the architect's neck.

When we finally made it to ICU, we could hear a commotion going on outside Penny's room. Billy was yelling, nurses yelling back. Fearing the worst, Skip and I ran down the hall and around the corner, just about knocking over an orderly carrying a stack of meal trays.

"I'm not leaving her," screamed Billy. "Just give me a splint. I'll put in on myself."

"What's your problem, young fella?" cried Skip, gripping his son by the shoulder.

"They want to take me downstairs, put a cast on me. Said my arm was broken. But, I'm not goin'. I'm not leavin' her."

"You get your ass down there and do as they say, boy," Skip ordered. "She's not goin' anywhere."

"But, Dad!"

"I don't want to hear anymore lip about it. You do as they say."

They stared at each other for a solid minute before Billy, growing paler and paler from the shock of his broken wing, finally backed down. An orderly brought over a wheel chair and took young Bill down to Orthopedics to get patched up. He was none too happy, and neither was the orderly, whom Billy ironically didn't know from Adam. Skip sighed, just as scared for Penny's well-being as his son and I.

We looked in on Penny as the nurses finished settling her in.

"She means everything to that boy," whispered Skip.

"She means everything to a lot of us," I replied.

Skip nodded in agreement. He'd always thought of Penny as the daughter he never had and it pained him to see her so wracked up. "She's got Moxie, though," he said, confident. "She'll pull through."

"Tough as nails," I sighed.

Skip stood sentry while I made the trip further upstairs to the Drug and Alcohol Dependency ward, passing through Geriatrics on the way. Colonel Pendlewaite was on the loose again and the nurses and orderlies were practically having a free-for-all trying to find him. Apparently, he'd left a trail of clothes behind and they caught up to him just as he was about to drop his drawers in front of an unsuspecting group of Bingo ladies. The gasps nearly sucked the oxygen right out of the room.

I found Ruthie curled up in a ball on her bed, shivering and crying like a little kitten caught in the rain. I knocked quietly on the doorframe, the attending nurse overseeing the exchange in case Ruthie was to suddenly fly out of control. The minute she spotted me, she jumped out of bed and dove at my feet, grabbing me round the knees and holding me tight. I crouched beside her and held her close, both of us wadded together like two crumpled pieces of newspaper. I motioned to the nurse that I was okay and she graciously granted us some privacy.

"Take me home, Daddy," Ruthie sobbed, rocking back and forth on the cold linoleum floor. "Take me home, please."

"I can't sweetheart. You have to stay. You have to get better."

"But, I'm so scared. I'm so scared. Mom's going to be so mad. I messed up so bad. I'm so messed up." She couldn't stop crying, couldn't stop rocking. I held her tight, rocking with her, just holding her, consoling her. There was little else I could do.

"Mom's not mad," I assured her. "She's just worried. She wants you to get better, just like I do."

"I keep getting sick. Why do I keep getting sick? I don't understand what's happening. I'm so scared."

"It's the drugs, honey. They're working their way out of your system. It's going to take a little while. Just hang in there."

"I can't. I can't. I feel like I'm going to die all the time. My skin is crawling all the time. I'm scared."

I held Ruthie for as long as I could until the nurse ordered me, twice, to leave. I didn't have the heart to tell her about Penny. She had enough going on as it was and she didn't need something else to worry about. When everything smoothed out, when everyone was on their way to recovery, then I'd tell her.

When I got back to ICU, Skip was nowhere to be found. After all that coffee, I thought at first he might be in the john until the nurse caught up to me and told me he was downstairs with his son. I couldn't blame him, really. Billy had been looking awfully peaked the last hour or so and he kept grabbing at his chest and adjusting the sling thrown over his left shoulder.

Soon they were wheeling in a stretcher with young Bill laid out prone and they parked him right next to Penny. He'd collapsed just as they finished putting his cast on and they had to toss a nitro tablet under his tongue to get him stabilized. Skip about had a coronary himself, the stress of the days coming together and mixing with the gallons of caffeine he'd consumed. He was shaking like a leaf.

"What happened?" I asked, leading him over to the bench outside the room.

"Guess it all finally caught up to him," replied Skip. "Catchin' up to me, too. Guess I shouldn't have had that last cup of coffee."

"Are you okay?" I asked, not wanting to see another man go down. "Can I get you something?"

"I don't know. I'm half starved to death. You must be, too, I should think."

I didn't realize it until he mentioned it, but I hadn't eaten for close to a day. My stomach was clawing away at my backbone and, as nervous as I was, I really needed something substantial. "I hate to leave," I said, "but I could at least use some soup or something right about now."

"Mr. Monaghan?"

"Right here," replied Skip, gathering himself up off the vinyl bench.

A young orderly came out to give us the news about Billy. Or at least that's who we thought he was.

"Your son's going to be fine," he said, jotting

something down on his official-looking aluminum clipboard. "He was a bit shocky from the trauma of his injuries. It puts a lot of stress on the heart. The nitro seems to have stabilized him, but we're going to keep him here a little while just to be sure."

"Where's the doctor?" asked Skip. "I'd like to ask him a few questions."

"I'm the doctor," replied the youth. "Malcolm MacHugh. Cardiology."

We both looked at each other, jaws agape. The guy still had acne and it was somewhat unclear whether or not his voice had completely changed. He stood there looking at us with this stupid toothy grin on his face that just begged for the attention of an orthodontist.

"You're twelve," sneered Skip.

"Not quite," he replied. "But, they say I'm very mature for my age."

"Well for chrissakes. And a goddamn Scotsman, too," he mumbled. He was clearly unnerved.

Skip ran his huge, weathered hand over his face, trying to wipe away a look that could kill. This was his son's life they were talking about, not some grade school, celery-and-coloured-water experiment. He took a deep breath and composed himself. "Well, you do what you gotta do, fella," he finally said. "Just keep him goin'. His mother'll take care of the rest."

"Is she here?"

It was all I could do to keep Skip from clocking the kid - excuse me, cardiologist. It was obvious he was from out of town and if Skip had any say in the matter he'd be out of town again - fast.

"She's everywhere," growled Skip. "And if you don't

take good care of *both* those kids, she'll be up your ass in spades. You got that?"

We left the poor little mouse of a doctor shaking in his dime store loafers. We could both tell he wasn't going to last long. After all, if he wasn't smart enough to buy a good pair of shoes, how smart could he be at all?

21

Skip finally went home to rest and take a shower at around midnight and I left shortly after. I couldn't remember the last time I'd slept and I was actually afraid to drive, not to mention the fact that I was getting a little ripe. I had two days growth of beard by that time and considered letting it grow out even further for the winter. Jaynie used to like me with a beard. When it got good and full, I'd throw on a turtleneck and wink at her. That was all it took and we'd be in the bedroom.

Jayne was sleeping when I got home, a fresh, nearly full bottle of Valium next to her on the nightstand. I was so exhausted. I lay down next to her to say hello and was sound asleep before I could even mumble. We both slept like logs until almost noon the next day, alarmed that the entire morning had just about passed us by. I took a quick shower then offered to make some soup and sandwiches, but Jaynie refused. "I'll just poach an egg later," she said, popping a pill.

It was so unlike Jayne to be this depressed. She was practically despondent. Sure she'd had her trials with the girls before and it went without saying that this was by far the worst. But, she had always been strong and stoic, handling everything like a trooper. It made me wonder if there wasn't something else eating at her.

I picked up her pill bottle and did a quick inventory. "I thought you were going to talk to the doctor about getting off these."

"I will. Just not now."

Jayne took the bottle and slid it into her robe pocket, then sauntered over to the couch. I sat down next to her and held her close. There was so little life in her. "Jaynie, honey, what is it? What's wrong?"

It took a while for her to answer, the words mixing round in her head as they tried to make their way to her tongue. She went through several tissues, a glass of water, another pill, and a mile of pacing before she could finally speak.

"I'm sorry," she quietly began. "I'm just so sorry."

"This wasn't your fault, sweetheart. It wasn't your fault at all."

"I'm sorry."

"For what?" I pleaded. "I don't understand."

"I'm so sorry. For everything. For the girls. For what I've done and haven't done. I'm sorry. I just can't do it anymore. I can't live this lie anymore."

"What lie, sweetheart?"

She seemed so broken. In all the years, I never once questioned her credibility as a loving mother and wife. She'd do anything for the girls and I. It was beyond me that she felt she'd somehow failed.

"It's true you know, what Donna said that day. She did take care of the family while you were away. She was always trying to find a nice boy for Ruthie. She worried about her so much. So did Penny. I should have done better with them. I should have been more supportive. But, I just couldn't do it by myself all the time. I was so lonely, Stephen. So lonely."

"I missed you, too, Jaynie. You know I wished I could have been here more."

"This was more than missing. It was deeper than that. I couldn't help it. When he asked to meet me for dinner, I hated to say yes. I hated it with all my heart. But, I couldn't stop myself. I needed someone. I don't know how else to explain it. I'm so sorry."

I was thrown for a loop. Never, ever, in all our years of marriage had I once even considered being unfaithful to Jaynie and never once thought she would be unfaithful to me. Yet, here she was confessing. At least that's how it sounded. My head was spinning and I felt myself being choked by my own stomach.

"Who asked you? What are you talking about?" I quietly urged.

"I loved you, Stephen. I still love you. I do. But, I can't live like this knowing what I've done to you."

I got up from the couch and began to pace the floor. How far had it gone? Was it still going on? Who was it? Did the girls know?

"I ended it a few years ago," she admitted, "and it's been eating at me ever since."

"Jesus, Jaynie. I don't know what to say."

"I was so torn every time you came home," she continued, trying in vain to hold it together. "I thought I could get angry with you, stay angry with you, maybe even get you to hate me for it. It was like asking for penance. Then we'd make love and I'd remember all over again why I fell in love with you in the first place. I love you, Stephen. I do. But I just can't bear the thought of knowing I've done something so hurtful."

Nothing strikes a man's ego quite so hard than to know that the woman he has loved with every fibre of his being somehow found it necessary to seek love elsewhere. All I wanted to do was provide for my family, but at what cost. Come to find out, the only thing they truly needed from me was love.

At this point I wasn't sure if it mattered, but I had to know, as if knowing would somehow lessen the sting.

"Who was it?" I reluctantly asked.

Jaynie paced away from me, grabbing up tissues from the box on the end table. She paused for the longest time, the din of silence almost unbearable. Finally, she gave in.

"Mike. It was Mike," she whispered.

"Mike Conners?"

"Yes," Jaynie nodded.

"That son of a bitch." At that very moment, I wanted to hate him. I wanted to hate everything he was, even everything he wasn't. I found myself tightening up all over, the very thought of another man touching my wife all but sending me into a palsy. "Did you sleep with him?" I asked.

"He wanted to. So did I, or so I thought," she shamefully admitted. "But I couldn't go through with it. All I could think of was you. How, if I *did* go through with it, I'd never be able to look you in the eye again - ever. It's hard enough as it is, having met with him. It all ended shortly after that. As much as I needed someone to hold me, it was all just too much. I loved you too much."

I suppose the fact that they hadn't slept together somewhat made up for the fact that they'd seen each other, but the fact remained that my wife cheated on me. And that was a tough pill to swallow.

Jayne and I sat at opposite ends of the couch in silence for close to an eternity. I didn't know what to say, didn't know what to do, didn't even know how to act. I'd waited years to get to this point in my life and now it was as if I couldn't wait for it to end.

The phone rang, breaking the relentless silence. Neither one of us got up at first until we both realized it could be the hospital calling with news about Penny or Ruth. It was disgraceful to think they hadn't been at the forefront of our minds.

"Hello?"

"Hey, sir. It's Billy. You're never gonna believe this, but Penny twitched. She twitched, sir. Isn't that great?"

I hung up the phone and grabbed my flannel shirt. I could barely look at Jayne and considered taking Penny's Nash to the hospital, not sure I could stand to have my unfaithful wife next to me in the front seat of a car. It was all so awkward.

Jayne, however, convinced me to drive the two of us in the Jag, worried what the neighbors would think if they saw us heading to the same destination in separate vehicles. It made me wonder if she ever considered what they'd think of her having dinner with Mike while I was out of town. Still, Jayne desperately wanted to go, having felt guilty for leaving the emergency room so suddenly yesterday and even guiltier that she hadn't once looked in on Ruth. It was an uncomfortable ride to say the least, each of us still unsure how to process the conversation prior.

Skip met us just outside ICU where Dr. Brice was conferring with a colleague from neurosurgery.

"How is she?" I asked, hopeful.

"Don't seem like much on the outside," Skip smiled, "but my boy and them doctors think it's pretty wicked."

Both Brice and Dr. Canyon noted that while a muscle twitch is often involuntary, the fact that it happened at the same moment Billy mentioned to Penny that he'd had a cardiac event gave them all the more reason to suspect that she may have some cognitive functioning going on. This was indeed promising.

They led us into the room where Billy, still dressed in his hospital jonnie, had himself practically chained to Penny's bedside. His colour was better and the smile on his face proved he was returning to good health.

"It was wild, sir," he beamed, whispering loud as if to not wake her. "You should've seen it."

I couldn't help but beam back. "That's great, son. That's great news."

Billy went on to talk about all he'd read on coma patients while recuperating from his spell. He urged us to bring in Penny's portable cassette player and some tapes they'd made of Ruthie singing, hoping it would spur the synapses of her brain. He said touch was equally important, sheepishly admitting to giving her a massage or two when no one was looking. "It wasn't like *that*, though, sir," he grinned. "I was cool about it."

Although she didn't move a muscle, Penny's heart monitor sped up for four or five beats, further indicating to the doctors that she may actually be aware of what was going on around her. Billy grinned from ear to ear, his face turning ten shades of red.

I squinted back at him, knowing full well he'd never do anything inappropriate with my daughter. Otherwise, he'd have to suffer *her* wrath followed by mine - a lethal combination to say the least.

His father squinted, too. "You're full of shit as a Christmas turkey. You know that, boy?"

Billy, still grinning, held up three fingers in a salute. "Scout's honor, sir. Swear to God. Scout's honor."

Jaynie decided to make the journey upstairs on her own to check on Ruth Anne while I stayed behind with Penny. Since she hadn't been up there as yet, I drew her a little map of how to get to the Dependency ward, noting any and all 'landmarks' so she wouldn't get lost, which I'd found out on numerous occasions was an easy thing to do.

After Jayne left, Billy and I talked about how we both got lost just coming back from the bathroom. We joked that in some part of this poorly designed building there must be a search party on stand-by for those who go missing for more than an hour. We parleyed back and forth, outlining the dispatch and retrieval of long lost souls.

Penny's monitor blipped two quick beats.

"She must be gettin' tired," said Billy.

I kissed her on the forehead and whispered in her ear. "Sorry, Peanut. We'll be quiet."

One quickened beat and her body seemed to settle, her pulse slowing ever so slightly. Billy took her hand in his and held it to his cheek as he stared at her still-battered face. He so wanted for her to be whole again, as did I.

A huge male nurse, first cousin to Willie Davis and just as menacing, came in with a plastic bag, a towel and a bar of soap. He walked right up to Billy, towering over him like Goliath over David. "This is the last time I'm askin' you, boy," he began, his voice deeper than the Mississippi. "Yo' ass is startin' to draw flies and we don't like flies 'round hea."

Billy just stared at him, defiant, readying his sling for battle. He was *not* going to leave his girl.

"He's right, son," said Skip, exaggeratedly wiping his nose with his blue bandana handkerchief. "Christ, I've had bait on board for the whole month of July smells better than you do."

Billy stared his father down then looked to me, but I wasn't giving him any sympathy either. The poor kid was developing his own atmosphere and it wasn't exactly a habitable one. Finally, he backed down.

"How far do I have to go?" he asked.

"Right across the hall. You can even leave the door open if it makes you feel better, although I don't think the nurses are gonna wanna to see yo' scrawny white ass. And I *sure* as hell don't wanna see it."

"Fresh clothes are in your duffle on the bench out there," added Skip. "Brought your razor, too, in case you wanna hack off them half dozen whiskers on your chin."

"I got more than you, old man," he grinned, mock jabbing his father on the chin.

"Yeah, well I about rubbed mine all off worryin' about you, you little fart. Now get in the bath like the man said before you give us all the dry heaves."

Billy grinned and gave Penny a gentle kiss on the forehead before reluctantly heading across the hall for the walk-in shower. Jerome, the nurse, wrapped his cast in the plastic bag to keep it from getting wet and brought him some shampoo to freshen his mop of hair. I wondered how long it would be before his lingering odor would start to fade from the room, if at all. He sure was pungent.

Skip took the opportunity to head to the cafeteria for a bite to eat and a gallon or two of coffee. He mentioned they had good fish-n-chips and I made a mental note to try some for supper.

I'd been alone no less than a minute when I heard a commotion down the hall and thought perhaps Donna had stopped by for a visit. It seemed whenever voices began to rise, you could pretty much bet she was in charge of the volume control. Sure enough, I won the pot.

"Well?" she sighed, peeking her head in the door. "Any change?"

"She twitched," I replied.

"Dead people can twitch. What's that have to do with her?"

Leave it to Donna to put everything in perspective. She was dressed in a business suit, which I thought odd, and was also carrying a small green plant, which I thought equally odd. I certainly could envision her bringing her sister a gift, but not one as ordinary as a potted plant.

"It happened because she was upset," I said. "Billy was talking to her and when he mentioned - "

"Wait a minute. He was talking to her? What was he talking to her for? I thought she was in a coma."

"She *is* in a coma. Just because her body isn't working doesn't mean her brain isn't. It's supposed to help stimulate activity."

"Preposterous."

"What's the plant for?" I finally asked.

"It's called a spider plant. Bob said it's supposed to act as an air cleaner. I brought one up to Ruth, too. They both could stand to use them in this place. What is that stench anyway?"

"Bob?" For the life of me I couldn't place who Bob might be, but then again I never could place any of Donna's friends. Penny and Billy's were hard enough to keep track of, but at least I knew a few of them.

"You know," she sighed, as if I should. "Reed's ex."

"Oh. Wait. His ex? When did that happen?"

Apparently, Reed had a roaming eye, and not just for my wife. Turns out he batted for both teams and took off for Reno with a cocktail waitress of questionable gender named Danni, leaving poor Bob and a number of unpaid bills in his wake. I found it funny that Jayne never mentioned it.

"Well, I've got to run," said Donna.

"You just got here."

"I know. See that she gets the plant, will you? Hopefully it won't die in this dungeon."

Donna handed me the little decorative pot and she was off. I couldn't imagine where she was going all decked out as if on her way to Wall Street. At least we didn't fight and she still didn't ask me for any money.

Billy, dressed only in a towel and dragging his duffle, raced back to the room. His hair was dripping, his nose running from the hot shower. He actually looked a mess, but he smelled much better.

"How's she doin' sir?" he whispered.

"Pretty much the same as she was five minutes ago," I replied. "You're dripping, by the way."

"Oh, yeah. Sorry."

Billy got behind a chair and clumsily pulled on his boxers and jeans, throwing the towel over his head as he dressed one-handed. He was having a terrible time with his shirt and I offered to help, carefully sliding one sleeve over his cast and feeding his good arm into the other. I could see him wince, but he tried like crazy to hide it. Like Penny, he was tough as nails.

I grabbed some paper towels from a dispenser by the sink and dabbed up the puddles in the room to avoid any slip-and-fall injuries. It was the last thing we needed. Billy lent a hand, too, sopping up the little lakes in the hallway that led from the shower to Penny's temporary digs. He may have toweled off when he stepped out of the shower, but that head of hair must have held at least ten gallons. I imagined an entire stand of trees being cut down to replenish the supply of paper towel we'd consumed soaking it up. I should have just commandeered a mop.

After having filled an entire trash can full of sopping wet towels, Billy sat down and began the arduous task of putting on his shoes and socks. I only watched him struggle for a minute, mumbling little obscenities under his breath, before I got up to help.

"This is a real pain in the ass, you know that, sir?"

"I can see that, son," I said, slipping a well-worn woolen sock over his calloused size nine foot. "But, just think. By the time you get the hang of it the cast will be off."

Jaynie appeared in the doorway, white as a ghost, alarming us both.

"Whoa. You okay, Mrs. Sheridan?"

"Jaynie, what's wrong? Has something happened to Ruth?"

It took her a minute to catch her breath, Billy scooting the chair underneath her. She fought to collect herself, taking deep breaths and letting them release slowly from between her pursed lips. I took a knee next to her, holding her trembling hand in mine.

"Ruth's fine," she finally exhaled as Billy handed her a glass of water. "Struggling, but fine."

"What's wrong then? What happened?" I asked, desperate for answers.

"Did somebody try to mug you, Mrs. Sheridan?" asked Billy, trying to keep his voice down.

"No, Billy. Nothing like that," she replied, still breathing and releasing, breathing and releasing, fumbling to open her pill bottle.

A thought came to mind. A terrible thought. A dreadful thought. In my attempt to be as thorough as possible in my directions to the Dependency ward, there had been one very important detail - an imposing "landmark", really - that I admittedly neglected to include.

The Colonel.

22

Jayne and I, both finally exhaling, sat quietly in the cafeteria. It seemed we were the only ones there. The lunch crowd had gone and the kitchen was in the early stages of dinner prep. Clinking dishes muffled our voices as we tried to make sense of the day.

"I'm sorry about that, Jaynie. I really should have warned you. Frankly, I thought by now they'd have figured out a way to keep him corralled."

"Well, they haven't," she sighed, taking another sip of her chamomile tea. "It was awful."

"I hope I don't look like that when I get to be his age," I emoted.

My ego was already a little deflated, but the thought that one day I, too, might be a wrinkled old coot like the Colonel really hit home. I perished the notion of becoming even more potbellied, a hump forming on my back as I slowly slumped into an "S", my testicles dangling down toward my knobby knees. Good god, what time does to you when you're not looking.

"Please, Stephen," Jayne reassured, "your posture's much too erect, not to mention the fact that you're far superior in other departments."

My smile broadened, hoping the other departments she was thinking of were the same ones I was thinking of. Jayne smiled, too, gradually calming from her traumatic experience in the Geriatrics ward. She tried to take another sip of tea, but a laugh got to her first. She tried to hide it, but it just wouldn't give up. Finally, it escaped in joyous delight.

I laughed, too, not able to help myself thinking of what it must have been like for her. What a sight he must have been, pith helmet and balls. It was the first time we'd shared a happy moment in weeks.

"I'm glad the girls are both doing better," she sighed.

"Me, too," I replied. "I'm beginning to really worry about Penny, though. It's been too long."

"Yes, I know. There's still a chance, though. Don't you think?"

"There has to be."

Another four days passed and Penny still had not regained consciousness. Although she managed to stave off an infection, fluid was beginning to build up in her lungs as pneumonia predictably, yet slowly settled in. If she didn't come to soon, it would be a sure bet that she wouldn't at all. Billy wasn't buying the prognosis, though, and continued his round-the-clock regiment of gentle massage, uplifting conversation, and unconditional love.

Jayne and I were beside ourselves wondering what we would do if we were to lose our baby daughter. Consoling each other was the most difficult of all, especially in light of

Jayne's recent confession. It was hard to ignore, harder still to put aside. I wanted to hold her, and she me, but all I could think of was Mike. It was tough putting on a brave front, but we did manage - especially in front of the girls.

Ruthie, although improving, wasn't going to be allowed any visitors for a full week after that evening. Apparently, it was part of the counseling process, something about deprogramming and, as much as we hated to, we were simply going to have to trust it. I stopped in to see her for a quick visit before her early evening curfew and gave her as much encouragement as I knew how to give. She was actually looking better, her wounds healing, the DT's subsiding. She even ate.

Ruthie asked several times about Chuck, almost obsessed at the thought that he would somehow find her and take her away, maybe even kill her. I assured her he was locked up in the county jail, the key all but thrown away, and wouldn't be released anytime soon. Not even his parents wanted him out, having themselves refused to pay the thousand dollars bail. I believe their exact words to the judge were, "He can rot in hell for all we care." Nice bunch of folks.

We still hadn't told Ruth about Penny and, with her coming session being so long, we thought it best to wait. Not even Donna spilled the beans, for which we were eternally grateful. Even she knew it would be cruel to pass on such information without any means for Ruth to following up. We all decided that whenever she asked about her little sister, the standard response would be: *she's fine*.

We'd noticed during the week that as Ruth began to feel better physically, she began to feel worse about her wardrobe. She asked if her mother could pick out some brighter dresses for her, maybe even some nice jeans and a pretty blouse.

"Please don't buy anything, though," she insisted. "If I have some old things in my closet, that will be fine. Or, maybe Donna has something she doesn't want anymore. I just don't think I like this dark look anymore."

I'm not sure what anyone else thought, but I took it as a pretty big breakthrough since all I'd seen her in for the past two years, including her make-up and hair, was blue-black, black on black, or just plain black. I promised her we'd bring a selection when the week-long session was complete and she could pick out what she liked. It seemed to cheer her.

Jayne and I stayed with Penny until around eight that evening. We took turns holding her hand, stroking her brow, talking to her; all the things Billy and the doctors told us were helpful. Her monitor would periodically blip, seemingly in response, which we still found promising. She'd also now and again twitch.

Billy never left Penny's side, except to go to the bathroom or eat a quick meal in the little family room across the hall. He and Penny knew several of the nurses' kids and younger siblings, too, and they all conspired to keep him hidden overnight so the two could be together. It was clearly evident that nothing was ever going to tear them apart.

When Jayne and I got home that night, we found Donna upstairs in her room going through what remained in her closets. Some clothes were thrown on the bed, others in boxes, still others in a suitcase.

"What are you doing, dear?" asked Jayne.

"I need to clean out this closet. Every time I go to look for something at Brian's it's here and every time I go to look for something here, it's at Brian's. It's extraordinarily inconvenient."

"Need some help?" I asked.

"I'm sure you'd love to get me out of here as soon as possible, wouldn't you," she sneered.

"That's not what I meant."

"Tea anyone?" asked Jayne, trying to ward off a fight.

"Love some," said Donna, grabbing articles of clothing piece by piece, giving each barely a nanosecond of a glance before tossing them on an appropriate pile.

I flopped on the bed next to a heap of assorted dresses, blouses, slacks and an oddly placed football jersey. "Going out for varsity this year?" I chided, holding the jersey up to my chest.

"That happens to have been a gift from Brian. He scored a touchdown wearing it," she said, tossing a chiffon blouse over my head.

"I'll bet he did."

"How's the brat?"

"The same," I frowned.

Donna pulled a dress out of the closet, the same dress she'd arrived in for the Chowder Cook-off. The same dress that matched Penny's. She held it up and stared at herself in the mirror, as if completely unsure which pile to put it in. Her lower lip began to quiver. Her eyes welled up and she began to sniffle, staring endlessly at the dress.

I tossed the jersey and blouse on the bed and joined her side. Something struck her, something about the dress, and it sent a shock wave through her entire body. Donna, unable to look at much else, placed a hand over her face then buried her head into my shoulder and wept like I'd never seen her weep before.

"Why did she have to do it, Daddy? Why?"

"What is it, sweetheart? What's wrong?"

For the life of me, I couldn't imagine the pain she must be harbouring, having felt so responsible for so much for so long. It likely equaled my own pain as I watched the family I so loved dissolve around me like a sandcastle in the rain. I held her close, running my hand over the back of her head to calm her. She trembled in my arms like a scared rabbit, the tears soaking every inch of my shoulder.

"Stupid brat. She was always so fearless," she began, "like nothing could stand in her way. I told her over and over again. Be careful. Don't go out if it's bad. She just wouldn't listen. Now what am I going to do?"

"Honey, it's okay. It's going to be okay," I whispered. "She's getting a little better each day."

"It's not enough, Daddy, and you know it. We all know it. She was supposed to be awake by now and she's not. She's not. What am I going to do? I hate her. I hate her for leaving me. I hate her for leaving us. I hate her."

"No you don't, sweetheart. No you don't."

Unable to carry the burden any longer, Donna collapsed to her knees. I sat next to her and held her in my arms like I did when she was a little girl. Finally, she began to calm, all the tears she had been saving for a decade having dispensed themselves in solid, steady streams. I gave her my handkerchief, smoothed the hair away from her dampened face.

"She was the one who took care of everything, you know. Not me. She worked, fixed things, called plumbers and electricians, made sure Ruth and Jayne were okay. I spent all my time trying to *look* important instead of actually *being* important. Now look where it's gotten me. Nowhere."

Poor Donna. I never thought I'd see the day when she

would admit to her own shortcomings, but she had. She'd demanded everyone act as her minion, and now that the minions were all grown up or sick of bowing to her demands, she had no one to rely but herself - and Brian, although I can't say as he counts for much.

She'd especially relied on Penny, more than anyone ever imagined really. And, now that the possibility existed that her sister might be trapped in an unconscious state for the rest of her life, Donna became suddenly and quite overwhelmingly lost.

Jayne, having come in with a tray and three cups of Earl Grey, startled at the sight of Donna and I slumped on the floor. She all but dropped the lot on the end of the bed, half-spilling the cream and most of the tea. "Good gracious, Donna. What's wrong, honey? Did you faint?"

"It's okay," replied Donna, rising slowly and wiping away the remains of her mascara. "I just had a moment, that's all."

Jayne hugged her tight and held her. "I know, honey. We've all had them. Some are worse than others. But they'll pass."

Jayne pulled a tissue from her sweater pocket and dabbed Donna's cheeks and the corners of her eyes. As awful as it was to see my daughter in such agony, it was nice to see her bond so tightly with her mother. Two stoic women, each mustering their own brand of courage in the face of fear.

"I hope that's real cream and not milk," said Donna, trying desperately to get back to her own sense of normalcy.

"Milk? How pedestrian," I teased, trying to be normal, too.

Donna, still sniffling, gave me a classic 'Donna' look, to

which I returned a grin in kind. I was determined to break through that platinum shell of hers come hell or high water.

"Please, Daddy. Don't be gauche," she snarled. "I have to go."

"What about your tea?" asked Jayne. "And your clothes?"

"Rain check. I'll pick these things up tomorrow."

And with that, she was off.

I slept on the couch that night - had been all week - still unsure what to make of Jayne's tryst. I was pretty sure I'd one day be able to forgive her. I just wasn't sure if I'd be able to forget.

When we arrived at the hospital the next morning, Jayne insisted on spending some time with Penny alone. I could see Billy quickly balking at the idea, but he backed down just as fast. He knew as well as I did that it was never a good idea to go against a Sheridan woman's demand and he and I both dutifully headed down to the cafeteria for coffee and breakfast.

"Is your father fishing this morning?" I asked as I pushed the elevator button for the ground floor.

"Yes, sir. He's gonna start haulin' some traps in before it gets too late in the season. He's startin' to hate the cold a little earlier each year."

"Have you given any more thought to going back to school?"

I knew it was a loaded question, but I had to know. He'd worked so hard for his scholarships and the chance to intern at the Marine Lab. I hated to see him miss a day and here he was working on a full week of absenteeism. Penny would be furious if she knew he was playing hooky, but then again she may very well want him at her side for the time being. It had to be tough on him.

"I'm thinkin' about it, sir," he replied. "My dad's startin' to get on my case a little, too, but I just can't leave her right now. I hate to get behind, though. I'm kinda torn."

In order to give Jayne ample time with Penny, we took the opportunity to order the cafeteria's equivalent to a full fry, which we both needed. Billy hadn't eaten a whole lot lately and he was starting to get a little thin around the middle. His belt was snugged up to the last available notch, yet he still had to hike his jeans up with his good hand about every three steps.

"You want this wrapped up, honey?" asked the aging checkout gal.

"No thanks, ma'am. We'll eat it here this mornin'."

A cute little candy-striper brought Billy's tray over to the table for him while I grabbed a couple of cups of coffee. I missed Dot's brew and longed for a plate of her fresh donuts. As good as the staff was here at the hospital, their cafeteria left much to be desired.

Billy dug right in, making quick work of his fried eggs, potatoes, bacon and sausage. Being half starved to death myself, I didn't waste any time either. I had to admit, it was actually good for a change. Billy wiped the toast crumbs off his half dozen whiskers, tossed the napkin on his plate and stared at it. He was deep in thought about something, and I just let him have his mental space.

"Sir?" he finally said.

"Yes."

"I don't know if this is the right time or the right place to be askin' this, but I think I better while I got the chance."

"What's on your mind, son?"

"Well, sir," he began, his words carefully chosen. "I've

been givin' this a lot of thought and... Well... You know I love your daughter more than anything in the world."

"Yes, I know. I love her, too."

"Yes, sir. Well, the thing is when Penny comes out of this - and I know she's gonna someday soon - anyway, when she comes out of this I'm not so sure I'm gonna be able to keep bein' her boyfriend anymore."

"I beg your pardon..."

I couldn't believe my ears. The one thing I never expected during this whole ordeal was to hear Billy say he was giving up. How could he? He seemed so hopeful on the one hand, yet unable to face the future on the other. On some level, I understood his reasoning. He was young, his whole life ahead of him. He had passions, dreams, so much to look forward to. Yet he still loved my daughter, despite the uncertainty of her fate, and I couldn't imagine him suddenly abandoning all they had invested. I held my breath, devastated.

"What I mean to say, sir," he continued, "what I mean is, I'm gonna want to be more than that. I'm gonna want to provide for her, to set up a home for her and our family if we're blessed to have one. I'm gonna want to be her husband, sir, and I want her to be my wife."

All at once, the seas parted, the clouds lifted and the angels rejoiced in full chorus. My god, I could have punched him for scaring me so badly. He'd never before given me cause to doubt him or his love for my daughter and I was ashamed that for that fleeting moment I thought he was going to prove me wrong. I was so quick to judge. Never again.

"With your permission, of course, sir," added Billy, gazing at me in anticipation.

I hid a smile behind my cupped hand, torturing him with a pregnant pause as I thought long and hard how to respond. After all, it wasn't a question of yes or no. More a question of how to phrase it.

"Well, Billy," I began.

"Yes, sir?" he replied, beads of sweat forming on his brow. I thought he was going to crush his coffee mug he was so tensed up waiting for my answer. In defense of the ceramic, I took a deep breath and continued.

"Of all the men in this world, those we've met and those we haven't, there isn't a single one I would choose to accept the hand of my daughter over you. You're everything to her and that means everything to me. And I would be honored to have you as my son-in-law."

Billy beamed from ear to ear. He stood out of respect, as did I, and shook my hand with great force, nearly dropping me in my tracks. I'd forgotten how strong he was and apparently he had, too.

"Easy, son," I gritted. "Save some of that grip for later."

"Sorry, sir," he smiled. "Guess I got carried away."

"No problem."

"I'll take good care of her, sir. You won't ever have to worry."

"I'm sure you will," I added.

Billy made quick work of gathering his tray and mine, handing it over, one-handed, to the candy striper. "Do you think maybe we could head back up now?"

"I guess we could peek in," I said, trying to massage the shape back into my hand, "maybe drop a hint or two that it's our turn."

"Thank you, sir," Billy said quietly. "For everything."

Neither one of us could wipe the smile off our faces as we headed back up to ICU. Billy promised to return to school the following week no matter what and planned to phone his professors to explain the situation. I encouraged him to stick with it, reminding him that Penny would probably kick his ass if he dropped out now, even if it was for just one semester.

"By the way, just wait until Penny's a little more sound before you ask her, will you?"

"Oh, yes, sir. Don't worry. I'll do it up right. You can count on that."

"Good man."

As we rounded the corner of the ICU, we noticed a group of nurses standing outside Penny's door and we both took off running. We practically had to muscle our way in past them to see what all the disturbance was about. Both of us were nervous as cats fearing the worst.

When we finally made it past the crowd of nurses, we then had to blitz our way through a perimetre of doctors all huddled round Penny's bed like a team of Rugby players in a scrummage. Jayne must have heard us in the commotion.

"Gentlemen, please!" she erupted, and motioned for them to let us through.

Finally realizing we'd arrived, the doctors parted the way to reveal the most astonishing sight they, or the nurses, or we, or the entire town for that matter, had ever witnessed.

"Are you seein' what I'm, seein', sir?"

"God, I hope so."

We both stared in amazement.

Penny

       was

            awake.

23

Billy arrived at the house early the next morning raring to go. He'd gotten pretty ripe again and Jayne demanded the night before that he go home and shower before he turned into a walking health hazard. She also wanted him to look in on his father, who missed him terribly, and convinced him that he should sleep in his own bed for once instead of the hospital-supplied recliner that doubled as a torture device.

"How's the arm this morning?" I asked.

"Not bad, sir," he replied. "It's a good thing it's my left. Otherwise, I'd have a helluva time scratchin' my balls in the mornin'. You know what I mean?"

"I know what you mean, son."

Billy sometimes forgot I was his girlfriend's father and not just some other guy, which I had to admit was kind of nice at times. He'd spent so much time with Penny over the years he'd become like family. Soon enough, he'd be a bona fide member.

"Did you call your friend up at school last night?" I asked as we hopped in the car.

"Yes, sir. I missed a few labs, but I should be able to make them up next week. I'm gonna call my professors today, too, and tell them what's goin' on. My buddy, Jake, gave them head's up."

We had a nice chat on the way to the hospital and it kind of helped calm my fears about what sort of life he and Penny had planned for the future. They'd thought of everything, right down to how many children they were going to have. They both wanted to work at the New England Aquarium - Billy in the research lab, Penny in engineering. They planned to have a nice home near the beach, a decent truck, and a good fishing boat. They also decided not to start having kids - one boy and one girl - until Penny was at least twenty-eight and he was thirty. This way they'd have plenty of time to develop their careers *and* have fun before the real serious stuff came into play.

The only thing they hadn't planned on was Penny's accident. Billy tried not to take it into account, but he knew he had to. Even though she'd come out of her coma, it was still unclear whether or not she would regain the full use of all her faculties. With that in mind, what was once all but written in stone was slowly dissolving into something no clearer than mud. Everything was now uncertain.

In spite of all that was unknown, Billy would not be dissuaded. "Don't worry, sir," he said as we drove into the hospital parking garage. "Penny got me through some pretty tight spots when I wasn't looking too good either. We'll be alright. We'll be just fine." Just the same, I couldn't help but feel a little sad.

There was a line at the reception area as we walked into

the lobby, but Thelma, the senior volunteer on duty, just waved us past. It got so we were on a first name basis with just about everyone from the custodians to the neurosurgeons. It kind of made me feel important, although there are plenty of other, less nerve wracking ways of becoming popular.

Even though it was only half past seven in the morning, Donna had already come and gone from the hospital. It was highly unusual for her to be up this early, let alone out and about. Penny had already eaten as well, but didn't remember that she had. Apparently, it was a side effect of the oxygen deprivation and may, over time, correct itself. She was delighted to see us and greeted us with open arms from the confines of her bed.

"Hi, Daddy. Hi, Billy. It's good to see you."

Her speech was a bit slurred, her motor skills a bit off, and she had a horrible wheeze, which we'd heard coming on over the past few days. Pneumonia had indeed set in and she wore a mask over her nose and mouth that pumped in oxygen and humidified medicines. The doctors were concerned, but not overly, since she possessed one of the best constitutions they'd ever seen. According to their assessments, she'd be fine in about a week or two.

"I'm going to have a bath this morning," she smiled, pulling the mask away so we could hear her.

"You already had it, dear. Remember?" said Jayne, placing the mask back on.

Billy stuffed his nose into Penny's hair and kissed her cheek. "She's right, babe. You smell wicked nice."

"Oh," she replied, her brows creasing to a curious point. "Did I eat, too?"

"Yes, dear. You did."

I could see Penny was getting frustrated at her forgetfulness and even more frustrated at her inability to hold a cup of water by herself. Billy assured her it was likely only temporary based on the many articles he'd read on the subject and the million and one questions he'd asked the doctors each time they came in to visit. He pulled a wadded up pamphlet from out of his back pocket entitled: *Taking Charge of Your Recovery – A guide to life after a serious illness or accident.* "A little R&R, some OT and PT and you'll be right as rain," he added. "It's all in this brochure."

"How about some PB&J, too?" she quipped, trying not to cough as she laughed to herself.

"Alright you two," piped Jayne. "I can see this is going to get out of hand so let's just quit while we're ahead."

Penny giggled and coughed some more, loosening up some of the junk that had settled in her lungs. I could tell it tired her and must have hurt, too. She closed her eyes, grimacing, and seemed to almost instantly fall asleep. The doctors said it might be a while before she regained much stamina.

Billy, scooting the chair as close to the bed as possible, laid his head next to Penny's and placed his hand on her shoulder. He, too, had been a little sleep deprived and rested his eyes while she slept.

Jayne mentioned that she and Penny had a talk after Donna left. She told her about Ruthie and the Drug Rehabilitation program and that she was doing well despite her terrible bout with the DT's. Penny cried, worried about her sister, but felt confident that she'd do well. After all, she was a Sheridan woman, too. There was nothing they couldn't do once they set their minds to it.

Dr. Brice came in to check on our little patient and

mentioned she'd probably get a regular room by the afternoon if all went well. The team was extraordinarily impressed with her recovery so far and didn't see much reason why she shouldn't continue to improve once her pneumonia cleared. He just kept shaking his head and smiling, overawed at her will to survive.

Penny stirred a few minutes later. She started to mumble, as if trying to come out of a dream, and called out for Billy.

"I'm here, babe," he said, rubbing her shoulder. "I'm right here."

Jayne and I rushed to her side and held her hand. "What is it, honey?" I asked. "Are you okay?"

The nurse had given Penny a pretty powerful pain killer for her broken leg and it sent her right down Stoned Street. In between being a little scared about what was going on, she'd laugh, cough, then close her eyes and jump back up as if she felt like she was falling. She said she felt the room begin to spin and, in no time, up came her breakfast.

Billy ran and got an orderly while Jayne grabbed a nurse. Penny began to sob, worried that since she threw up they might not let her move to a regular room. Although she'd been awake less than twenty-four hours, she desperately missed seeing the sunshine and needed some fresh air just as badly. The room was like a tomb and she wanted out.

"Can't I just go home?" she coughed.

"Soon, sweetheart," I said. "It won't be long."

After Penny was cleaned up and calmed down, Jayne and I decided to go have some lunch. We both needed a little break and we could see that Billy wanted to spend some time with his girl alone. They couldn't stop staring at one another. I was hoping he wouldn't propose to her while we were gone, but I wouldn't have been surprised if he did.

"Be good while we're gone you two," I ordered. "No monkey business."

"Okay," smiled Penny. "We'll just go in the broom closet and make out."

Billy turned his typical ten shades of red and poked Penny in the ribs. She jabbed him back in the arm, his broken one, to remind him that it still hurt. She laughed and coughed and laughed and fell fast asleep. We were hesitant to leave, but Billy gave a reassuring wave and we were reluctantly off.

I was surprised Jayne was willing to take the time to go out. We still weren't speaking to each other much, except about the girls, but I felt if we were going to do it at all, it would be a good time to start burying our hatchets. Besides, my back was killing me from sleeping on the couch and I missed holding her close. I did still love her. Mostly, I was getting worried about her dependency on Valium. She kept telling me it was perfectly safe, but I still had my doubts.

We decided to skip the cafeteria and instead ventured over to the new French Bistro that Donna recommended. We had a lovely meal of quiche and salad and even split a dessert. I have to admit, though, we got off to an awkward start. But, after a glass of wine - or two - we finally began to relax and enjoy ourselves.

I hated to spoil the mood, but I really needed to break the ice regarding Jaynie's dependency. I knew she'd never forgive me if I mentioned it in public, so I suggested we go for a walk in the quiet park across the street.

"It's a very low dose," she assured. "It's not much different than the glass of wine we had."

"I know, honey, but it's the fact that you take five or six a day that alarms me."

Jayne and I walked in silence around the entire perimeter of the park before finally taking a seat on a secluded bench.

"It alarms me, too," she finally admitted. "I just don't know what to do sometimes. I always relied on some sort of sedative to help me cope while you were away. Now, with all that's happened, I'm relying on them even more."

"Why don't you talk to Dr. Fenton at the hospital? I'm sure he can recommend something - or someone. Maybe even a program like Ruth's."

"Oh, god, Stephen, I couldn't. What would people think?"

It should have dawned on me that when it came to Jayne, what people thought was always the principal consideration with regard to everything.

"You wouldn't have to stay there, I'm sure," I said. "There's got to be some sort of outpatient thing you could go to."

She hemmed and hawed. It would be easy to attend a program while the girls were in the hospital, I argued. No one would be the wiser. And if it went on longer than that, we'd just say she was visiting a patient we'd come to know - the Colonel.

With that agreed, we stopped to take a quick peek in the window of the travel agency before heading to the car. They had a very inviting display showcasing Paris with all the trimmings and it made me think of my sister and her art studio. Jayne had always wanted to go, too, having dreamt her whole life of climbing the Eiffel Tower. I looked at her and smiled. Timid, she smiled back, perhaps still savouring the idea.

Our fantasy was quite unexpectedly squelched, however, when Mike Conners showed up from out of the blue. He was dashing out of the cobblers next door to the travel bureau and almost ran right into me, scaring the shit out of us both.

"Oh, hey," he squealed. "Hey. Steve. Jayne. How are you?"

At that moment, I couldn't even speak for fear I'd say what I really wanted to. Jayne was speechless, too, and looked to me for direction, squeezing my arm tighter than a blood pressure cuff. I gritted my teeth. As much as I wanted to avoid this, I knew I had to face it or it would eat at me for the rest of my life.

"I need to talk to you," I said sternly.

"Oh, well, I can't just now," stammered Mike. "I've, uh, got a meeting."

"Don't worry. This won't take long."

I handed Jaynie the keys and asked her to wait for me in the car. She stared at me, frightened I might do something rash. I gave her a nod to say I'd keep my cool, which I'm not sure she entirely believed - nor did I. When I saw she was safe inside the car, I faced Mike directly, my fists clenched at my sides just in case.

"I really have to go," Mike said. I could tell he was about ready to piss himself. He started to walk past me, but I stopped him with a firm grip to the shoulder.

"You're not going anywhere until I talk to you," I said, coaxing him back in front of me.

"Listen," he began, clutching his shoebox in one hand, covering his balls with the other, "I didn't mean to... I mean... We never..."

"Shut up. Just shut the hell up."

"Please don't hit me," he whimpered.

"For chrissakes, Mike. I'm not going to hit you, although the thought had crossed my mind."

He shuffled his shoebox back and forth under each arm, jockeyed for position, looked around for an exit that didn't exist. "Yeah, well, I guess you've got a right," he mumbled.

He started to walk past again and again I stopped him.

"This is over, right?" I asked, my hand firmly gripping his boney shoulder.

He was absolutely paralyzed. Even his sweat was too afraid to emerge from the protective confines of his pores.

"Yeah," he managed. "It's over."

"Good."

I stared at him another few seconds, just letting him stew a bit longer, then released my grip. He walked past and headed for his car, throwing the shoebox through the open window. I was stunned when he spoke again, his voice more than a little shaky, his hand poised on the door handle ready to jump in should I decide to charge him.

"You know," he began. I turned, my fists still clenched, and looked him square in the eye, not sure what direction he was taking the conversation. He opened his car door, hoisted a leg in. "She loves you," he courageously continued. "A lot. I just thought you should know that."

I didn't say a word.

I still wanted to clock him, but not as much as before, and I actually thought there might come a day when I might *not* want to clock him. I had to give him credit, though. It took some balls to face me and I was glad he possessed a set that could handle it.

I hopped in the car and stared at the steering wheel as Mike took off down the street. Jayne, seated in the centre of the bench seat, put her hand on my thigh. "Thank you for not doing what I thought you were going to do."

I returned the gesture, turning my gaze to the display in the travel bureau window. "You want to run away to Paris when all this is over?"

Jayne eked out a coy smile. "Maybe we could start with a trip to the Cape."

"The Cape it is."

Jayne started to scoot over to the passenger side of the seat, but I kept my hand firmly planted on her inner thigh, letting her know her company was more than welcome. She sidled back up next to me and moved my hand onto the steering wheel as she tried to hide her blushing cheeks. "Wouldn't want to get into any accidents," she cautioned.

When we got back to the hospital, Billy and Penny were gone from the room and a cleaning crew was busy disinfecting and changing linens. "Excuse me," I said, "where's my daughter?"

"They don't tell us where they're going, sir," replied the custodian, "just that they're gone."

The nurses had just changed shifts, too, and no one seemed to know for sure where Penny was. Finally, Marge, the head nurse, came on the scene. She shook her head, frustrated that it was easier to fill out mortgage paperwork than it was to process the forms required when a patient moves from one ward to the next.

"She's downstairs on three," she sighed, blowing a stray hair out of her face. "It's kind of a maze on that floor, so just go to the desk when you get off the elevator. Karen will help you."

It was a maze everywhere, I thought to myself. Why should "three" be any different? All I hoped was that there'd be windows, and lots of them.

It took us a good ten minutes to find Penny's room, but she wasn't there either. Turns out, "three" had a solarium that made the entire place look more like a greenhouse than a recovery wing, and that's where the Peanut ultimately gravitated.

She was so overjoyed to see the outdoors, even if it was behind a pane of glass. You'd have thought she'd been in a concentration camp the way she was going on and on about it. She had her face plastered up against the big picture window, her hands outstretched and pasted alongside as she craned her body away from the wheelchair. It was like someone had thrown her against the glass like a strand of wet spaghetti. She was stuck to it like glue.

"There you are, dear," cried Jayne. "We've been looking everywhere for you."

"Sorry, Mrs. Sheridan," said Billy. "They said she could go so we didn't waste any time."

"A person could get rickets up there," added Penny, her speech still slurred, but improving. "I thought I was going to have to start asking for a daily ration of limes."

It was good to see her start to act like her old self again, cutting up and smiling at her own humour. The fact that her pain pill had worn off was a help, but to see the sun again and feel its warmth would do her more good than anyone could imagine. No wonder flowers look so joyous when in bloom.

24

Penny had a good week and was growing stronger by the day. Her pneumonia was clearing and it looked as if she may be released the following Tuesday or Wednesday. Her therapy was also going remarkably well. She had two fairly intensive sessions a day to help build back her short-term memory and strengthen her motor skills. Her memory was improving the fastest and she could now not only remember that she'd eaten, but could recall for the most part what she'd had. Lunch was the easiest, since she seemed to order the creamed chipped beef every day.

"Ooh, S.O.S.," she'd swoon, "my favourite."

Truthfully, it was also the only thing on the menu, besides the fish and chips, that was palatable. I'd love to know what they put in hospital food that makes everything taste like disinfectant so I can avoid it in my own cooking at all costs. It would certainly top the list of anyone's *Culinary Secrets Best Avoided.*

Even though it was only Friday, I ordered what amounted to the full fry from the cafeteria and brought it up to Penny for a treat. She was tired of the poached eggs and porridge and the doctor said it was okay if she indulged. Jaynie made a mouth-watering batch of homemade scones that morning, too, and we brought enough to last the day. I could eat my weight in them.

Billy called earlier from Salem to say "see you tonight, babe" before reluctantly heading back to class. It about killed him to be away from Penny all week, but she let him know in her own indomitable way that she would indeed personally kick his ass if he dropped out of school now. I thought they were actually going to get into a full-fledged fight about it, but they both backed down before it came to blows. As Penny so vehemently argued, the fact that she'd suffered a setback was no reason for him to abandon ship. A plan was a plan. Finis.

Along with the scones, Janie also brought in a nice selection of clothes for Ruthie to pick out. Her week-long session was now complete and we were set to go up and visit after Penny's morning therapy session and bath which, because of her cast and huge mane of unruly curls, was a forty-five minute production in itself. It would be the first time the two girls had seen each other since Penny's accident and her mother and I were eager to have them reunited.

We were hoping Donna would stop by, too, since we'd seen so little of her over the past week. It was odd for her to be so aloof. Penny was concerned that she may be getting jealous of all the attention that was being shown to her and Ruth and that Donna might be retaliating using her weapons of mass indifference.

"You know she's always been the centre of the

Universe," she explained. "But, I'm sure she'll get over it once the planets line up again."

I suddenly realized, too, that Donna hadn't asked me for any money lately, or even to reopen the credit card account. The wedding was coming up soon and I was sure there must be thousands more to be spent. Then there was the whole business suit thing. I'd seen her in three different ensembles the few times she flew through to drop something off for one of her sisters. Jayne even said she was asking what type of shoes I recommended, having forgotten the popular brand I swore by. Something was definitely amiss and neither one of us could figure out what she was scheming.

While Penny was in her physical therapy session, Jayne and I went down to the gift shop to pick out a nice card and something pretty to decorate Ruthie's hospital room. She had at least another full week to go and we wanted her to feel comfortable in her surroundings away from home. Jayne also picked out some earrings for her, little pearls, and a matching necklace. For gift shop jewelry they were surprisingly nice quality.

"She always did prefer these over diamonds," noted Jayne.

"And you?" I asked, hoping I knew the right answer.

"Oh, Stephen. You know for me it's the thought that counts and I'm thankful that you've thought of me and the girls so often. It's one of the reasons why we all love you so dearly. That and the fact that you look so damn good in a turtleneck."

I drew her close and kissed her tenderly right there in the gift shop in front of God and everybody. You'd have thought we were on a honeymoon the way we looked at each other, held each other, not even caring that people were staring. I just couldn't help myself and I didn't care what anyone thought. My Jaynie was coming back to me and I was never going to let her go.

Penny was having her bath when we got upstairs and Jayne offered to brush her hair when she got out. The nurse was grateful, having dreaded the thought of tackling those stubborn ringlets. A heavy dose of cream rinse was definitely in order.

"Well?" resounded a familiar voice. "Where's the brat?"

Donna, dressed in a handsome pinstripe suit, stood in the doorway, hand on hip. I could tell she had on good shoes, too, although I couldn't tell what brand, and I wondered if perhaps she'd been busy negotiating some sort of free trade agreement.

"Oh, hi, honey," replied Jayne. "We were just talking about you."

"I'll bet," she scoffed, tossing her head to the side. "So what's happening? Where is she?"

"Taking a bath. She should be out in a minute if you'd like to wait."

"Can't. I have to run."

"What's the rush? You just got here," I said, chiming in while I had the chance. "And what's with the suits? I mean, they look very nice. It's just a different look for you."

"This suit happens to have set me back two-hundred dollars," she sneered. "And by the way, I've actually been here twenty-five minutes. It took me that long just to track you people down. Ludicrous."

"It set *you* back? Or it set *me* back?" I asked, the one corner of my mouth raising the same degree as my one eyebrow.

"You'll see. By the way, I was going to stop over to the house tonight to discuss some things with you if you were going to be home."

"What kinds of things?" I asked. I could feel my wallet getting lighter by the second, the notion of hundred-dollar-a-piece table favours zipping back and forth across my synapses like a pinball.

"You know," she predictably replied. "The credit card. I have a proposition. But right now I have to go. See you tonight."

Donna gave Jayne and I a quick kiss a piece and she was off, tossing a pink enveloped greeting card on the bed on her way out. I cringed at the thought of her proposition, whatever it may be, knowing the hospital bills for her two sisters were going to seem like a walk in the park compared to her wedding. I couldn't imagine her taking over the payments. What I could imagine was her making them higher.

Penny emerged from the bathroom with her hair wrapped in a huge towel. I couldn't help but laugh and neither could she. She looked like some sort of crazed out Indian mystic in a terry turban. I half expected her to whip out a flute and start charming snakes.

Jayne pulled the towel off and gave Penny's hair a good rubbing. "Better you than me," said the nurse as she handed Jayne the hairbrush and wide-toothed comb. "I'd have sprained a wrist trying to get through that mop."

Jayne smiled and attacked slowly from the bottom up. The cream rinse did wonders, making the work far less agonizing than predicted. Penny enjoyed having her hair combed and closed her eyes while her mother tamed her mane.

"Maybe you could run upstairs to see if Ruthie's ready for us," said Jayne.

"They said around eleven," I replied. "I think it would be nice if we all went up together. Don't you? It's nearly eleven now."

"Then maybe you could go downstairs or in the sunroom and get a cup of coffee," she added, eyeing me like I was supposed to be picking up on some subtle hint. Penny opened an eye and gave me a sarcastic glare, then closed it up tight smiling that little impish smile of hers.

I was by no means an expert on reading women's thoughts, but over the years I'd at least learned to pick up on certain cues. Sometimes it took me a minute, but I eventually got it. For instance, whenever Jaynie would start off a sentence with, "Maybe you could go do *something*...", it usually meant, "Okay, you need to get lost for a while." So, off to the sunroom I went.

I was greeted in the solarium by a little girl of about seven and her slightly younger sister. They reminded me of Donna and Ruthie when they were little and I couldn't help but smile.

"Our mommy's having a baby," crooned the younger of the two.

"How wonderful," I exclaimed. "Are you going to be having a little brother or a little sister?"

"We haven't decided yet," remarked the elder. "We've been weighing the pros and cons for weeks. It's looking good for another sister, though. Boys can be so uncouth."

Shades of Donna for sure.

The father, holding a tiny football, weighed in from his seat. "I'm hoping for a boy."

"I know what you mean," I added. "I've got three girls

myself. Still, I wouldn't trade a one of them for all the world."

I had a nice chat with the father-to-be and before long the nurse was there to tell him he was again being outnumbered. "Yeah," shouted the girls. "Crap," mumbled the Dad. I assured him it would be an easy road so long as he kept them happy.

"Just don't forget which one likes diamonds and which one likes pearls," I commented. "They'll dote on you for life."

He left the football behind and took a girl in each hand as they shuffled off to the maternity ward on the second floor. I wished him well, knowing he'd have a challenging, yet worthwhile journey ahead of him.

I barely finished my coffee and I, myself, was being summoned. Penny looked fresh as a daisy, her hair all shiny and neat, her jammies and robe all sparkly clean. "Let's go make some trouble, shall we?" she grinned.

I explained to her that we had to pass through Geriatrics on the way and that she should shield her eyes in case a resident decided to share more than just a few pictures of their grandkids. "He's right, dear," added Jayne. "There are things in that ward that no woman should have to bare witness to."

"Then we must go immediately!" she shouted, fist thrusting the air like Napoleon's Josephine aboard her trusty steed.

Without incident, we made it up to the Dependency ward and were greeted by Dr. Fenton, the head honcho. He gave us a quick run down on Ruthie's progress, which was quite promising. He mentioned that if she continued on this same track, she could be released next Friday. It would be so nice to bring her home, we all thought. Nicer still to see her well.

While Penny and I went to look for Ruthie, Jayne took the opportunity to line up some counseling sessions for herself. She was nervous and full of reservation, but was assured by Dr. Fenton that the utmost discretion would be employed. "Not even your hairdresser will know," I believe is how he put it.

Ruthie was more than happy to see us, but alarmed at the sight of Penny in a wheelchair and dressed in hospital garb, her leg in a cast from hip to toe. "What did you do?" she cried. "What happened?"

"Long story," said Penny, nonchalant and stifling a cough. "How are you feeling?"

"Better."

Jayne, toting the little suitcase, soon joined us and gave Ruthie a welcomed hug and kiss. "You look well, dear. Are you eating?"

"Yes. The food isn't very good, but I'm trying. Are those clothes?" she asked, pointing to the valise.

"Yes. I can pick some other things if you don't like what I brought," said Jayne, opening the case.

"Did you bring some make-up, too?"

"Just a few things," Jayne replied, handing her a tiny travel cosmetic pouch. "I got you a new foundation and Donna picked out a nice blush and lipstick."

"That's all?" frowned Ruthie.

"I don't know why you think you need it at all," added Penny. "You look so much better without all that eyeliner and shadow."

Ruthie stared down at her folded hands resting in her lap. "I don't know."

"She's right, dear," said Jayne, sitting down next to Ruth and pulling her curly black hair away from her face. "You look so beautiful just the way you are and I'm sorry I didn't tell you that more often."

I sat down on the other side of Ruth and put my arm round her. "You could always light up a room, sweetheart." I kissed her on the temple and thought for a moment that she might be trying to smile. Penny couldn't help but chime in.

"Geez, what am I? Chopped liver?"

"Chopped bait, you mean," said Ruthie, chiming right back, her smile finally emerging. "You still didn't tell me what happened to you."

"Well, let's see. I fell overboard, busted my leg in two places, wracked up my knee," she recounted, pointing to the location of each fracture and sprain, "almost drowned, went into a coma, got pneumonia from the drowning part, lost my short-term memory for a while - that was after the coma part - puked a couple of times, couldn't pick up a glass of water, hmmm, I think that's about it." Cough. "But, I'm on the mend." Cough, cough.

Ruthie's eyes were the size of little pizza pans, her mouth agape. "You drowned?"

"Almost," corrected Penny. "I think they said I was actually dead for something like ten minutes. Isn't that right?" she asked, looking to me for verification.

"I think it was closer to eight," I commented, trying not to seem alarmed by the gravity of it all. "But who's counting."

Ruthie still hadn't blinked and I could see a tear forming in her eye. "Why didn't anyone tell me?" she asked quietly. "You died and nobody bothered to tell me? Why?"

"We didn't want you to be upset, sweetheart," I said.

"You had enough on your plate as it was. We didn't want you to have to deal with this, too."

"But, Daddy…"

"Honey," added Jayne, holding Ruth close, "Penny had a very rough time of it. We didn't know for the longest time if she was even going to… Well, let's just say we didn't want to bring you news until we knew what sort of news to bring."

Ruthie looked at Penny as if she hadn't seen her for a decade, not sure what to make of the ordeal she'd been through. "So are you okay?" she finally managed, still staring.

Penny, knowing neither she nor her sister were yet whole, held back a tear. "I'm getting there," she quietly replied, her slur still faintly detectable. "It's slow. Real slow. But, I'm getting there."

Ruthie suddenly burst into quiet tears herself and rushed to Penny, hugging her tight as best she could. I don't think Penny had yet acknowledged the fact that she had actually died and the possible consequences of it all hit her quite suddenly, forcing her into a sea of tears along with her sister.

"I thought about you," said Penny quietly, "when I was under the water."

Ruthie looked Penny in the eye, both of them wiping away the other's tears as they each wept.

"I worried about who was going to protect you," she continued. "I just wanted you to be safe. And happy. I just wanted us all to be happy. That's all. I just wanted us to be happy."

It's a strange feeling one gets when an epiphany strikes, like a glass of water suddenly bestowed with an Alka-Seltzer. A surge of energy fizzles through your body, followed by a slow, soothing calm. I held Jayne close to me as she, too, began to weep. She realized, as did I, that Penny's often futile attempts to garner a simple smile from her mother and sisters were rooted in her deep desire for universal peace. Penny did have something worthwhile to always be cheery about. The simple joy of plain, old-fashioned happiness.

25

Donna barreled in at around eight-thirty carrying a cardboard banker's box. "It's getting cold out there," she barked as she kicked the door shut with her heel and dropped the box on the table. "I hope you've thought about what you're going to do for firewood. I doubt Penny's going to be able to split it for you this year."

"Maybe I'll hire Brian," I quipped. "He *is* looking for work, isn't he?"

"Deliver me, please," she sighed, pulling off her kangaroo hide gloves.

"Speaking of which, you never did tell me why the sudden interest in business attire. Have you been interviewing?"

"If you must know," she began, hand on hip as she slapped her gloves on the table, "I happen to be working."

My jaw dropped to the ground and I felt my body seize as if in a great shock. "Working?" I shrieked, my voice

265

cracking like an adolescent on the brink of puberty. "Where?"

"Filene's. I don't know why they haven't at least made me an assistant manager," she continued, although I found it remarkable that I even heard another word after *I* and *working* came out of her mouth in the same sentence. "I know more about fashion than just about anyone in that store. They really should make me a buyer, although that would mean traveling to New York several times a year. Brian despises New York."

I found myself still staring, still paralyzed. Donna stared back, hand still on hip. I shook my head, rattling my brain back into action. "Say that again."

"Say what?" she asked, only a little incensed that she should have to repeat herself.

"*I'm working.* Say that again," I teased, snickering.

"I know. You're shocked beyond all belief. But, I'll have you know I'm not doing it forever. I have my limits."

As if that wasn't enough, Donna also laid out in great detail her proposed plan regarding the credit card account, which included exchanging high-priced party favours for more sensible ones and using the credit on the account toward her dress and shoes. She went on and on, showing me charts she'd done up outlining what she'd bought vs. what she actually needed. The way she had it calculated, she could pay for everything with the credits earned from returned merchandise and claimed I'd still have enough leftover to take Jayne to Nantucket or the Cape for a weekend getaway. I don't think I blinked once during her entire presentation.

"I know the hospital bills for Penny and Ruth Anne are probably going to set you back a bit and I didn't want Jayne to have to suffer because of it. She deserves a little break from this place you know. Besides, to be completely honest, it's a bit humbling when one suddenly realizes that they're a perfectly capable adult and still asking their parents for money. It's time I paid my own way. At least until Brian does something productive."

You could have knocked me over with a feather. Talk about an epiphany. I thought for sure that Donna must have had a personal visit from the Almighty Himself it was so profound. I was so proud of her. I took her in my arms and hugged her tight. "Thank you, honey."

"For what?" she sighed.

"For thinking of your mother."

Of course she had to leave immediately. She wouldn't even stay for a cup of coffee, even though I'd just made a fresh pot of decaf in her honor. She couldn't even stay for Jayne, who was due to be home any minute.

"I have to go," was all the more she said and away she went. She never was big on sentiments.

Jayne arrived home from her evening orientation session at the hospital shortly after. Penny, she reported, was apparently developing some sort of infection, likely in her knee, and had to be put on an antibiotic drip to stop it in its tracks. They'd know more in the morning after the test results. Since she still had a slight case of pneumonia, the infection would likely delay her homecoming, which was originally set for Tuesday morning. Jayne and I were both heartbroken.

"At least they caught it early," she added.

It was a beautiful night and we both needed some fresh air after being cooped up in the hospital's stale, disinfected environment for the past week. I knew it was getting late, but I suggested a warm brandy and a stroll down to the beach, since it was too cold for a drive with the top down. Jayne was surprisingly receptive to the idea and went to get a cashmere throw from the cedar trunk in our room.

It had been a while since we had a chance to just sit and relax and be alone with each other. Although Penny was having a setback, we still felt at ease knowing she was in good hands and would be on the mend in a day or two. Ruthie was doing remarkably well, too, and was set to come home late Friday afternoon. Then there was Donna.

We'd settled ourselves up against a steep sand dune and snuggled in close under the blanket, our brandies still a little warm. "Did you know she was working?" I asked Jayne.

"Did I know *who* was working?"

"Your daughter. Donna."

Jayne gave me a look. I've seen that look, although I usually try to avoid it. It's the one she gets when she can't believe I've gone and said something completely absurd like, *I suppose I ought to mow the lawn*, when the grass has grown so tall a small child could get lost in it. But instead of scoffing at me like I half-expected her to, she just laughed. Not really out loud mind you. But, I clearly detected a laugh.

"I know," I said, laughing along with her. "I couldn't believe it myself."

"Where?" asked Jayne, still in disbelief. "Doing what?"

"Filene's. Selling Better Sportswear, apparently. She said something about becoming a buyer. I bet she'd be pretty good at that," I said. And I genuinely meant it.

"Well," smiled Jayne as she took a sip of her brandy. "I never would have imagined it."

"You and me both," I replied, holding her close.

It was so beautiful out, the air crisp and clean, the

heavens bright with stars. It felt so good to have Jaynie close to me again and I couldn't help but draw her in for a kiss. She took my glass and set it in the sand next to hers then put her hand to my cheek.

"Do you think things will ever be the same between us?" she quietly asked.

"No," I replied, kissing her softly as I pulled her coiled frame into my lap. "They're going to be much better."

Had it not been so cold that night, I would have made love to her right there on the beach. As it was, we retired to the bedroom and rekindled the flame that had once nearly been extinguished. Never again would I let the woman of my dreams slip so far away.

Penny showed signs of improvement that following Monday morning and was back on schedule to head home the next day. Although she'd still have to make the daily trip back to the hospital for physical therapy, we didn't mind in the least. It was the perfect excuse for Jayne and gave me the chance to work in the darkroom.

We started reading over the *Taking Charge of Your Recovery at Home* pamphlet that the orderly left and got to the section on *Comfort and Accommodations*. Jayne instantly panicked, wondering what sort of special sleeping arrangements we'd have to make, being that Penny was still in a cast up to her hip. We knew she'd want to sleep upstairs in her room - with the window open, of course - but that was clearly out of the question. "I can't believe I didn't think of it sooner," she gasped.

"Billy can carry me upstairs," she argued.

"Billy's up at school, sweetheart," I argued back.

It was like a tennis match, one argument after

counterargument being volleyed over a virtual net, until Jayne finally called it.

"You'll sleep in the den," she forcefully began. "It faces the ocean, which is the whole point, and no one will have to fall victim to a hernia to get you there."

Penny couldn't help but mumble under her breath. "Brian could carry me," she jeered. "He's strong."

While it was common knowledge that Brian had single-handedly upended a stationwagon during a fraternity fund raiser and could easily heft all ninety-two pounds of Penny up to nearly any elevation, the fact remained that Jayne and I weren't about to become domestic mountaineers ourselves running up and down flights of stairs to wait on her day and night.

"You'll sleep in the den," Jayne demanded.

"Shit," huffed Penny.

And that was that.

It was pretty evident that Penny was going to have to drop out of college for the semester but, according to Dr. Brice, there was a good chance she'd be able to attend in the spring. For now, she needed to focus on regaining her motor skills and healing from her injuries. College or no college, we were happy to have her coming home.

After Jayne and I talked to Brice and the therapists, we took a quick jaunt upstairs to see Ruthie, miraculously passing through Geriatrics again without incident. Ronnie York, the local police rookie, was there with her and had brought a nice bouquet of fresh flowers. They were both sitting on the bed talking and holding hands when we arrived, so entranced with each other they didn't even notice us walk in.

"Good morning," I finally announced.

The two of them about jumped out of their skin, both flying off the bed in opposite directions like a couple of teenagers who just got caught making out on the couch.

"Oh!" squealed Ruth. "Hi, Mom. Hi, Dad."

"Good morning, dear," replied Jayne, giving her a hug and kiss. "Who's your friend?"

"Ron York, ma'am," he said, delicately shaking Jayne's hand. "I just thought I'd stop in and see how Ruthie was doing."

"That's very nice of you, Ron. Donna mentioned you had an interest."

Jayne had a unique way of screening boys - and now men - that left no doubt in their minds that they'd have to deal with her personally if they were ever to break one of her daughters' hearts. It wasn't so much what was said, but what wasn't said that made it painfully obvious. Chuck had been the only one not to get the "interview".

Ronnie, blushing at this point and suddenly realizing he'd been "off radio" for an extended period of time, diplomatically excused himself. I could tell he wanted to kiss Ruth, and she him, but he was very gentlemanly about it and just gave her hand a squeeze on his way out. Ruth held back a smile, unable to contain her own blush, and sat back down on the bed.

"He seems nice," I said.

"Yeah," she swooned.

Jayne read the card next to the flowers:

Get well soon, Love, Ronnie.

"He has good taste, too," she noted.

"Yeah."

We were hesitant at first to tell her that Penny was going home the next day, since the thought that we may not be around as often might upset her. However, we were told that it was important that she learn to face the truth and the truth was we were never more than a phone call away.

We mentioned, too, that we wanted to throw her a homecoming party that Friday night to celebrate her success. We promised it wouldn't be big or showy, just family and close friends. Ruthie was a little nervous about it, though, feeling more embarrassed than anything that the reason she'd been away was because she had a drug problem. However, once we explained that the whole point was to show her how much we all loved and supported her, she felt a little more receptive to the idea.

Ruth was somewhat fearful about leaving the safety of the hospital, though, still worried that Chuck was going to hunt her down. She shared those feelings with Ronnie, who assured her that Chuck wasn't going to be going anywhere soon. He promised to check in on her often and I had a feeling he would hold true to that promise for quite some time, if not for good. It was pretty apparent that he was *very* interested.

Donna, dressed in a turtleneck sweater and denim jumper, stopped by with a new dress for Ruth.

"Day off?" I asked.

"Day off from what?" asked Ruth, not yet knowing the ruse her sister had been playing on us all.

"Work," replied Donna.

Ruthie laughed to herself. "No, really," ha, ha.

"Why is it that everyone finds it so remarkable that I'm gainfully employed?" she snapped.

"Because you're Donna," giggled Ruth.

Jayne thought it funny, too, and we all tried to stifle our laughter. Even Donna, her epiphany having far reaching effects, managed to find the humour in it all and tried like hell not to smile.

"Fine. This is for you for when you get out," she sighed, handing Ruth the pretty print dress. "I have to run."

"But..." began Jayne.

"I know. But it is my day off and I have a million things to do."

And off she went to do her million things.

Ruth pulled the plastic Filene's bag off the dress and held it up to herself as she looked in the mirror. She smiled, the green in the print bringing out the green in her bright eyes. I could tell she was pleased with Donna's selection. She did know fashion.

Jayne stood behind her and placed a hand on her shoulder. "It'll look beautiful on you, dear."

"I like the colours in it."

"I'm very proud of you," she added. "It's nice to see you well."

Ruth turned to her and smiled, tears forming in her eyes. She hugged her mother tight. "Thank you, Mom. I love you."

"I love you, too, honey."

All my women had come so far over the past months. Of all the directions they could have gone during their journeys, I was pleased they'd chosen the better paths.

I phoned Page that afternoon to give her an update on the girls' progress. It seemed ages since we'd spoken and it was good to hear her voice. Better still, there was so much *good* news to tell. We must have talked a full two hours. It was refreshing not to feel lost.

273

"Love to the women," she said in closing.

"Love to you, too," I replied.

Billy arrived home from school around noon the next day to help us get Penny settled in the den. He only had two classes in the morning, so it worked out well. Brian and Donna were there, too, which was a good thing since we needed Brian's brawn to move the bed down from upstairs. It was bad enough we were refusing to let Penny stay in her own room. We weren't going to make her sleep on a davenport, too. Billy tried to help, but had a terrible time with his arm still in a cast. It frustrated him to no end to feel so helpless.

"Don't worry about it, sis," joked Brian as he grabbed the mattress. "Besides, I wouldn't want you to bust a nut."

"Bust a nut my ass, you fuckin' no-neck," said Billy, jockeying around like a boxer in the ring, completely unaware that he had an audience.

"Alright, boys," piped Jayne.

Billy stopped dead in his tracks. "Oh, shit. Sorry, Mrs. Sheridan. I thought you were in the other room."

Jayne went back in the kitchen to make some sandwiches and I thought it a good time to give both the boys a little advice from someone who knew better.

"By the way," I began, "she's never in the other room when you say something stupid or uncouth, so mind your P's and Q's."

"Yes, sir," piped Billy.

Brian just stood there with his mouth open, staring that deer-in-the-headlights stare he so often gets when you use "big people words". Even though I had at least three unabridged dictionaries in the den, I seriously doubted he'd make use of one and left him to inquire from Billy what the hell *uncouth* meant.

Donna was heading out the door just as I returned to the kitchen to help Jayne. "Don't tell me you're going," I cried.

"I just have to get something out of the car," she said. "Then I'm going. I work two to close."

"What is it with that girl that she can never stay in one place for more than five minutes?" I asked Jayne as I stole a slice of ham.

"I have no idea. But don't you feel honored that she at least bestows us that much?" she replied, tongue firmly planted in cheek. She slapped my hand as I reached for a slice of provolone.

I eased my way around behind her and held her close around the waist, nuzzling my nose into the nape of her soft neck. "God, you smell good." Jaynie smiled and continued making sandwiches as if having me hold her was the most natural thing on earth.

"It must be the new perfume you gave me. Do you like it?"

"Love it."

Donna flew back in carrying a dress that looked just like the one she'd bought Ruthie. "Here. I have to go," she predictably announced. "See that the brat gets this, will you? I'd like to see her wear it to Ruth Anne's homecoming party."

Jayne and I were both perplexed to say the least. "Isn't that the same dress you bought Ruth?" asked Jayne.

"Exactly," she replied.

"You didn't buy one for yourself, too, did you?" I asked, never imagining in all my life that she'd do such a thing of her own free will.

"As a matter of fact, I did. We got them in on a special purchase. Plus, I used my employee discount. Working does have its privileges, you know."

Jayne and I stood there speechless for the longest time. We simply didn't know what to say.

"It's meant to be a joke," cried Donna. "Would it be asking too much to play along?"

She waited for a reply we were too *stupefied* to extend and off to work she went.

Jayne and I looked at each other and burst into laughter. We couldn't believe that this was the same girl who practically went into apoplexy whenever anyone so much as wore the same colour, let alone an identical ensemble. We both weren't afraid to admit that Donna truly had changed and it was certainly for the better.

After lunch, Brian headed home while Jayne and Billy and I made our way to the hospital to pick up Penny. Billy was beside himself he was so happy and couldn't wait to surprise her. I knew it was going to tear him apart to leave her behind that night, but the good news was he'd be back Friday evening and every weekend after.

As we made the trek out of our village and down Hancock Street, I couldn't help but be thankful as I reflected on all we'd been through over the past several weeks. Despite the rollercoaster of emotions, the near loss of love and life, and the seemingly endless uncertainties that we faced, I was grateful that at the end of the day my family still cared deeply for each other with a fierce determination not to be undone by life's extraordinary challenges. Strong women leading strong and willful lives. What better example for me as a man to follow.

26

Friday arrived before we knew it. It was a crisp fall day, the leaves just beginning to show their colour as we all but said goodbye to September. Penny was doing great, although she frustrated easily that she couldn't navigate as well as she wanted to in her wheelchair. Frankly, I was surprised she hadn't ventured out into the barn to hack off her cast with the first implement she could get her hands on. "Friggin' useless thing! Where are my crutches?!" she'd yell, wheeling into the door casing for the fourteenth time. "Son of a..." She was always so delicate.

As directed by the rehab counselors, Jayne and I had spent a full day and a half going through every cabinet in the house searching for stashes of drugs and paraphernalia. It was important that Ruth not have any temptations during the first weeks of her release and we made sure there wasn't anything left behind that might entice her to use again. We even made sure that the party would be alcohol-free and stocked up on sodas and juice, which would be best for Jayne, too, we found out.

"Did you check the attic?" asked Penny. "There's more nooks and crannies up there than an English muffin. Of course I'd go up there myself if it wasn't for this albatross." She couldn't wait to get out of that cast.

"Are you going to behave yourself while we go get Ruth Anne?" I asked. "Or should I have Dot come over with her twelve-gauge and stand guard."

"Very funny," she sneered. "Billy will be here soon, so you don't have to worry. His last class gets out in about fifteen minutes, so I'm sure he'll be on the road right after that."

"I should help you with your dress before we leave, don't you think?" asked Jayne. "That way you'll be ready."

"Billy can help me. Besides, the party isn't for another couple of hours. I don't want to get all sparkly yet."

"I'm sure he'll be more than eager to assist," I said, glaring at her with my fiercest Dad-glare.

"Oh, Daddy, come on. Give it a rest."

"I know. I get it," I emoted. "You're eighteen. Excuse me! Practically nineteen!"

"Two weeks to go!"

"Yes, I know. Two weeks."

Penny stuck her tongue out at me and practically bit her lip trying to contain a grin. I stuck mine out at her, too, but was caught by Jayne. We both got the Mom-glare, which is far worse than any Dad-glare, and immediately ceased and desisted. However, and quite unexpectedly, Jayne gave us both the tongue right back.

Penny was shocked and so was I. She started laughing, her eyes wide with delight. She gave me a look, then her mother, then me again. Then, that little impish smile of hers overtook her face and I dreaded what was about to come next. Although oxygen deprivation had temporarily affected much of her faculties, it was apparent it did nothing to negate her acute extra-sensory perception.

"Have you two been fooling around?" she cunningly hissed.

"What?" What else was I supposed to say? It's not something you openly admit, and certainly not to your daughter. "What!?"

Jayne didn't have any better reply either and grabbed her coat and handbag. "Behave yourself, young lady," she ordered. "And stay in the house. We don't want to come back to find you stuck in a sand dune somewhere." And she bolted out the door.

I grabbed my coat and hat and pointed a shaky finger at her like James Cagney when he's about to say, "*You dirty rat.*" That impish little grin was still plastered on her face and she pointed right back at me. With the exception of her broken leg, which was more of an inconvenience than anything at this point, it was evident her recovery was full and complete.

Jayne and I couldn't help but smile the entire way to the hospital. It was good to see her taking Penny's jest in stride, and she didn't even need a pill to do it. It was true, though. We had been fooling around and we were loving every minute of it.

We gave a quick hello to Thelma at the reception desk and headed directly for the elevators. It was like we were on auto-pilot, the same right, then a quick left down the corridors, the same elevator buttons to push, the same song piped in over the little speaker. But, as much as it had become a part of our routine, we welcomed the day when we could retire it.

We passed through Geriatrics where the nurses and orderlies were on their usual hunt for the Colonel. We kept an eye peeled ourselves, hoping we wouldn't run into him in his altogetherness. Jayne and I both agreed he was probably a fairly interesting person and likely had some wonderful old war stories to tell. It was the whole unpredictable disrobing thing that kind of put a damper on engaging him in conversation.

As we made our way down the hall to Ruth's room, we couldn't help but detect a familiar voice resonating through the corridor. It was the sound of a young woman singing, beautifully, like an angel. It was Ruth. She was joined in chorus by another voice, a male tenor, equally angelic, although much older it would seem. They were singing *My Wild Irish Rose* in close harmony and we couldn't help but stop still to listen.

As we paused taking it all in, Jayne and I both simultaneously experienced a sudden, frightening premonition. An orderly from Geriatrics was heard talking to a nurse just behind us and confirmed our most dreaded fear. We looked at one another and sang out in unison: "The Colonel!"

We ran as fast as we could down the hall, the orderly and nurse right behind us dashing full bore. The four of us screeched to a halt in front of Ruthie's door just as she and the Colonel finished their final coda. We were all amazed, and gratefully relieved, to find Ruthie safe and sound, graciously accompanied by Colonel Reginald Q. Pendlewaite dressed in full British Army regalia right down to his military-issue patent-leather boots.

"Good day, town folk," he bellowed, standing at

attention, his riding crop tucked deftly under his right arm, his posture true as a flagpole in May. "I say, this child sings like an angel. Wouldn't you agree?"

"We certainly would, Colonel," exhaled the orderly. "Now, how about we go on back to the regiment and report our findings to the commanding officer in charge."

"Ah, yes," he replied. "Kipling is it?"

"That's right," said the orderly, taking the Colonel gently by the arm and leading him back down the hall.

"Mousy chap. Tells a damn good story, as I recall," he added, not able at that point to tell the difference between fact and fiction.

"That's right, sir…"

It was the last we'd see of the great Colonel, who died in his sleep that night of natural causes. I thought to myself what a wonderful comfort he must have felt, hearing the voices of heaven before actually arriving at the pearly gates. Ruthie had been blessed with such a beautiful voice and she was honored to have shared it with such a welcoming audience.

"Are you okay, sweetheart?" asked Jayne. "He didn't do anything strange, did he?"

"No," she replied, her brows creased to a curious point. "Why would he? He was just going around saying hello to people. It was actually kind of fun."

"You really did sound like an angel," I added. "It's nice to hear you sing again."

"I'm surprised I could make a sound at all after all the screaming I'd been doing in all those bars. It was kind of nice just to sing something quiet for a change."

Dr. Fenton popped his head in the room and gave a little wave. "Ruth Anne? Are you ready for your final session?"

"I hope so," she smiled.

We joined other parents and their sons and daughters who were also graduating from the program that day. One young girl was only about fourteen and looked like she'd been to hell and back. Another boy, on his third trip through the program, was only nineteen.

As for Ruth Anne, she was one of the success stories. She was determined to beat the demons that had taken over her life in such a paramount way, so much so she could barely see the light at the end of the tunnel. But now, with new found hope and aspirations for a better future, the light shines bright inside her once again.

"Congratulations, Ruth Anne," said Dr. Fenton, shaking her hand and presenting her with her certificate. "You did very, very well and we wish you all the best."

I thought Jayne and I were both going to cry, but we kept it in. We were so proud of her and all she'd gone through to arrive where she had that day. It was indeed an accomplishment.

Ronnie York met us in the hospital lobby, his squad car parked just outside in the police zone. We'd invited him to the party and asked him to show up in case Ruth had any reservations about leaving the safety of the hospital.

"Hey, Ronnie. What are you doing here?" asked Ruth, obviously delighted to see him.

"I thought you might like a police escort," he smiled. "You know. For the big homecoming and all."

"Oh, I don't know," Ruthie replied, hesitant. "I don't want to get you in trouble or anything. Besides, I didn't want this to be a big deal. It's not like I'm coming home from the Peace Corp."

"It's no trouble. I just got off duty. What do you say? Your folks did invite me."

"I don't know, Ronnie," she looked at us, biting her lip and looking for some direction. "What would the neighbors think?"

"You can go if you want, honey," I said. "We'll follow you."

"It's perfectly fine, dear," added Jayne. "And it *is* a big deal. To us."

"Well, okay," she said. "But promise you won't blow the sirens or anything. My mother will have a fit."

"Oh, Ruth Anne..." chided Jayne.

"I promise," Ronnie assured. "Nice dress, by the way. You look really pretty."

"Thanks. Donna bought it for me."

The two really hit it off. He was such a gentleman, too. Jayne and I both approved. I could tell I wasn't going to have to stay up late worrying about her like I did when she was with Chuck. Ronnie had nothing but good intentions.

When we all got home, Billy and Penny greeted Ruthie with another little green spider plant and a huge bouquet of sunflowers, her favourite. The girls both commented on each other's matching dress almost immediately, none the wiser that their sister - and mother - had conspired against them.

"Mom," shouted Penny. "Didn't you know Donna bought this same dress for Ruthie? We'll never hear the end of it."

Jayne just rolled her eyes. It was hard for us to keep it all a secret, but we knew how much trouble Donna had gone through to make her joke a success and we didn't want to be the ones to spoil it.

"I know its mean, but I can't wait to see her face," squealed Ruthie. "I think it's funny."

While the two of them explained the family tradition to Ronnie, Billy and I brought soft drinks in from the cooler on the patio deck.

"I take it you were on your best behavior with my daughter while we were away," I said.

"Oh, yes, sir. You know it," Billy replied, trying to look serious. "I kept my eyes closed the whole time while I was helpin' with her dress, too."

"Uh, huh." We both couldn't help but smile. He was a good man and I knew it.

By the time everyone arrived, we had enough food to feed a small army. Dot and her husband came by with a green salad and a piping hot casserole that smelled delicious. Skip brought lobster rolls and Bob, who was now the official Sheridan family florist, concocted a home-made chocolate dessert that was to die for. Donna finally arrived on the scene, fashionably late of course, and brought quiche and a seafood bisque she'd picked up at the French Bistro. Three guesses what she was wearing.

"Oh, my god!" she dramatically feigned as she caught sight of her 'twin' sisters. "I don't believe this. Is there no fashion justice at all in the world?"

"You can't be serious?" Ruthie chortled. "How many of these did you buy?"

"I did it as a joke," she confessed. "Didn't Mom tell you?"

Mom… She called her mother, *Mom*. Jayne caught it, too, and beamed with joy. She didn't exactly mind being called Jayne, but Mom was a title earned and she was proud to wear the badge.

"That's it," cried Penny. "Officer York, arrest this woman. She's an imposter!"

It was all uphill from there.

And as the night went on, I couldn't help but think to myself: *This was what it was supposed to be like.* This was what I'd work so hard for, what I'd dreamed of providing. The laughing. The singing. And all the love in between. This was what it was all about.

Later on, when no one was looking, I took Jayne by the hand and we slipped out the kitchen door. We walked down to the beach arm in arm, the crisp night air kissing our blushing cheeks. We turned and looked back up at the house, watching all the happiness unfold through the big picture window, and we held each other close.

Epilogue

"All right everyone. If I could have your attention, please!" shouted Jayne. The Fifteenth Annual Sheridan Family Chowder Cook-off was about to begin and I was ready as ever to best my daughter with another soon-to-be-famous chowder recipe.

Penny, confident as always, took a whiff of my brew. "Still haven't figured it out, have you," she jeered.

"Oh, I've got it figured out," I snidely replied. "You'll see."

"No, you don't," she sneered, dipping her finger in for a taste. "You had me on my deathbed once, you know. You should have asked me then. It would have saved you an awful lot of trouble."

That little shit. She was right, though. She *was* on her deathbed once upon a time. So were Ruth and her mother, it seemed. Looking back, I couldn't believe that nine summers had come and gone since then. It really had been all uphill from there and I couldn't be a happier man.

As planned, Donna married Brian that November and actually came in under budget. It was a gorgeous wedding and everyone, including the Groverton's, had a fabulous time. We all danced until dawn with Ruthie singing her heart out at the reception with the hired band and Penny running a confetti machine that she rigged up using a mini Shop Vac. As promised, I even had money left over to take Jayne to the Cape for a weekend getaway. We called it our second honeymoon.

Predictably, ever-feisty Donna was quickly promoted to buyer at Filene's and moved to New York where Brian, who'd dodged the draft because of his bum knee, became a personal trainer at an upscale gym in Manhattan. While they still haven't decided whether or not to have children, they do spend a lot of time happily doting on their nieces and nephews.

Ruthie, still clean and sober, eventually married Ronnie York and became the Activities Director at the local nursing home. Something about the Colonel must have struck a chord with her that summer in the rehab ward since she always closes their Bingo night with a touching rendition of *My Wild Irish Rose.*

She and Ronnie, unable to have children of their own, adopted a special-needs boy about five years ago. Rudy, now seven, was born with Downs Syndrome and I must say he is the most loving child on the face of the planet. He's just so full of life. His smile is contagious, as is his laugh, and one can't help but hug him tight and love him. Every Saturday he comes over to help me in the darkroom. He's got a keen eye for photography and I can tell he's going to be a great artist one day. We've become great pals.

Billy proposed to Penny on Christmas Eve the winter after her accident, claiming he wanted to give Santa the opportunity to redeem himself for not bringing him his mother and brother. All he wanted that year was a *yes* from his best girl. He got his wish and then some.

According to plan, the two had a backyard wedding the following summer and sailed to Bermuda for their honeymoon. Billy landed a lucrative job at the New England Aquarium after his subsequent completion of Graduate school while Penny freelances as an Engineer on special projects. They bought a modest home on the beach, along with sensible autos, and even had kids. Lots of them.

Although they didn't run in either family, Penny and Billy managed to produce two sets of identical twins: Otis and Derry, now three and a half; and Haley and Hannah, now eleven months. All four have unruly manes of curly hair; impish smiles; and, much to Billy's relief, strong healthy hearts. Grampa Skip lovingly refers to them as "the little boogers" and keeps a picture of the lot laminated to the dash of his boat. As for myself, I about turn inside out every time I see them. They're quite the brood.

As for Jayne and I, we grow closer every day. She bravely gave up Valium shortly after that rollercoaster summer, switching instead to high-potent doses of love and affection from her husband and family. She also gave up her decorating business, much to the dismay of her wealthy clients who were eager to take advantage of her. I was pleased to see her stick up for herself, no longer concerned what the neighbors would think. It made me admire her all the more.

As part of our new routine, we take a spring vacation each year to someplace romantic so we can remind ourselves why it was we fell so madly in love. I always try to pick someplace cold so I can wear a turtleneck until I start to think about what Jaynie looks like in a swimsuit. This year we chose the best of both worlds – a resort in the desert southwest. Hot during the day, cold at night. Boy, did we keep busy.

We've been to Paris twice now, too, to visit my sister and to climb the Eiffel Tower. We're planning on going again next year for our anniversary and we're already getting excited about it. I have to admit, there's nothing like making love to the woman of your dreams in Paris. There's just something about the place that makes you melt.

But, as Penny so often reminds me, there's always going to be a little yin to go with the yang.

Page, my dearest friend in all the world, passed away last year after a brief illness. She'd lost her husband, Cedric, not three months prior and it was said she died of a broken heart. The two had known each other since primary school and were lovers to the end.

Jayne and I flew to London to attend the funeral and were met by both Mr. Donovan and Mr. Davis. Davis couldn't stop crying and Donovan looked like he was going to have a nervous breakdown. They'd kept Page on the payroll after her retirement and had her come in two days a week to keep things running smoothly in the secretarial office, which they didn't the other three days. They were beside themselves wondering how they were ever going to replace her.

"I'm sorry to break it to you gentlemen," I began, "but Page Reynolds cannot be replaced. She's one of a kind. So if you're looking to find someone who can match her, you'd better aim your sights pretty high. Personally, I'd start with a miracle worker. You can take it from there."

Page, the Queen of Candor, would have been proud.

I'll never forget the phrase she always left me with whenever we spoke: "Love to the women." She was so right and so deserving of that love as much as any woman. Where would we be without them?

"Come on, Dad! It's time for the vote!"

Acknowledgments

I would like to give a huge thanks to my number one go-to guy for all things literary, David Edmonds. Your advice and mentorship has been invaluable and I am truly blessed. Without you, this book would not have been published.

To my son, Charles Maximus, I tip my hat to you, bud, for being so understanding while I banged away at the keyboard, often losing track of the time and totally forgetting about lunch. I commend you and your imagination, which kept you occupied while I spent hours and hours trying to get a scene just right, a line just right, a page formatted just right. You are my Rock Star.

I would be remiss not to acknowledge my parents, as well, for their love and support while I pursued my dream of telling stories. You've always been encouraging, letting me know in your own small way that perhaps I ought to be doing this. I ought to write.

My mother has always been my toughest critic, and to that I owe her a great debt. After reading an early draft of *Love to the Women*, she simply said, "I think you did it." It was all I needed. I thank you and I love you.

To my father, Dave, I thank you for selflessly sharing your vast knowledge of everything important. You taught me how to bait a hook, how to solve an algebraic equation, even how to change my own oil and run a table saw. You have always been my greatest teacher. You made me feel empowered.

My father was at the forefront of my mind as I developed the character, Skip Monaghan. Not unlike Skip, Dad was always working to build a faster boat, a faster car, a faster plane, a faster anything-he-could-get-his-hands-on. In 1990, he built and raced *Evolution*, a beautiful 32-foot lobster boat, at the Harpswell, Maine, lobster boat races. He beat out the competition by a landslide, but was subsequently disqualified for not having a lobster license. Later that summer, however, the fine gentlemen of the racing committee decided to award him with an honorary 1st place trophy since he'd been such a good sport about the whole thing.

Dad's still designing and building to this day, having recently completed a little racing craft he christened, *Maximus*. She sure turns heads every time he launches her down at the local boat ramp and it goes without saying, naturally, that she'll go faster than the hammers of hell. It scares my mother to death.

I used to dream of being a screenwriter, always hoping to see my stories presented on the big screen – maybe even the little screen. However, as friends and family read my work, I began to see a pattern emerging in their critiques: "Hey, this would make a great book." It took a while, but I finally listened.

I hope I can one day present you with another equally captivating story that will make you laugh, make you cry, or maybe just plain get your Irish up. And who knows. After all that, someday, someone, somewhere, might even say, "Hey, this would make a great movie." The spirits dost move in mysterious ways.

I humbly thank you for your readership. God Bless and Safe Journey...

-h.t.